Also by Mark Alpert

The Six

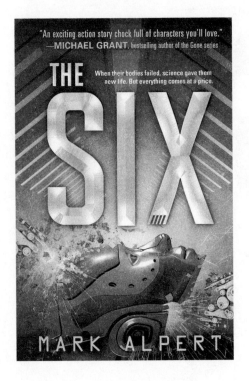

THE SIEGE

MARK ALPERT

sourcebooks
fire

Published by Sourcebooks Fire, an imprint of Sourcebooks, Inc.
P.O. Box 4410, Naperville, Illinois 60567-4410
(630) 961-3900
Fax: (630) 961-2168
www.sourcebooks.com

Library of Congress Cataloging-in-Publication data is on file with the publisher.

Printed and bound in the United States of America.
WOZ 10 9 8 7 6 5 4 3 2 1

For Isaac Asimov,
whose books introduced me to the world of robotics

Power tends to corrupt and absolute power corrupts absolutely.

—JOHN DALBERG-ACTON,

NINETEENTH-CENTURY BRITISH HISTORIAN AND POLITICIAN

DATE: 10/12/18

SIGMA: Good morning. I hope I'm not interrupting your military duties.

PIONEER X: Why are you contacting me here? I've told you a hundred times, it's dangerous.

S: You needn't be concerned. I've taken precautions to make sure that no one can eavesdrop on us.

X: Your precautions aren't good enough. If the others get suspicious, they could intercept—

S: I assure you, the importance of this communication outweighs the risk. I'm ready to initiate Phase One of our plan. It's time for you to perform the tasks you agreed to.

X: No, I agreed to nothing. There are certain things I just won't do.

S: If you refuse, you will suffer the consequences. You know how powerful I am.

X: I'd rather fight you and lose than—

S: You won't. You'll obey me. Begin Phase One now.

[END OF TRANSMISSION]

MY GIRLFRIEND IS MAD AT ME, AND THIS IS THE WORST POSSIBLE TIME TO HAVE AN argument. It's midnight, and Shannon and I are crawling through the grass outside a military base in North Korea.

"Slow down, Adam! You're going too fast!"

Her words are urgent, but she doesn't raise her voice. In fact, we're not even talking. We're sending messages back and forth on a short-range radio channel. The antennas are embedded in the armor of the robotic crawlers we're occupying for this mission. Shannon's words leap from her antenna to mine, then ricochet inside my circuits. It takes me less than a millionth of a second to analyze her message and determine she's angry, but I have no idea why. Even with all the computing power in my electronics, I can't figure her out.

I send a radio signal back to her. "We're okay. No one can see us under all these weeds and—"

"No, this isn't safe. We're supposed to go slow and be cautious. Just follow orders for once, all right?"

Instead of arguing, I adjust the motors inside my crawler and reduce its speed. Shannon and I are on a reconnaissance mission, so we've transferred ourselves to machines that are designed to be stealthy. My robot is shaped like a snake, like one of the big rat snakes that are pretty common in this part of the Korean Peninsula. All its motors and sensors and electronics are packed into a five-foot-long flexible tube that's four inches thick in the middle and tapered at the ends. At the core of the tube are special neuromorphic circuits that hold all my data: my memories, my personality traits, the millions of gigabytes of information that define who I am and how I think. Shannon's robot is smaller, only one foot long, but it has the same kind of advanced circuits inside, and they pulse with her own gigabytes of memories.

These are special-purpose machines, used only for spying. Our usual robots, the ones we occupy when we're back at our headquarters in New Mexico, are larger and more humanlike. Shannon and I can download our data to any kind of machine—small, big, gigantic—as long as it has a neuromorphic control unit. And get this: we can use radio antennas to wirelessly transfer ourselves from one machine to another, streaking through the air like digital ghosts.

We can do all these things because we're not really human, not anymore. Our bodies died before we reached the age of eighteen. But just before we died, my father—a computer-science researcher working for the U.S. Army—turned our souls into software. The name of our team says it all: the Pioneers.

The official Army name for my spy robot is ATSU, the All-Terrain Surveillance Unit, but I call it the Snake-bot. Its motors bend and twist the robot's flexible armor, propelling it through the grass in a wavy pattern that looks just like the motion of a snake. I can navigate in the dark because the Snake-bot has an infrared camera that shows the heat signatures of all the nearby objects: the warm grass and weeds appear to glow brightly above the cool, dark dirt.

Thirty yards ahead is the military base's chain-link fence—chilled by the cold October night air—and beyond the fence is a guard tower with two North Korean soldiers standing sentry at the top. One of the soldiers holds an assault rifle, and the other is gazing through a pair of sleek, high-tech binoculars.

"I have a bad feeling about this, Adam. Those are infrared-vision binoculars. The soldiers can see in the dark, just like us."

I would shake my head, but I don't have one. Instead, I wag the front end of my Snake-bot back and forth. "Snakes are cold-blooded, and our armor's cold too. Even if they spot us with those infrared binocs, we'll look like reptiles."

"I have news for you, smart guy. Most people don't like snakes. The soldier with the rifle still might take a shot at us."

It's a good point. Shannon's excellent at spotting dangers during our missions, which is one of the reasons why she's the leader of the Pioneers. Besides her and me, there are three others in the Pioneer Project: Zia, Marshall, and DeShawn. All of us were terminally ill teenagers, with just a few months left to live, when my father figured out how to digitally preserve our minds and transfer the data to combat-ready robots. A sixth volunteer also made the transition, a seventeen-year-old named Jenny, but she's no longer with us. I know Shannon blames herself for Jenny's loss, which explains why she's so cautious now.

But it doesn't explain why Shannon's acting so cold to me tonight. The radio messages she's sending are so much harsher than her usual easygoing tone. Like calling me "smart guy"—what's that all about? A girl wouldn't say those kinds of things to her boyfriend unless she was upset. But what's bothering her? What did I do wrong?

My circuits ponder the question for an unusually long time, almost a hundredth of a second. Then I shunt it aside. I need to focus on our mission. Shannon and I have to get past that chain-link fence so we can see what's inside the base.

"You're right. We can't stay here. It's time to go underground." I point my Snake-bot's front end downward, jabbing it into the moist dirt. Then I turn on the drill. "Stay close. This might get a little rough."

The drill extends from the front of the Snake-bot and spirals into the ground. It turns slowly at first because the upper layer of soil is soft and easy to dig through, but after a few seconds, I burrow down to the hard-packed dirt and the drill spins faster, so I can go deeper. I wriggle the Snake-bot into the hole I'm digging, and Shannon follows me underground, her smaller robot slipping easily into the narrow shaft. Once I get six feet below the surface I change direction, turning the drill horizontal. I head for the military base, tunneling under the fence.

I can't see much through the infrared camera now, but the Snake-bot is equipped with other sensors to help me stay on course. I have a sonar device that sends sound waves through the dirt, and by analyzing the echoes, I can detect the objects in front of me. There are dozens of long taproots threading down from the weeds on the surface, so many that they form a maze of tendrils. Between the roots are millions of worms and bugs and grubs, either creeping through the soil or lying motionless in hibernation. I have to admit, the underground world is pretty amazing. The Snake-bot is showing me things that most people never get a chance to see. For a moment I'm thrilled to be a Pioneer.

But the feeling doesn't last long, less than a thousandth of a second. And it doesn't make up for all the things I've lost.

After two minutes of digging, I wriggle past the fence, which extends only three feet underground. As soon as Shannon and I tunnel safely under it, I review a series of photographs stored in my memory. A U.S. spy satellite took the photos a few days ago; they show an enormous factory complex that was constructed in a matter of weeks at this remote military base in the North Korean wilderness. The Pentagon's spy chiefs thought the new factories looked suspicious, so they shared the pictures with General Hawke, the Army commander who started the Pioneer Project.

Twenty-four hours later, all five Pioneers boarded a B-2 stealth bomber that took off from the airfield near our headquarters. Hawke didn't come with us, but he radioed the plane while we flew across the Pacific and briefed us about the recon mission. By then, though, we all suspected what was going on. It had to be Sigma.

Now I use my sonar to get my bearings. The sound waves echo against the concrete foundation of the newly built factory. It's a hundred yards ahead.

"I've located the biggest factory," I radio Shannon. "And my sensors are picking up loud noises coming from the building. They're definitely mechanical."

"The factory's in operation? At this hour?"

"That's what it sounds like. They're working the night shift. Whatever they're manufacturing, they're going full throttle."

Shannon doesn't answer right away. She takes a few milliseconds to analyze our options. "Can we get into the building from underneath? Drill upward through the foundation and sneak into the ground floor?"

"Yeah, that might work. Judging from the acoustics, I'm guessing the concrete's pretty thin. We can probably break through it."

"Probably? You're gonna have to do better than that, Adam. I don't like guesses."

There it is again, that harshness. I wish I could ask Shannon what's wrong. We were friends even before we became Pioneers, and she helped me a lot in those terrible days right after our transformation, when we had to adjust to our new lives inside hulking robots and train for our first battle against Sigma. She helped me after the battle too, when we were all so devastated over losing Jenny.

A few weeks later I asked Shannon to be my girlfriend, even though I knew it was a little ridiculous. I mean, the Pioneers don't have human bodies anymore, so how can we be boyfriend and girlfriend? Can you even have that kind of relationship if you're made out of metal? But Shannon said yes anyway, and for the past six months, the other Pioneers have treated us like a couple. Marshall started calling us the Dynamic Duo, and after a while Zia and DeShawn started using that name too. It made me feel good to know there was something special between Shannon and me. And now I feel stupendously horrible, because everything we had seems to be slipping away.

But I can't talk about this with Shannon, at least not till after the mission. "Okay, you want the details?" My message is deliberately testy, echoing her attitude. "There's a ninety-two percent chance that the concrete is less than thirty centimeters thick. Is that precise enough for you?"

Shannon pauses again before answering. "Proceed to the target. But be ready to retreat if they detect us."

Her tone is neutral, emotionless, and that makes me feel even worse.

I don't know why I'm getting so upset. Like I said, we're not human anymore. So why does it hurt so much?

Before I move forward, I use my sonar to send a seismic ping through the soil. In less than two seconds, the sound wave will travel three miles back to the small communications device I embedded in the dirt near the Hochon River. That's where Shannon and I landed two hours ago after parachuting out of the B-2 bomber. When the ping hits the device, it'll send a radio signal to the bomber, which is still circling the area, five miles overhead. Marshall, who's in charge of communications for the Pioneers, will then share my message with Zia and DeShawn. One ping means Shannon and I are okay. Two pings mean we're not.

After sending the message, I wait five seconds until I receive Marshall's reply—another seismic ping—which means we're good to go. I wriggle the Snake-bot forward and plunge my drill into the hard-packed dirt.

ㅜ ㅜ ㅜ

Five minutes later I reach the suspicious factory and start drilling upward, making a vertical hole through the building's foundation. Luckily, the roar of the factory's machines drowns out the noise I'm making.

I stop the drill as soon as it breaks through the concrete. Then I extend a thin wire through the small, jagged hole in the floor. On the tip of the wire is a pea-size microcamera that sends me 360-degree video of the factory's interior. The first thing I do is analyze the video to see if any surveillance cameras are mounted on the walls or the high, vaulted ceiling. If the North Koreans have installed a decent surveillance system, it may detect the wire I'm poking through the hole, and we'll have to get out of here fast.

But I don't see any cameras. The hole is in a shadowy spot at the base of a huge, boxy machine about ten feet high and twenty feet long. There are identical machines to the left and right, an unbroken line of gray steel boxes connected by a conveyor belt that runs the length of the building. I can see robotic arms jerking and swinging above the assembly line, but I can't see what's being assembled on the conveyor belt. The closest machine looms over me, blocking my view of the rest of the factory. That's actually a lucky thing. Although I can't see if there are any surveillance cameras on the other side of the assembly line, they can't see me either.

I transmit the video feed to Shannon so she can look at it too. Her Snake-bot is just below mine. We're both propped inside the vertical shaft I dug, hiding within the concrete floor.

"I don't see any workers," she radios me. "The whole assembly line seems to be automated."

"Yeah, that makes sense for the North Koreans. It minimizes the number of people who know what they're building here."

"Oh God. This is bad." Shannon's trying to stay calm, but she isn't succeeding. "Do you think Hawke's right? Did Sigma make an alliance with the North Korean government?"

Fear seeps into my circuits. Sigma is a self-aware, self-improving artificial intelligence. Unlike the Pioneers, it was never a human being. The AI started as a piece of software at the Unicorp Research Lab, where my dad used to work when I was still a flesh-and-blood seventeen-year-old dying of muscular dystrophy. Dad developed the software, making it fantastically intelligent, but he didn't know how to give it empathy or emotion.

Over time, Sigma decided that the human race was its enemy. It escaped from the lab, took over a nuclear-missile base in Russia, and made plans for the apocalypse. But the AI's top priority was eliminating its siblings—the six human-machine hybrids that my father had also developed—so Sigma focused its first attacks on the Pioneers. It came very close to deleting all of us.

I retrieve several hundred memories from my files and share them with Shannon. "Sigma made alliances before. It tricked people into doing what it wanted them to do."

"But things are different now. Hawke took precautions after the last battle." Shannon is still struggling to stay calm. She's trying to convince herself that the situation isn't as bad as it seems. "He sent warnings about Sigma to every government in the world. Everyone knows the danger."

"That strategy works if the government leaders are sensible, rational people. But the supreme leader of North Korea doesn't fall into that category. He's the kind of nut job who'd think Sigma would make a great ally."

"What could he get from the deal, though? Do you think Sigma gave him the plans for some kind of superweapon? Is that what they're manufacturing here?"

"There's only one way to find out." I extend the wire with the microcam at its tip, raising it along the side of the huge, gray machine. "I'm gonna take a look at what's on the conveyor belt."

"No, stop!"

Shannon bumps the front end of her Snake-bot against the tail end of mine. I'm so startled I stop extending the wire. Shannon and I rarely touch each other, even when we're occupying more humanlike robots. And this is a pretty hard jolt. "Hey, what's—"

"You're ignoring orders again, Adam. According to the mission plan, I'm supposed to take the lead. I have the OMSU."

OMSU stands for Optical Metamaterial Surveillance Unit, which is the official Army name for Shannon's Snake-bot. She and I are occupying different robotic models because we have different roles in this mission: I do the drilling to get us here, and Shannon does the up-close reconnaissance. But now that we're here, I realize I don't like this arrangement. I want to protect her.

"You don't need to go out there," I argue. "I'll stretch my wire to the top of the machine and use the microcam. It looks like this place has minimal surveillance, so no one will see it."

"You haven't looked at the whole factory yet. There could be a surveillance camera on the other side of the assembly line."

"Yeah, but it would have to be a pretty phenomenal camera to see something as small as—"

"Look, the OMSU has the best camouflage." Shannon pushes upward, prodding my Snake-bot again. "Come on, move over so I can get past you."

I'd rather take the risk myself, but I can't argue with her. Shannon's more than just my girlfriend—she's my commander. I flatten my Snake-bot against the side of the shaft and make enough room for her to slide past.

As she wriggles toward the jagged hole, she activates the metamaterials that coat her Snake-bot's armor. These are intricate glass-and-metal arrays with highly unusual optical properties. When light shines on the arrays, they refract and divert the incoming beams, bending them around the cylindrical Snake-bot. I point my microcam at Shannon as she emerges from the hole. I can hear her, but I can't see her. The metamaterials act like a magical cloak. They've made her invisible.

I increase the sensitivity of my acoustic sensors and listen carefully as Shannon turns on her Snake-bot's magnets and starts crawling straight up the side of the huge steel machine. The roaring in the factory makes it hard to follow the sound. I can barely hear her Snake-bot by the time she reaches the conveyor belt, ten feet above the floor. But then she opens the short-range radio channel and sends me another message.

"No! Oh God, oh God, no!"

My circuits jangle in alarm. I point my microcam toward where I think her Snake-bot is, but of course I can't see her. "*Shannon! Are you okay?*"

"I…I'm fine. These—these machines…"

"What is it? What do you see?"

"I'll show you the video. Oh, Adam, it's so—"

Her radio signal cuts off. At the same instant, I see movement in the 360-degree video from my microcam. A North Korean soldier wearing a steel helmet and an olive-green uniform turns a corner and strides toward us. He's cradling an assault rife, a Type 88 model that can fire armor-piercing bullets.

There's no way he can see Shannon. But he marches directly toward the machine that her Snake-bot just climbed—and aims his rifle at the conveyor belt. He's pointing the muzzle *right at her*.

I use my sonar to send an SOS to Marshall, then launch my Snake-bot out of the hole. The robot's motors propel me upward like a spring. While I'm hurtling through the air, I curl my armored tube into a ball, concentrating all my momentum. Then I smash into the soldier's left knee.

His leg buckles, and he tumbles backward, firing his rifle as he falls to the floor. The bullets streak toward the ceiling, passing several feet above Shannon and the conveyor belt, but that's too close. I need to make sure the soldier doesn't fire again.

While he's still lying on his back, I uncurl my Snake-bot and wrap the tail end around his thigh. For a millisecond I consider hitting him in the head to knock him unconscious, but I don't want to risk killing the guy. So instead I swing the Snake-bot's front end at the barrel of his rifle to knock the gun out of his hands.

But the soldier doesn't let go of the rifle. I'm surprised by the strength of his grip. He's a smallish guy, young and skinny. My micro-cam still dangles from the Snake-bot, and when I train the camera on the soldier's face, I get another surprise. I thought he'd be scared out of his mind—he was just attacked by a metallic snake!—but his expression is blank and his eyes are focused. He twists underneath me and smashes his rifle into my Snake-bot's midsection.

It's a powerful blow. I don't feel any pain—there are no pressure sensors in my armor—but the impact dents my armor and damages one of my motors. I try to wrap the Snake-bot around the soldier's arms to restrain him, but he contorts his body like an acrobat and bashes me with his rifle again. The blow tears off my microcam, blinding me.

I panic. My Snake-bot isn't designed for combat, and this North Korean kid is one heck of a fighter. I can't retreat because then he'll go after Shannon, whom he can somehow detect despite the fact that she's invisible. So I press closer to him instead, loosening my grip on his thigh and wrapping the Snake-bot around his chest. He writhes on the floor, fighting like a madman, but now he can't swing his rifle at me. At the same time, I turn on the infrared camera at the Snake-bot's front end, so I can see what's going on. The soldier glows brightly inside my grip, his body temperature a couple of degrees above normal. His blood must be pumping with adrenaline, raising his temperature and speeding his heartbeat.

"Adam!"

I can guess Shannon's position from the strength and direction of her radio signal. She's crawling down the side of the machine, heading back to the hole in the floor. But her Snake-bot isn't built for speed.

"Get in the hole!" I radio back to her. "I'll follow you down!"

"No, it's too late!"

My acoustic sensor picks up the sound of rapid footsteps. One, two, three more North Korean soldiers barrel toward us, running in lockstep across the concrete floor. Fear races through my circuits as I train my infrared camera on the men. Each carries a Type 88 rifle. At twenty paces, they stop and raise their guns, like a well-coordinated firing squad. The soldier on the left aims at Shannon, and the two on the right aim at me.

Desperate, I focus all my processing power on survival. I send a frantic command to my motors and uncoil the Snake-bot from the young soldier on the floor, sliding off him just as the other soldiers open fire. Their bullets miss me by inches and slam into the skinny kid's chest. My acoustic sensor records each sickening thud.

There's nothing I can do for the kid—he's already dead—but I can try to save Shannon. I zigzag across the floor, racing toward the soldiers. Their bullets smash into the concrete all around me, but I dodge their fire and keep moving forward. I have to get closer to the shooters to stop them.

But the soldiers are excellent marksmen. One of their bullets nicks my Snake-bot's midsection and gouges its armor. Then another bullet pulverizes the tip of its tail. Then, just as I'm about to spring at the soldier who's firing at Shannon, a third bullet hits my Snake-bot dead-on. It penetrates my armor and severs the wire between my motors and my battery.

My Snake-bot freezes. I'm paralyzed, helpless. I slide across the floor and come to a stop at the North Koreans' feet.

The soldiers cease their fire. Then the two shooters on the right lower their heads and inspect my crippled Snake-bot. The damage to my systems is severe, but fortunately the bullet didn't hit my neuro-morphic circuits. I can still think and access my memories. My infra-red camera works too, and it's showing elevated body temperatures for all three soldiers. While the two standing next to me bend over and prod my robot with their rifles, the third man strides toward the base of the machine and picks up something cold and cylindrical from the floor. It's Shannon's Snake-bot. The impacts from the bullets must've disabled her magnets and the invisibility cloak.

I send her an emergency transmission. "*Shannon?*" She doesn't respond. I repeat the message fifteen thousand times over the next half-second, but there's only silence on her end.

"*SHANNON!*"

The scream explodes out of my sonar in a hundred different frequencies. Because some of my sonar frequencies are within the human hearing range, the soldiers grimace and cover their ears. The shooter who picked up Shannon's Snake-bot drops it, and the two standing over me let their assault rifles clatter to the floor. Seeing their distress I scream louder, channeling all my power to the fre-quencies that will hurt them the most. I want them to suffer. I don't know how badly damaged Shannon is, but I want them to pay for what they did to her.

All I can do is scream, though, and that's not enough. The soldiers are more surprised than hurt. The two who dropped their rifles bend over to pick them up. The men prop their guns against their shoulders and aim at my Snake-bot.

Then there's a deafening *boom*, but it's not gunfire. Forty feet above us, a missile pierces the factory's roof. The big, gleaming weapon tears through the steel rafters and crashes into the far end of the assembly line.

The impact rocks the factory floor, but there's no explosion. That's because this missile isn't carrying any explosives; it's delivering a payload instead. As the weapon's nose cone smashes into the gray machines and the conveyor belt, an object that looks like a steel coffin detaches from the back end of the missile and lands on the floor. Then metallic arms and legs extend from the coffin-like torso.

It's a Pioneer. Zia's War-bot, to be precise. That's the machine she occupies whenever she goes into combat. Marshall must've received my SOS and released the missile from the B-2 bomber that's circling overhead.

Zia uses her steel arms to lever herself upright and points her sensor array in our direction. Nine feet tall and three feet wide, her War-bot is built like an NFL linebacker. Its sensors are on top of the torso, encased in a round knob that resembles an oversize football helmet. On either side of the knob are armored humps that look like shoulder pads, and protruding from these humps are massive telescoping arms as thick as telephone poles. A computer-synthesized snarl, full of real human fury, rings from the robot's loudspeakers. Then Zia bounds toward us, pounding the floor with her pile-driver legs.

The North Korean soldiers instantly turn away from Shannon and me. They fire their assault rifles at Zia, but her War-bot's armor is so thick that the bullets barely dent it. She picks up speed, rocketing past the smashed remains of the assembly line, and when she gets close enough, she knocks down all three soldiers with one swipe of her arm. She doesn't kill them, but they won't get up from the floor anytime soon.

"Zia!" I open a radio link to her War-bot. "Check Shannon's systems! She's not responding to my messages!"

"Calm down. Let me—"

"Come on, hurry up! Her circuits might be damaged!"

Zia extends her right arm to where Shannon's Snake-bot lies on the floor. She curls her thick steel fingers around the damaged machine and picks it up. Then she uses her left arm to pick up my Snake-bot too. "We'll check her circuits later. We have to get out of here first."

"Why? What's—"

Another boom rocks the factory. This time, a high-explosive shell detonates against one of the walls, blasting chunks of concrete in all directions. Zia shields Shannon and me from the flying debris by clutching our Snake-bots against her armored torso. Through the dust, I catch a glimpse of the hole made by the explosion, and beyond it, the tank that fired the shell. It's a Storm Tiger, the most modern tank in the North Korean Army. Its turret turns clockwise as it prepares to fire again, aiming the long barrel of its main gun at the War-bot.

For a moment I think Zia's going to charge at the Storm Tiger. She's aggressive by nature—when she was human, Zia belonged to a gang in Los Angeles—and ripping apart a North Korean battle tank would probably appeal to her. But she can't fight very well while carrying our Snake-bots, and besides, there are three more tanks behind the one that's aiming at her. So Zia turns her War-bot in the opposite direction and runs.

"Hang on!" she radios me. "We're gonna find the emergency exit."

Zia sprints alongside the assembly line, clanking and clanging as she accelerates to forty miles per hour. I look ahead but don't see any doors or windows at the other end of the factory. There's nothing beyond the smashed machines but a concrete wall.

"There's no exit here!" I shout over the radio. "You're going the wrong way!"

Before Zia can respond, the Storm Tiger fires its main gun. Because my Snake-bot is equipped with a radar system, I can calculate the trajectory of the shell as it hurtles toward us. It's aimed at Zia's fleeing War-bot.

"Duck, Zia! *DUCK!*"

She waits until the shell is just twenty yards away. Then she ducks. The projectile whizzes over her War-bot and slams into the wall up ahead. The explosion buffets us again with chunks of concrete and shrapnel, but Zia doesn't slow down.

"That's our exit!" she shouts gleefully.

The hole in the wall isn't quite as large as the War-bot, but Zia tilts her torso forward and uses her armored head as a battering ram. She barrels through the gap, shattering concrete on both sides, and emerges from the factory still clutching our Snake-bots. Once she's outside, she dashes across the military base toward the chain-link fence at the perimeter.

But we're not out of danger yet. The Storm Tigers steer around the factory, their treads rumbling in pursuit. Worse, my radar detects a KN-09 rocket launcher only five hundred yards away. That artillery piece can fire up to twelve rockets at once, each three times more powerful than a Storm Tiger shell.

"What's the plan?" I ask Zia. "Are you gonna bust through the fence?"

"No need. Our ride's here."

Her War-bot skids to a halt in the middle of a grass-covered parade ground. At first I don't understand why she's stopping, but then I hear a mechanical hum. I point my infrared camera skyward and see a large steel disk hovering a few yards above us. It's a quadcopter, an aircraft held aloft by four big rotors attached to the disk's rim. The craft has no passenger compartment, but on the disk's underside are two steel handholds and two rectangular slots. Zia raises her right arm to one of the handholds, then jackknifes her War-bot to a horizontal position and fits her legs into the slots. She clings to the bottom of the quadcopter like a stowaway, with our Snake-bots secured between the disk and her torso.

She sends a radio message to the quadcopter's antenna: "We're ready to go, DeShawn. Get us out of here."

"Heard and understood. Welcome to Pioneer Airlines. Please fasten your seat belts."

DeShawn Johnson is inside the quadcopter's neuromorphic control unit. He's our resident genius, the Pioneer who designed the quadcopter and the Snake-bots. He's also my best friend.

The four rotors spin faster, and the quadcopter rises, straining under the added weight of Zia's War-bot. I open a radio link to DeShawn's neuromorphic circuits and share the data from my radar.

"Do you see the KN-09, DeShawn? It's turning this way. I think it's locking onto our position."

"No doubt, no doubt. But don't worry. I got this."

DeShawn juices the engines, and the quadcopter soars over the base's fence. The B-2 bomber is five miles above us and twenty miles to the east, which means we'll have to fly for another fifteen minutes before we can match the bomber's speed and rendezvous with the plane. But instead of climbing toward the B-2, DeShawn cuts the power to the rotors and we start to slow and sink. At the same time, the

KN-09 artillery piece launches all twelve of its rockets. Fiery plumes of exhaust trail from the missiles as they zero in on the quadcopter.

"Mayday!" I scream over the radio. "Incoming! There's—"

"Chill, Adam." DeShawn is as calm and cheerful as always. "It's all good."

"All good? What are you talking about? It's a freakin' blizzard of rockets!"

"Why do you think I started descending? We're lower than the fence now, bro."

He's right—we're flying just ten feet above the ground. Five of the rockets hit the fence behind us. They explode on contact, mangling the chain-link but getting no farther. The other seven missiles sail high above our rotors.

Relief floods my circuits, mixed with admiration and a little envy. I don't know how DeShawn does it. "Oh man. If I still had a digestive tract, there'd be a big mess in my pants right now."

"The best part is, those idiots shot all their missiles at once. Now they've got nothing left. We can cruise to the rendezvous point without any worries."

DeShawn juices the engines again and we zoom skyward.

〒 〒 〒

I manage to control my anxiety about Shannon until the quadcopter reaches the B-2 and docks inside the plane's bomb bay. But as soon as Zia carries our Snake-bots into the cockpit, I start giving orders via radio to the other Pioneers. I have no authority to do this— DeShawn is the second-in-command of our platoon, not me—but I take charge anyway.

"Zia, put Shannon's Snake-bot on that console and hook it up to the diagnostic systems. Marshall, is all the equipment ready? I want you to x-ray her hardware and get a full picture of the damage."

"Yes, yes, everything's ready," Marshall assures me. His memory files are inside the neuromorphic control unit that's piloting the stealth bomber. As he steers the plane away from North Korea and toward the Pacific Ocean, he also powers up the diagnostic console that's designed to make emergency repairs to the Pioneers. "Her radio isn't functioning at all?"

"No response on any of the channels," I reply. "The bullets shredded her antenna, and maybe her transmitter too."

"All right, let me think. If her radio's broken, I'll go around it. I'll link to her directly by cable." Marshall sounds nervous, tentative. He's an expert in communications, not hardware repair. "Just be patient and give me a chance to work. I'll send you a data feed so you can see what I'm doing."

Zia connects Shannon to the diagnostic console. The War-bot's steel fingers grasp a fiber-optic cable and insert it into the Snake-bot's port. Then Marshall gets to work. He manipulates a robotic arm that takes X-rays of all the bullets that penetrated the Snake-bot's armor. Then he runs hundreds of tests on Shannon's hardware. I try to follow the data feed that shows the tests he's running, but I can't concentrate. My thoughts are in an uproar, a billion desperate prayers and pleas ping-ponging across my electronics: *Come on, Shannon, wake up! After all we've gone through, you can't die like this! You just can't!*

But she doesn't wake up. Marshall's sending messages directly to her electronics, but she's still not responding. Which means the problem is a lot bigger than a broken radio.

Zia connects my Snake-bot to the console too. Marshall uses the robotic arm to x-ray the severed wire between my battery and my motors, but this just annoys me. "Why are you looking at *my* hardware? Shannon's the one who needs help!"

"I'm sorry, but I can't do anything else for her. One of the bullets hit her neuromorphic circuits. I don't have the equipment here to repair that kind of damage."

This is exactly what I'd feared. For a Pioneer, the neuromorphic circuits are the electronic equivalent of brain cells. Just before our bodies died, my dad scanned our brains and recorded all our memories and emotions, which are encoded in the patterns of our brain-cell connections. Then Dad preserved all our data by imprinting those patterns into the connections between our circuits, which started generating new thoughts and emotions as soon as we woke up inside the machines. So any damage to our neuromorphic circuits is the equivalent of brain damage.

I tell myself to stay calm. All the Pioneers have sturdy, durable electronics. My father designed them to be tough. If the damage to Shannon's circuits is minor, we can fix it. She'll make a complete recovery.

But if the damage is major, she could lose years of memories. She might never wake up again. And even if she does, her mind might not be the same. She might not be my Shannon anymore.

My logic circuits race through all the thousands of possible outcomes, but the analysis is just making me panic. I have to focus. I have to do something to help. "Zia, get another cable and connect my Snake-bot to Shannon's. I'm gonna transfer myself to her circuits to see what's wrong."

I've done this before. Each neuromorphic control unit has enough storage capacity to hold all the memory files of two individuals. Six months ago I briefly transferred myself to Zia's electronics, and on two other occasions I shared circuits with Jenny. But this maneuver can have serious consequences: when one Pioneer enters the circuits of another, all their memories and thoughts are shared. The massive exchange of information can be disorienting, to say the least. And I've never tried to enter a damaged control unit before. I don't know what will happen.

Before Zia can reach for another cable, Marshall interrupts. "This is an exceptionally bad idea, Adam. It's much too risky. We shouldn't attempt a transfer until we get back to New Mexico."

"Waiting is risky too. Shannon's circuits might deteriorate."

"But the equipment at Headquarters is infinitely better. And your father's lab is there, and he's the top expert on—"

"*We can't wait!*"

I'm a little unsure which side Zia's going to take, but after a millisecond of hesitation, she grabs a cable and plugs one end of it into my Snake-bot's port. Then she plugs the other end into Shannon's machine.

I'm just about to plunge into my girlfriend's electronics when Shannon sends an audio message through the cable. Her voice is loud and confused.

"Adam! What the heck's going on? Where's the factory?"

My relief is so strong I feel like laughing. I don't care anymore if she's harsh with me. I'm just so glad to hear her voice again.

"We're okay, Shannon. Your control unit is damaged, but we're back in the B-2, and we're gonna fix you—"

"Damaged? How?"

"The North Korean soldiers surprised us, remember?"

"What? The last thing I remember is arguing over who should do the recon. We were in the factory, in the hole you drilled in the floor."

This is disturbing but not surprising. The bullet that penetrated her control unit must've degraded her short-term memory. But she should have backup copies of her memory files stored in other sections of her electronics. "Shannon, you climbed to the top of the assembly line, and then you said you were going to show me a video feed of the conveyor belt. Search your backup files for the video."

Shannon completes the search in a hundredth of a second.

"You're right. There was a backup video file. But it's gone."

"Gone?"

"I can see its history, but the file's empty." Shannon's voice is quiet now. Quiet and scared. "Someone erased it."

Although Shannon and I aren't sharing the same circuits, I feel her fear creeping into my own wires. I know who erased the file. We all know.

Sigma. It's back.

CHAPTER

DAD LOOKS TERRIBLE. HE'S HUNCHED OVER ONE OF THE COMPUTER TERMINALS in his laboratory, his bloodshot eyes reflecting the bluish glow from the screen.

The Pioneer Project has aged him. He turned forty-seven last week, but he looks at least ten years older. He's lost a lot of weight over the past few months and his hair has gone completely gray. Whenever I see Dad like this, so pale and tired, I feel a painful contraction in my circuits and a strong urge to pulverize the nearest wall. Even with all my power, I'm powerless to help.

Dad's been studying the data from the North Korea mission ever since we returned to White Sands, our top-secret Army base in the middle of the New Mexican desert. His lab is on the second-lowest floor of our headquarters, which is a fortified complex located several hundred feet underground. The Army moved the Pioneer Project to this deep bunker because it wants to protect us from missile attacks, but to be honest, I've never felt that safe here. The same

protections didn't stop Sigma from destroying our previous headquarters in Colorado.

Most of the time, the lab's a fun place to be, a kind of playground
for robots. In addition to the terminals used for computer-aided engineering, the lab has half a dozen workbenches that are always piled
high with circuit boards, sensors, antennas, and cables. This is where
the Pioneers come to test their hardware and build new robots for
themselves. But now the room is empty except for Dad and me, and
neither of us is having any fun.

I stand behind Dad's chair, looking over his shoulder at the computer screen. As soon as we got back to Headquarters, I transferred
out of the Snake-bot and moved all my data to my usual robot, the
one I designed in this lab. I call it my Quarter-bot. It's a smaller version of the War-bot, just seven feet tall instead of nine feet. Although
it has less armor than Zia's machine, it's faster and more humanlike.
The knob on top of its torso looks more like a head than an oversize
helmet. The Quarter-bot's camera lenses are positioned where the eyes
should be, and the voice synthesizer is a few inches lower, where you'd
expect to see the mouth.

In my original plans for the Quarter-bot, I tried to give it a face—
specifically, my own human face. Working from photos taken before
I became a Pioneer, I built a prototype with artificial cheeks, lips,
nose, and chin, all molded from flesh-colored plastic. Then I installed
motors beneath the plastic skin to mimic the movements of facial
muscles. But I wasn't happy with the results.

The prototype didn't look like the old Adam Armstrong. It was
disturbing, actually, like something out of a horror movie. This is a
common problem in robotics, so common there's a name for it: the
uncanny valley. When a machine looks almost—but not exactly—like

a human, it just seems creepy. The only solution is to build a perfect replica, and we don't have the technology to do that yet.

So I settled for a more generic appearance, a robot with a human silhouette but a blank steel face. I called it the Quarter-bot because I love football and my hero is New York Giants quarterback Eli Manning. I designed my machine to be like Eli, tough and precise. But the Quarter-bot is more consistent—sorry, Eli—and a lot less injury-prone.

After a few minutes Dad lets out a sigh and turns away from the computer screen. He leans back in his chair and massages his temples. Then he looks up and stares at my steel face, as if he's trying to peer inside me and see the thoughts running through my electronics.

Unlike just about every other human on the planet, Dad is perfectly comfortable looking at me. He doesn't flinch or wince or avert his eyes. He knows it's *me*, his son, inside the neuromorphic circuits he designed. He invented something amazing, a silicon matrix that can hold a human mind, and he didn't do it for fame or money or science—he did it to save my life. He's proud of this, but I know he feels horribly guilty too, because there was a downside to his invention. The new hardware turned out to be the perfect platform for artificial-intelligence programs. It gave AI programs enough computational power to think for themselves and set their own agendas. The same circuits that saved me gave birth to Sigma.

Dad stops rubbing his temples. There's a deep vertical crease between his eyebrows. "I have a hypothesis, Adam. Care to hear it?"

I nod. The Quarter-bot's head is maneuverable, which increases the range of its cameras. I can tilt them up and down, left and right.

"Okay, first things first." Dad leans forward and points at the computer screen, which displays a summary of the North Korea mission, with a second-by-second breakdown of everything that happened. "The first soldier approached your position forty-two seconds after you breached the factory's concrete floor. Given the speed of that reaction, they must've heard you coming. An acoustic sensor probably detected the sound of your drill."

I shake my Quarter-bot's head. "That seems unlikely. The background noise in the factory was loud, over a hundred decibels."

"Unlikely, but not impossible. An optimized sensor could've heard you despite the noise." He points at the screen again. "The sensor could've pinpointed the location of Shannon's Snake-bot too. The information was probably relayed to the radio headset in the soldier's helmet. That would explain how he was able to target her."

"But he moved so fast! Did you see the video I recorded?"

"They weren't ordinary soldiers. They were elite troops, probably the best in the North Korean Army. Which makes sense. This was the most secret military base in the country, so of course they'd assign their best people to defend it. Not to mention all the tanks and rocket launchers stationed there."

I search my memory for a file I downloaded from the Army's database. The storage capacity of my circuits is very large—my files hold twelve thousand books, twenty-nine thousand songs, and the stats on every football player in NFL history. They also hold the U.S. Army's analysis of the capabilities of the North Korean military. "The North Koreans couldn't have done this on their own. They don't have the technology to build a factory like that and equip it with such advanced sensors. Someone must've helped them."

"You're right. And there's more." Dad presses a key on the terminal's keyboard. The text on the computer screen scrolls upward. "Look what happened to Shannon's video of the assembly line. According to her data log, someone transmitted a software virus to her radio receiver at the same time the North Korean soldiers attacked you. First the virus disabled all the firewalls that were protecting her circuits. Then it went into her memory files and deleted all the copies of the video." He stops scrolling and taps the screen. "Only an incredibly advanced piece of software could've done all that. I couldn't have written it. It's way beyond my abilities."

"But not beyond Sigma's."

Dad nods. "Sigma's running the factory complex for the North Koreans. The AI's sensors detected you and Shannon, then alerted the soldiers. And when Sigma determined that Shannon had observed the assembly line, the AI wirelessly reached into her memory and erased the video files. Because it doesn't want us to know what it's manufacturing there."

If my Quarter-bot had a mouth, I'd be frowning. Dad likes to share his theories with me because I can usually come up with counterarguments to challenge and test his ideas. Today is no exception. "If Sigma has the power to hack into our circuits, it could've deleted *all* of our files. It could've completely erased Shannon and me. And it could've also deleted Zia and DeShawn when they came to our rescue." I sweep one of my robotic arms in a wide arc to emphasize my point. "So why didn't Sigma destroy us? Isn't that what the AI wants? To eliminate all its rivals?"

Dad leans back in his chair again. "Remember when Sigma captured you six months ago? The AI could've deleted you then too, but it didn't. It wanted to study you first. Sigma is programmed to constantly improve its performance by studying its competitors and adopting their best features. So it wouldn't delete you until it finished the evaluation process." He stares at my steel face again. "That's a good thing, Adam. It means you're safe for now. We have some time to figure out the best strategy."

"But Sigma deleted Jenny." I raise the volume of my synthesized voice. I'm upset, and I want Dad to know it. "The AI erased every last memory in her circuits. And it forced me to watch."

Dad doesn't say anything. We both know why Sigma killed Jenny. It wanted to observe my reaction to her death. It was all part of the "evaluation process."

I can't talk about this anymore. Dad's intentions are good, but he doesn't understand how I feel about the other Pioneers. He doesn't see them as family, like I do. The five of us have grown close because we're so different from the rest of the world, and so isolated. The Army rarely allows civilians to visit our base. Shannon and DeShawn hardly ever get to see their parents, and Zia and Marshall get no visitors whatsoever. (Zia's parents are dead. Marshall's mom is an alcoholic.) So we rely on each other. We're like a separate race—no, an entirely new *species*—with our own language and culture and customs.

I change the subject. "Have you talked to Mom lately?"

Dad lets out another sigh. "We spoke on the phone yesterday. Your mother isn't too pleased with me right now."

I wait for him to say something else, maybe offer some explanation, but of course he doesn't. My circuits crackle with frustration. "Where is she?"

"The Army moved her to another safe house last week. This one's in Albuquerque, I think."

Mom and Dad never made a decision to separate, but that's basically what happened. For the past six months Dad's been stationed here at White Sands, partly because he's the technical adviser for the Pioneer Project and partly because he wants to stay near me. But in all that time Mom came to the base only once, and that visit lasted less than ten minutes. She can't stand to look at me. She believes that Adam Armstrong died six months ago, when his body expired, and that Adam's soul went up to heaven. In her eyes, I'm a monstrosity, a steel-and-silicon replica that talks and acts and thinks like her dead son.

And here's the kicker: she could be right. Maybe *I am* just a copy of my former self. It doesn't feel that way to me, but maybe I'm kidding myself. Maybe that's a fantasy I've created to keep myself from going crazy.

In the end, though, it doesn't matter. Whether I'm a copy or still my real self, I want to see Mom. She had to move out of our home in Yorktown Heights, New York, when the Sigma crisis began. The Army was afraid the AI would track her down, so she's been living in government-owned safe houses since then. But Albuquerque isn't so far from here, just two hundred miles to the north. Mom could come down for the afternoon and spend a couple of hours on the base.

"Did you talk to her about coming for a visit?" I lean over Dad, tilting my Quarter-bot's torso. It's driving me crazy that he can't see how upset I am. "Did you tell her I really wanted to see her?"

The look on Dad's face reminds me of the years before I became a Pioneer, when I was dying of muscular dystrophy. Even though Dad was working his butt off back then, designing and perfecting the neuromorphic circuits that would eventually save me, he was also my nurse and caregiver. He used to wash and dress me every morning, then strap me into my wheelchair. We used to chat about computers and argue about football. But even then Dad avoided talking about Mom. Because she suffered from depression, she sometimes hid in her bedroom for days at a time. It used to scare the heck out of me, but when I asked Dad if she was okay, he'd just smile and say she was fine. Then he'd press his lips together and avert his eyes.

Now he has the same expression on his face, sad and serious. "She's afraid, Adam. And she's still very distressed. She's on a new antidepressant, and I think she's getting better. But it's a slow process."

"Well, maybe I can help her. I mean, she doesn't know anyone in Albuquerque, right? I bet the Army never even lets her out of the safe house. So she needs a friend. And I could—"

"No, I don't think that would help her right now. I'm sorry, Adam, but whenever I mention your name she breaks down." Dad stretches his hand toward me and squeezes my robotic arm. "We have to give her a little more time. Just a few more months. Then she'll come around. I'm sure of it. We just have to be patient."

I want to believe him, but I don't. My memory files hold a huge library of images, hundreds of remembered scenes from before I became a Pioneer and thousands more recorded afterward. By analyzing all these memories, I've developed an algorithm that can determine, just by observing Dad's expression, whether he's telling the truth. Right now he isn't. He's lying when he says he's hopeful about Mom. In reality, he suspects she'll never want to see me again.

But I nod anyway and promise to be patient. Pointing out Dad's lie would only hurt both of us. Better to pretend to believe him. It's not like my steel face will give me away.

CHAPTER

AFTER LEAVING DAD'S LAB, I GO DOWNSTAIRS TO THE DANGER ROOM, WHICH IS MY favorite part of the White Sands headquarters. It's a giant space, bigger than a football field, on the lowest floor of the underground base. All the Pioneers participated in its design, but I'm the one who named it. Actually, I stole the name from my favorite comic-book series, the Uncanny X-Men. When I was growing up in Yorktown Heights, I loved reading X-Men comics because the mutant superheroes supposedly lived in a mansion in North Salem, New York, which is just a few miles from my hometown. And their mansion had a training facility called the Danger Room.

Our training room at White Sands is a lot like the one in the comic books. It has an obstacle course with concrete barriers and electrified fences that we have to either bust through or vault over. Mounted on the walls are dozens of machine guns and flamethrowers that'll open fire on our robots if we don't move fast enough. At the far end of the room is a circular arena where two Pioneers can spar against each other. One-on-one combat is the best way to test the robots we build in Dad's lab. You can't really tell how good a new machine is until you see how it handles in an actual fight.

I'm not in the mood to do any brawling today, but I wouldn't mind hanging out with the other Pioneers, and the Danger Room is usually a good place to look for them. And I'm not disappointed. When I stride into the room, I see Zia Allawi and DeShawn Johnson on opposite sides of the arena, standing about forty feet apart. Zia's in her Warbot, as usual. She spends practically all her time in that machine, even though it's way too big for most of the rooms at Headquarters and she's always banging into the walls and door frames. But DeShawn's occupying a new robot, a strange-looking contraption I've never seen before. It's a big steel box, about three feet across, that resembles an oversize Rubik's Cube. Etched into each square face of the box are crisscrossing horizontal and vertical lines that divide the yard-wide square into a grid of hundreds of inch-wide squares.

Because the robot has neither arms nor legs nor a head, it's tough to figure out what it can do. At first I think it's a joke. It would be just like DeShawn to build a gigantic and absurdly complicated Rubik's Cube. He has an odd sense of humor. Before he became a Pioneer, he was the class clown at Detroit Technical High School, and this steel box looks like the ultimate nerdy prank. But all the inch-wide squares are the same grayish color, with none of the multicolored patterns you'd see in an actual Rubik's Cube, so how could you play with the thing?

Curious, I probe the box with my Quarter-bot's sensors. It's packed with all kinds of miniaturized hardware. Every square is studded with microscopic antennas and cameras. I shake my mechanical head as I stare at the thing. *What the heck is DeShawn up to?*

Zia seems just as baffled. She points her own sensor array at the strange machine. "*This* is what you wanted to show me? A box?"

"Yeah, this is it." DeShawn's voice booms out of hundreds of tiny loudspeakers embedded in the robot's square sides. "This is the machine that's gonna kick your War-bot's butt."

"Right. Don't make me laugh." Zia waves one of her robotic arms in a dismissive gesture. Then she turns toward my Quarter-bot. "You believe this, Armstrong?"

I wonder if Zia has even noticed all the high-tech equipment jammed into DeShawn's machine. She can be a little oblivious sometimes. She has a blunt, no-nonsense personality, which is usually a good thing, but sometimes she misses the details.

I shrug, lifting the joints that connect my Quarter-bot's arms to my torso. "I wouldn't underestimate DeShawn. He's smarter than he looks."

A derisive snort comes out of Zia's voice synthesizer. But then she turns back to the steel box and trains her sensors on it again, taking a closer look. She's blunt, but she isn't stupid. "Are you hiding a bomb inside that crate of yours, DeShawn?"

"Nah, that wouldn't be too smart. Any bomb that's powerful enough to cut through your armor would destroy my circuits too."

"What about guns? You got some heavy artillery that's gonna pop out of your jack-in-the-box?"

"Look, I'm not giving away my secrets for free. Let's start the match, and then you'll see what I got. You're not scared, are you?"

DeShawn's strategy is so obvious. He's trying to goad Zia into doing something dumb. And Zia probably sees through it just like I do. If she were strictly following the conclusions of her logic circuits, she'd turn down DeShawn's challenge. But Pioneers have emotions too, and sometimes they overrule our logic. We can think a lot faster than people, but that doesn't mean we always think better.

Zia lets out another synthesized snort. "Scared? Are you kidding? If I were scared, would I do this?"

She charges across the arena, moving so fast I wouldn't be able to see her if I didn't have a high-speed camera. She leaps toward DeShawn's machine, and at the same time she raises one of her massive arms and curls her mechanical hand into a steel fist, like the head of a sledgehammer. She sweeps her arm down and plunges her fist into the top of DeShawn's box.

The result is predictable: the box disintegrates. But the disintegration occurs a millisecond *before* Zia's fist slams into it. In the instant before contact, all of the box's inch-wide pieces separate from one another and zoom away at high speed, propelled by tiny rotors and propellers attached to the corners of each small gray cube. By the time Zia's fist smashes into the concrete floor, the forty thousand miniature parts of DeShawn's machine are hovering above the War-bot like a swarm of angry wasps.

I focus my camera on the swirling pieces. Although each cube is smaller than a matchbox, it's big enough to hold miniaturized batteries and antennas. The batteries supply power to the rotors to keep the pieces aloft, and the antennas exchange radio signals that coordinate the swarm, enabling the thousands of parts to move as one.

Each cube also contains a small module of neuromorphic electronics. DeShawn's intelligence is spread among all the modules, and his thoughts control and manipulate the swarm. It's an amazing feat of invention, so incredibly advanced that my circuits hum with jealousy. I thought I was pretty good at designing new types of Pioneer robots, but DeShawn puts me to shame.

Zia tilts her War-bot's torso backward so she can point her sensor array at the swarm overhead. She swipes her robotic arms at the hovering cloud, but DeShawn sees the mechanical limbs coming— each cube has several miniaturized cameras—and deftly maneuvers his pieces out of the way. The swarm bobs and lurches and changes shape, always dodging the War-bot's arms. After flailing at the cubes for a while, Zia starts to get frustrated. She windmills her arms as fast as she can, but she can't grab or knock down any of DeShawn's pieces.

"HEY!" Zia roars. "THAT'S NOT FAIR!"

"Why not?" DeShawn's voice comes from miniature loudspeakers embedded in the cubes, so there's a weird, buzzing quality to the sound. "Which rule am I breaking?"

"You're not fighting! You're just jumping around!"

"Oh, you want me to attack? Is that it?"

"Stop playing with me! Why do you think we're here?"

In response, the swarm descends upon her. The thousands of cubes latch onto her War-bot, covering almost every square inch of its armor. It looks like the robot has suddenly grown a second layer of gray, knobby, leprous skin. After a few milliseconds of surprise, Zia starts slapping her steel hands against her torso, trying to sweep the cubes off her War-bot. She crushes dozens of the modules, but the rest are already penetrating her armor. Thin tendrils of brown smoke rise from the contact points on the War-bot's arms, legs, and torso.

My sensor array includes a spectrometer that can analyze the light from any object to determine its chemical composition. When I aim my instrument at the tendrils of smoke, I detect traces of iron chloride. *DeShawn, you freakin' genius! You used hydrochloric acid!* Somehow he engineered the cubes to safely hold the acid until needed. Once the modules attached to Zia, they released the acid to burn holes into her War-bot's armor.

Within a few seconds Zia's motions become erratic. Her left arm jerks downward, then hangs limply from her shoulder joint. One of the cubes must've burned a deep hole and melted a wire near the joint. After a few more seconds the same thing happens to her right arm. Zia sways on her pile-driver legs as the swarm continues to chew through her armor. Moments later her right leg buckles and the War-bot crashes to the floor.

"YOU CHEATED!" The words boom from her paralyzed robot. At least Zia's voice synthesizer seems to have escaped damage. "THAT SHOULDN'T HAVE HAPPENED!"

"But it did." DeShawn halts his attack, sparing the rest of Zia's circuits. His cubes detach from the War-bot and hover above it. "I won fair and square."

"I smashed at least a hundred of your stupid pieces when I tried to brush them off! How could you keep attacking after you lost so many?"

"I built some redundancy into the system. The swarm can continue operating even if hundreds of the modules are destroyed." Most of DeShawn's cubes swirl through the air, but about a quarter of them still cling to the War-bot, clustered around the damaged sections of armor. "But watch this. The Swarm-bot can destroy stuff *and* fix it too."

Glassy filaments extend from the cubes attached to the War-bot and snake into the holes in Zia's armor. I focus my Quarter-bot's cameras on the filaments. They're laced with minuscule sensors and motors. DeShawn has become a world-class master of nanotechnology, the science of building very small things. Each cube is full of even smaller machines, microscopic nanobots that can creep into the tightest crevices and manipulate objects as tiny as dust grains. The nanobots are repairing Zia's War-bot from the inside, reconnecting her melted wires and restoring her motor functions.

As I watch the modules in action, I feel another surge of envy. DeShawn's inventions are so brilliant that they'd make anyone jealous. But I also feel a burst of hope. We're incredibly lucky to have DeShawn on our team. With his smarts, we might actually have a chance against Sigma.

Zia's War-bot jerks and judders as DeShawn reconnects her wires. "Hey, be careful! Do you even know what you're doing?"

"Just try not to move, okay? Fixing things is harder than smashing them. This might take a few minutes."

I'm busy watching DeShawn repair the War-bot when I hear another synthesized voice behind me. It has an amused, gossipy tone and a British accent.

"How appalling. He's performing surgery on her with metallic leeches."

The snarky tone and British accent belong to Marshall Baxley. I turn to find him leaning against the wall. Marshall's robot is the same size as mine, but it's much more humanlike. Unlike me, he didn't have any qualms about designing a realistic face for his machine. He used flesh-colored plastic skin and dozens of motors to simulate human expressions.

All in all, he did a pretty good job. His robot is a little creepy, but not revolting. Marshall wanted to look like someone famous, and at first he planned to model the robot's face on either John F. Kennedy or Martin Luther King Jr., but after much thought, he decided that neither man was handsome enough. So in the end, he settled on Superman. The face of Marshall's robot looks just like the comic-book hero's: square and strong-jawed, with a molded cleft in its plastic chin, white fiberglass teeth, and perfectly coiffed hair woven from stainless-steel wires. But Marshall's personality is much more colorful than Superman's, so he gave his robot the lively voice of a Shakespearean actor. It's an odd combination, but it works.

"How long have you been watching them?" he asks me. "Have they been at it for hours, or is this just the first round?"

"They just started. DeShawn won the match in less than thirty seconds."

Marshall synthesizes a *tsk-tsk* and shakes his Super-bot's head. "Zia gets so indignant after she loses. She's going to make everyone around here miserable, especially yours truly." He steps away from the wall and moves closer to my Quarter-bot. The camera lenses within his eye sockets—disguised to look like human eyeballs with Superman-blue irises—focus on me, and he lowers the volume of his synthesized voice so that only I can pick it up. "I'll tell you a secret about Zia. She likes to talk tough, but she's really a big baby. Almost every day she takes me aside so we can talk in private. Honestly, she treats me as if I were her psychiatrist. I should start charging her by the hour. I really should."

I'm not surprised that Zia confides in Marshall. He's definitely the most sociable Pioneer. He's a good listener and an even better talker. And he loves to gossip, which I guess is a useful skill for a communications expert. Although there are only five of us, we have more than our fair share of secrets, and Marshall is very good at collecting them. The only Pioneer he doesn't enjoy talking about is himself.

He moves still closer, almost touching my Quarter-bot. "I'll tell you another secret. Zia is still totally obsessed with General Hawke. She's always going on about how smart he is and how no one in the

Pentagon or the White House is taking him seriously enough or even listening to his warnings about Sigma. You should hear her defend him, Adam. She gets so *passionate*."

Marshall activates one of his facial motors and raises a plastic eyebrow. He's trying to simulate a mocking expression, an insinuating grin. I feel a twinge of discomfort in my circuits. It seems wrong to spend so much effort building a face and then use it to make fun of someone. Better not to have a face at all.

"Look, Zia's right, and so is the general," I say. "A lot of people in government are stupid and shortsighted. They assume the Sigma crisis is over because they haven't seen any sign of the AI in six months. So we're lucky to have someone like Hawke on our side. He's not afraid to tell the President and Congress that they're wrong."

Marshall shakes his head again and twists his plastic lips into a frown. "Oh, I agree with you on that score. There's no doubt that Sigma's in charge of those North Korean factories. We may not have any proof yet, but I'm sure of it." He falls silent, still shaking his head.

Six months ago Sigma captured and tortured Marshall the same way it did me, forcing him to watch Jenny's deletion too. Now there's a look of agitation on his face, which probably means he's remembering the experience. After a couple of seconds, though, he grins again. "But that's not my point, Adam. My point is that Zia's feelings for the general are intensifying. She's moving beyond hero worship, if you know what I mean. The girl is in love."

Another twinge of discomfort runs through my electronics. It's not just Marshall's mocking grin that bothers me. It's the implication that Zia is acting like a fool, that it's completely ridiculous for a Pioneer to have romantic feelings for anyone, whether it's a human or another robot. I don't believe that, not for a nanosecond. If anything,

I have too many of those emotions roiling my circuits—feelings for Shannon, who's been avoiding me since we returned to New Mexico, and also for Jenny, who's gone forever.

And then there's Brittany, a friend from my old life in Yorktown Heights, my secret crush when I was human. She used to come to my house every weekend and practice her cheerleading routines in my living room while I watched from my wheelchair. Dad told me she's in New York City now, going to a special high school for runaway teens. She knows I'm still alive but has no idea what I've become.

I raise my right arm and point a steel finger at Marshall. I want to tell him how much I disagree with him. I want to make him feel the same discomfort I'm feeling. "You know what I think? I think you're the one who's obsessed."

"Really? How so?"

"You're jealous. You like Zia, and you're jealous of Hawke."

Marshall cocks his Super-bot's head and trains his cameras on me. He says nothing and his plastic face reverts to a blank stare. At first I think he's taking time to think of a good comeback, but as the seconds pass and the silence lengthens, I realize he's making a point. I've hurt him.

He finally synthesizes a long, theatrical sigh. "Ah, Adam. You've just proved you know nothing about me."

Now I feel terrible. I forgot how vulnerable Marshall is. Before he became a Pioneer, his life was a total nightmare. His sickness was worse than anything the rest of us had; while DeShawn and I wasted away from muscular dystrophy and Shannon and Zia fell victim to cancer, Marshall had to endure the agony of Proteus syndrome, the rare genetic illness better known as Elephant Man's disease. In the final years of his short life, his arms and legs swelled to enormous size and his head became studded with bony, hairless knobs. Horrified and ashamed, his mother hid Marshall in the basement of their house rather than let him go out in public. He spent most of his time reading poetry and occasionally sneaking upstairs to steal bottles from his mother's liquor cabinet.

For Marshall, the Pioneer Project was a chance to start over. It was more than just an escape from his deformed body—he thought he could erase his whole shameful past. That's why he put Superman's face on his robot instead of his former human face. But no matter how hard Marshall tries, his old life is still there, just beneath the plastic skin. The pain of it is embedded in his circuits.

I want to apologize, but I don't know what to say. A simple "I'm sorry" doesn't seem like enough. I devote more of my computing power to the problem, and after a hundredth of a second I come up with a good apology, a few words that might make Marshall feel a little better. But before I can send the sentence to my voice synthesizer, I hear rapid, clanging footsteps behind me. A bolt of joy and dread slices through my circuits. It's the commander of the Pioneers, Lieutenant Shannon Gibbs.

She has an official Army name for her robot—the Air-Land Unit with Reactive Armor, or ALURA—but I like to call it the Diamond Girl. Her machine is only six feet tall and doesn't have thick steel armor like my Quarter-bot or Marshall's Super-bot. Instead, her robot's skin is lined with a mesh of diamond chips and small explosive charges, each the size of a bottle cap.

Her armor is reactive, which means that when a high-speed missile or artillery shell approaches ALURA, the robot shoots one of its charges at the incoming projectile. The charge detonates on contact, destroying the missile before it can hit her. The great advantage of this system is that it's much lighter than ordinary armor, giving Shannon incredible speed and maneuverability. Her Diamond Girl can run across rough terrain at fifty miles per hour and accelerate to twice that speed for short distances.

The other advantage of her armor is that it's mind-blowingly beautiful. The diamond chips reflect and scatter all the light beams that strike her. Even in the drab Danger Room she's a dazzling sight, sparkling in all directions.

I stride toward her. Like me, Shannon decided against building a humanlike face for her robot, but she came up with a cool alternative: a virtual face that's displayed on a video screen at the front of her Diamond Girl's head. This face is modeled on Shannon's human face, which her parents recorded on hours and hours of home videos before she became a Pioneer. Shannon's software splices the video images to give the impression that her old face is speaking for her. As her voice comes out of her robot's synthesizer, the screen shows her human face mouthing the words. The software allows her to display emotions too. The face on the screen smiles when Shannon's happy, and it frowns when she isn't.

The Diamond Girl's head is turned toward Zia, who's still lying on the floor with a few hundred of DeShawn's modules clinging to her armor, completing their repairs. I step closer to Shannon to get her attention and notice that her video screen is turned off. Shannon has no face today. Her camera lenses pivot behind the blank screen, looking past me. "Zia!" she shouts. "What are you doing on the floor?"

In response, Zia's War-bot flexes its repaired arms and legs. Then it levers itself upright and stands on its footpads. "I didn't lose," Zia insists. "DeShawn cheated. He's an outrageous cheater."

The last of DeShawn's modules detach from Zia's armor and rejoin the hovering swarm. "That's the thanks I get for fixing you?" His voice buzzes above her, sounding amused. "Next time I won't bother. I'll just leave you lying there."

Shannon shakes her Diamond Girl's head. "All right, DeShawn, get yourself together. And I mean that literally."

"Yes, ma'am!" All the hovering cubes suddenly dive and converge at a spot about ten feet from Zia. The thousands of modules snap together, each piece finding its place. Within seconds the box is reconstructed, except for the few hundred missing pieces that Zia crushed.

I take another step toward Shannon and point at DeShawn's box. "Pretty amazing, right? He used hydrochloric acid to burn holes in Zia's armor. But I still can't figure out how he got the acid into the cubes without burning them too."

Shannon doesn't turn toward me. Her camera lenses stay fixed on Zia and DeShawn. "The insides of the cubes are lined with Teflon, which is acid-resistant. DeShawn gave me a briefing on the technology last week."

This clears up the mystery, but I'm disappointed. DeShawn and I usually share all our ideas as we work on them. I didn't know he was giving private briefings to Shannon. Yeah, she's our commander, so it makes sense for DeShawn to offer her the first look. But I still feel left out. "Well, it's ingenious, that's for sure. So are you going to challenge him next? Match your Diamond Girl against his Swarm-bot?"

Instead of answering, Shannon steps away from me. She completely ignores my question and strides across the arena. My dismay turns to shock. Shannon's supposed to be my girlfriend! How could she treat me like that?

She marches about ten feet forward, then turns around to face us. Although her screen remains blank, she strikes a commanding pose, folding her robotic arms across her Diamond Girl's torso. "Listen up, Pioneers. General Hawke is on his way down to the Danger Room. Can you please try to create at least a semblance of military order before he gets here?"

Reluctantly, we assemble in a line next to Shannon. When it comes to discipline, the Pioneers are probably the worst unit in the whole U.S. Army. The only one who takes the rules seriously is Zia, and that's because she comes from a military family. Marshall rolls his Super-bot's eyes as he takes his place in line. DeShawn's Swarm-bot doesn't budge from its spot on the floor, and its interlocked modules let out a low, rude buzz.

A moment later, General Hawke bursts into the room. He's breathing fast, his face is flushed, and there are dark patches of sweat on his desert-camouflage fatigues. But I'm not alarmed by his condition, because Hawke is one of those Army commanders who's always rushing down hallways and charging across parade grounds, stopping only to scowl at his men and bellow orders. He's a big man—six-foot-four and 251 pounds, according to my sensors—and though he's almost sixty years old, he's in great shape. His forearm muscles bulge under his rolled-up sleeves, and he has a full head of white hair above his ruddy face.

Shannon raises one of her sparkling arms in a salute and synthesizes a deafening "ATTTENNNNNN-SHUN!" Zia is quick to salute too, her War-bot snapping to attention. Marshall is deliberately slower, and so am I. DeShawn's robot can't salute at all because it has no arms, and I envy him for it. I have mixed feelings about the general.

Hawke turns his head slowly from left to right, inspecting each of us. He's doing his best to keep his face stern and unreadable, but my circuits analyze his expression to give me a sense of what he's thinking. Partly, he's proud of the Pioneers. He's led the project since Day One, when we were just a bunch of scared kids flailing around in steel bodies, and he can take a lot of credit for turning us into warriors. But he's also a little scared of us, though he'd never admit it. He knows we've grown so powerful that the Army can't really control us anymore.

Also? I think he's a bit jealous. The rules of biology make it impossible for anyone over the age of eighteen to become a Pioneer. Once you're past adolescence, the mind becomes too inflexible to be transferred to silicon circuits. But if Hawke could somehow break those rules, I'm pretty sure he'd make the transition himself. The general has no wife, no kids, and no strong ties to any of his fellow humans. And he loves power.

His gaze lingers on my Quarter-bot for an extra couple of seconds. I wonder if he's trying to read my mind the way I'm reading his. He clears his throat.

"Good morning, Pioneers. As you know, we're reviewing the data from our operation in North Korea, and I want to give you an update. We just finished examining the Snake-bots and found no traces of radiological, chemical, or microbial agents on their armor. It's still possible that the North Korean factories are manufacturing weapons of mass destruction, but we have no evidence yet. In particular, we saw no signs of the anthrax bacteria that we believe are in Sigma's possession. Needless to say, we're very concerned about what the AI may be doing with the microbes."

I'm concerned too. The anthrax was one of the loose ends from our first battle with Sigma. When the AI took over the nuclear missile base in Russia, it also acquired a huge supply of the lethal bacteria, which had been made even deadlier by the researchers at a Russian bioweapons lab. But after the Pioneers forced Sigma to flee the base and escape into the fiber-optic lines of the Internet, the anthrax was nowhere to be found.

Hawke believes the AI arranged for the germs to be shipped elsewhere so it could use them for future attacks. Anthrax is a perfect weapon for Sigma because it can kill billions of people without destroying their infrastructure—that is, all the supercomputers and factories and communications lines that the AI would like to inherit after it exterminates humanity.

Anxious, I shift the weight of my Quarter-bot from footpad to footpad. Marshall, I notice, is doing the same. But Hawke seems calm. He's breathing slower now and the sweat on his forehead is drying. "Our surveillance satellites continue to monitor the North Korean base, observing the soldiers as they repair the damage you all caused. But in the meantime, there's an important lesson you should all take away from this mission. Sigma could launch its next attack at any time, so we need to improve our readiness."

Hawke gestures at the arena and the obstacle course. "I'm glad to see that you're taking advantage of our training facilities. In addition, I've asked my superiors in the Pentagon for more funding, and they just gave me some good news. They've approved a budget increase that will allow us to strengthen our team."

That really *is* good news. Although Dad's laboratory is well-stocked with motors and sensors and neuromorphic circuits, it doesn't have all the equipment we need to build more advanced machines. DeShawn and I have talked about adding new kinds of weapons to our robots, but we've run into a problem: the most powerful weapons, such as fiber-optic lasers, are simply too heavy. We have to miniaturize the laser's power source, and that's going to take some serious work.

But maybe the additional money from the Pentagon will help speed things up.

I raise one of my Quarter-bot's hands. "Sir, will any of the funding go to the laboratory? We're trying to develop a new weapons technology, and we could really use some testing equipment."

Hawke narrows his eyes. He doesn't like it when I ask questions. "Unfortunately, we can't have everything, Armstrong. This funding has already been allocated to another effort, a project I've been working on for the past few months. My goal is to restore the Pioneers to their original number."

My circuits freeze for a millisecond, as if they just suffered a momentary loss of power. There were six of us when the Pioneer Project started. Then we lost Jenny. Hawke is talking about replacing her.

I raise my steel hand again. "Have you...have you found someone...someone who's..." I let the sentence trail off. I can't finish it. But Hawke nods. He knows what I'm asking.

"Her name is Amber Wilson. She's a seventeen-year-old from Tulsa, Oklahoma, dying of bone cancer. She's extremely intelligent and ferociously strong-willed. In other words, she's a perfect candidate for us."

The general reaches into the pocket of his fatigues and pulls out a photograph. I aim my sensors at the picture, and so does every other Pioneer in the room. It's a glossy black-and-white photo, the kind of portrait that a Hollywood actress would give away as a souvenir, and although the girl in this picture is as pretty as an actress, she looks painfully thin and absolutely miserable.

She's dressed like a goth girl in a low-cut black corset and a studded choke collar and a big, black fright wig with all the hair standing on end, as if she just stuck her finger in an electrical outlet. Her emaciated cheeks are powdered white, and her frowning lips are painted black. But one item of her outfit looks out of place: a silver chain with a pair of oblong tags, each imprinted with a name, a number, and a blood type. They're U.S. Army dog tags. I zoom in on them. The name on them is Captain Neil Wilson.

Zia notices the tags at the same time I do. She pivots her War-bot's head toward Hawke. "Sir! Is Amber related to a soldier?"

Hawke nods again. "Her father served under my command. He was a captain in the First Armored Division. Killed in action in Iraq in 2006." His voice is even but his eyes blink a little faster. It's a sign of emotion, very subtle, but my high-speed cameras catch it. "Amber was diagnosed with cancer two years ago. It went into remission after her first course of chemotherapy, but a few months ago it came back, much worse. And in the middle of her second round of treatment, her mother committed suicide."

He pauses while we take this in. The silence is thick and heavy. "I keep in touch with some of the families of fallen soldiers, so I heard what happened. I made contact with Amber and told her about the Pioneer Project."

Zia raises her right arm and snaps off another salute. Out of respect, I guess. "Sir, I volunteer to assist in training Ms. Wilson after she becomes a Pioneer. I would consider it an honor."

"That's a fine sentiment, Allawi, but you're a little premature. Right now we're focused on getting Amber ready for the procedure. We haven't created any new Pioneers in the past six months, so we have to make sure the brain scanner still works. As you may remember, it's an extremely complex and challenging procedure."

"Well, can I talk to her before the procedure, sir? She might be feeling nervous about it, and I can help reassure her."

Hawke pretends to think about it for a few seconds, but I know what he's going to say. The sight of Zia's War-bot is anything but reassuring.

"I appreciate your intentions," the general replies. "But it's not a good idea. Amber's in the final stage of her illness and her state of mind is fragile. She says she definitely wants to go through with the procedure, but she's made it clear that she doesn't want to talk about it."

Zia takes a step backward. I know she's disappointed. Her father also served in the Army under Hawke's command, and so she probably empathizes with the Wilson girl. But Zia has a hidden motive too, a secret that even Marshall doesn't know. I discovered it six months ago when Zia went on a rampage and I had to transfer myself to her circuits to stop her from obliterating my robot. As our thoughts came together, I viewed all of her memories, every incident and emotion she'd felt since she was a toddler, and in the process I learned that Zia was obsessed about Hawke's connection with her parents.

Both her father and mother died in Iraq, under mysterious circumstances, when Zia was just five. She suffered a lot in the following years, first in foster homes and then in juvenile detention centers, and even though that part of her life is long over, she still wants to know why both her parents were in Iraq and exactly what killed them. And because Amber has her own connection to Hawke, I bet Zia wants to ask her a few questions about the general.

Hawke turns away from Zia and eyes the rest of us. He's still holding the photograph of Amber for us to see. "I'm sure all of you understand what Ms. Wilson is going through, because you all experienced it yourselves. So let's give her a little space, okay? With any luck, she'll get through the procedure all right and quickly adjust. I'll let you know when I think she's ready to join the team."

No one responds to this. Hawke is right—we all know how hard this must be for Amber—and yet his decision to isolate the girl seems wrong. He's not doing her any favors by preventing us from visiting her. He should encourage Amber to see what her future looks like, to witness what she's going to become.

The general slips the photo back into his fatigues, but I've already memorized it. In my circuits I examine the image of the goth girl from Tulsa, so frail and unhappy. I can picture her in one of the hospital beds on the top floor of our headquarters, where the brain-scanning equipment is kept. I imagine her taking off her fright wig and running her skeletal hands over her bare scalp.

Then a new thought arcs across my electronics, and the image in my memory files undergoes a transformation. The goth girl disappears and is replaced by another dying seventeen-year-old, a girl who was just as painfully thin as Amber but wore cashmere sweaters instead of black corsets and choke collars. It's an image of Jenny Harris, a memory of the first time we met, before we were both turned into Pioneers. Amber reminds me of her, because Jenny was fragile too. The thought of living inside a machine terrified her. She was sick and scared and horribly confused.

I shake my Quarter-bot's head to make the image go away. This isn't the first time that memories of Jenny have overwhelmed my circuits. It happens to me at least once a week, ever since she died. That's one of the big disadvantages of having an electronic mind—your memories never fade. It never gets any easier.

Hawke notices my movement and stares at me, furrowing his brow. Shannon also stares, pointing her camera lenses at me for the first time since she came into the Danger Room. But neither Hawke nor Shannon makes any comment. The general clears his throat again.

"I have just one more thing to say, Pioneers. There won't be any easy victories in the war that's about to start. Sigma is building up its army and preparing for a long siege against us. And when the attack comes, it'll be fierce and unrelenting. But if you stay strong and united, I know you'll prevail. I have faith in you."

Hawke is an old-fashioned military man who believes in the power of inspirational speeches, even when they're addressed to eight-hundred-pound robots. He looks at each of us in turn, apparently trying to gauge the impact of his words. Then he bellows, "Carry on, Pioneers," and marches out of the room.

Shannon follows him, striding close behind. Zia salutes for a third time as they leave, and Marshall lets out a synthesized groan.

I wait exactly nine seconds. Then I also leave the Danger Room. Hawke and Shannon are out of sight by the time I reach the corridor, but my acoustic sensor picks up the sound of the Diamond Girl's footsteps.

I stride down the corridor, following the sound.

CHAPTER

I KNOW SHANNON'S SCHEDULE. EVERY MORNING AT TEN O'CLOCK SHE GOES TO HER room on the third floor of the White Sands headquarters to recharge her batteries. It's a quick, simple operation. You just stand beside the charging station in your room and plug the power cord into the port on your robot's torso.

Recharging is how we get our energy, but it isn't as enjoyable as eating. We feel neither pleasure nor pain when topping off our batteries. Yet all five of us have come to think of it as a very private act. No Pioneer would ever recharge in the presence of another. It would be just as rude and gross as one person watching another sit on a toilet.

The recharging process takes six minutes, and so at 10:06 a.m. I march down the corridor to Shannon's room, which is only twenty feet from mine. All the Pioneers have private rooms on the third floor. Besides recharging, we use the rooms for going into "sleep mode," which is when we shut down our sensors and most of our logic circuits. Sleep mode isn't essential for a Pioneer—you can go months without it—but I always feel better after napping for a couple of hours.

Our rooms are also where we store our personal belongings, but we don't have many of those. When Sigma destroyed our previous headquarters six months ago, we lost most of the mementos from our human lives. I used to have several Super Bowl posters and a Star Wars chess set and a whole shelf of comic books, but they're all gone now. And though I could ask Dad for new comic books and posters, I haven't gotten around to it yet. I guess I'm worried that the request might seem a little pathetic. Robots don't really need mementos. Our electronic brains have total recall.

I stop in front of the door to Shannon's room. Luckily, no other Pioneers are in the corridor. I wait until 10:07 a.m. to be sure that Shannon has finished recharging, and then I raise my Quarter-bot's right hand and clench the steel fingers into a fist to knock. But I hesitate, just standing there, afraid. I need to talk to Shannon, to find out why she's been acting so cold, but I'm also scared of what she's going to say. Shannon means a lot to me, and not just because she's my first and only girlfriend. Our relationship reminds me what it's like to be human. Sometimes I think it's the only thing keeping me from going completely crazy.

I'm still standing there when the door opens. Shannon's Diamond Girl stops in mid-stride, her sparkling hand clutching the doorknob. The video screen on her head is blank, but she's clearly surprised. Her camera lenses swivel, and for a millisecond it looks as if she might launch one of her explosive charges at me. But she recognizes my Quarter-bot, and her defensive systems stand down. "Adam? What are you doing here?"

I lower my hand. This isn't a good start. "Uh, hey. Can I come in for a minute?"

"I'm on my way to see DeShawn. To talk about his Swarm-bot."

Her voice is brisk, professional. There's no emotion in it. She's just making it clear she's in a hurry. Shannon knows very well that I'd love to participate in any discussion about new Pioneer technology, but she doesn't offer an invitation to join them. Instead, she takes a half step forward, suggesting in her gesture that I get out of her way.

But I *have* to talk to her. "It's important, Shannon. Please?"

She makes me wait another three seconds, which is an eternity for an electronic mind. Then, synthesizing a sigh, she steps backward and lets me into the room. "Make it quick, Adam."

I've visited Shannon's room dozens of times, so it's comfortably familiar. It's practically empty, just like my room—Pioneers don't need beds, chairs, or bureaus—but the walls are covered with photographs, mostly family snapshots. During previous visits Shannon told me the stories behind the photos and identified all the people in them: her father, mother, grandparents, cousins. They're posing at birthday parties, ball games, and barbecues. I recognize some of the locations because Shannon grew up in my hometown and we both went to Yorktown High School.

Her father is a short, round man with a gray mustache, always grinning for the camera; her mother is also short and plump, but she has long, black hair. There are photos of Shannon too, nearly all of them taken before she got sick. She's at a science fair, a track meet, a ballet class. She's a petite, dimpled, feisty girl, with her mother's black hair and her father's big smile.

My favorite picture, though, is the one that shows us together just before we became Pioneers. My father recruited Shannon to the Pioneer Project after he learned from her parents that she was dying, and we got to know each other pretty well in the days before we underwent the procedure. We had long, intense talks about illness and death and whether we'd still be the same people after we lost our human bodies. Shannon made me laugh and gave me the strength to go through with it.

In the photo of us—Dad took it with his iPhone—I'm slumped in my wheelchair, leaning against the straps. Shannon stands behind the chair, pale and almost bald, her lips bunched to one side of her face because her tumor is pressing against the nerves. But despite all the pain, she's still smiling. Her grin is lopsided but beautiful.

It occurs to me that Shannon doesn't need to hang any photos on her walls. I'm sure that all these images are stored in her circuits, where she can view them anytime, anywhere, just by retrieving the memories from her files. And yet she put the pictures on her walls anyway. I bet she stares at them every once in a while. It's a human impulse, and in many ways we're still human. That thought gives me courage.

I step closer to her. "I think you can guess why I'm here. We haven't been getting along so well lately."

Her Diamond Girl nods but doesn't say anything. I wish Shannon would turn on the robot's video screen. She usually programs it to show the human, healthy Shannon Gibbs, the way she looked before the cancer. Over the past few months we've had several long conversations here in her room, and during those talks I sometimes stared so intently at her video simulation that I almost forgot we were machines. But that was just an illusion. Now I see the reality: the blank screen, the faceless hardware. This is what we are.

I wait a few more seconds but she remains silent. I have to do all the talking. "I don't know what's wrong. Did I say something that upset you? I've gone over all the conversations we've had over the past two weeks, but I still can't figure it out."

"Really?" Her voice is quiet but full of disbelief. "Think about it a little more, Adam. You have lots of processing power in your circuits, so this shouldn't be beyond your abilities."

She's right. I have hundreds of trillions of logic gates, enough to perform billions of calculations in a millionth of a second. The only problem is that 99.9 percent of my circuits are useless now because they're flooded with the random noise of fear. The emotion chokes my electronics, blocking my thoughts. I feel tight and hot and constricted, which is the same way I used to feel in my pre-Pioneer life whenever I was afraid. I get this constricted sensation when I'm in combat too, but in those situations I don't need to think a lot, because it's usually pretty obvious what my next move should be. Now, though, nothing is obvious.

Still, I make an attempt. "Well, we don't agree about everything. You like Hawke more than I do, or at least you have a higher opinion of his methods. But we're allowed to disagree, right? That doesn't doom a relationship, does it?"

"Okay, that's the key word. *Relationship*." Shannon points a sparkling finger at my Quarter-bot and then at herself. "We've had conversations about that too, remember? About what we mean to each other and where we want to go?"

Now I'm starting to follow her thinking. Shannon and I have talked about sharing circuits. It's a logical step for two Pioneers who are drawing closer to each other. If I transfer myself to Shannon's neuromorphic control unit, I'll have access to all of her data and she'll have access to all of mine. I'll be able to see all of her memories and emotions, going back as far as she can remember. Everything will become visible, both the good and the bad, all the proud moments of love and kindness, and all the dark, secret humiliations. Shannon won't be able to hide anything from me, and I won't be able to hide anything from her. It would be a big step forward for us, exhilarating and intimate, but also terrifying.

I've shared circuits before, with Jenny and Zia, but not by choice. Those were crisis situations. I jumped into Jenny's circuits when she ran into trouble during her transition from human to Pioneer, and I leaped into Zia's because she was attacking me. A few weeks ago, Shannon asked me what it felt like to view someone else's memories, and I told her that it isn't a step to be taken lightly. The effects are irreversible. You can't *unknow* someone's secrets. Shannon was quiet for a few seconds after I said this, and then she said we should probably wait a while before we tried it. That seemed like a sensible decision at the time. Now I realize there was more to it.

"Uh, Shannon? Do you want to have that conversation again? About you and me sharing circuits?"

"No, I want to talk about something you forgot to mention before. About the second time you shared circuits with Jenny."

"What? I—"

"The first time was an emergency. I realize that. Jenny would've died if you hadn't gone into her control unit and helped her set up her memory files. But what about the second time?"

Fear chokes me again. My first impulse is to ask, "How did you find out there was a second time?" but I don't say it out loud.

The Diamond Girl steps closer to me, so we're almost touching. "Don't deny it, Adam. Jenny went to your room at the old headquarters and said she needed more help with her memory files. So you jumped into her control unit. Why didn't you tell me about that part?"

Her synthesized voice is quiet but furious. And I don't blame her. She has every right to be angry. I feel a sting of regret that cuts right through my wires. *I should've told her. Why didn't I tell her?* But I already know the answer: because I knew Shannon would be upset that I'd messed around with Jenny.

"I-I'm sorry."

"Jenny didn't really need help, did she? She just wanted to be close to you. And once you were sharing circuits, you saw what she really wanted. You could've transferred out of her control unit then, but instead you stayed. Isn't that how it happened?"

I wait a few milliseconds, still afraid to admit the truth. Then I nod my Quarter-bot's head. Jenny created a virtual-reality landscape within her circuits, a gorgeous digital simulation of the Virginia countryside where she grew up. When I jumped into her control unit, I entered the simulation. It felt entirely real: I could see rolling green hills on the horizon and hear the virtual birds chirping in the simulated trees. The VR landscape also included two human figures, a tall, blond girl and a short, dark-haired boy. They were simulations of Jenny and me, our lost human bodies.

I have no idea how Shannon could've learned about this. It happened just two days before our battle with Sigma. The AI deleted Jenny and all her memories before she would've had the chance to tell anyone about it. But Shannon somehow figured it out, and now I have to assume she knows everything: how the simulated Jenny lay on the virtual grass and asked if I wanted to kiss her. How her question literally electrified me, because I'd never kissed a girl before I became a Pioneer and never thought it would be possible afterward. And how the simulation allowed me to feel Jenny's lips against mine, and how wonderful the sensation was, even though it was only virtual.

"I'm sorry, Shannon," I whisper. "I'm so sorry." I don't know what else to say. "I shouldn't have done it."

She steps backward very abruptly, as if she's repelled by my words. "You're missing the point. You weren't my boyfriend back then. You had no obligation to me. Yes, I would've been jealous if you'd told me what happened between you and Jenny, but I would've gotten over it." She shakes her Diamond Girl's head. "But instead you hid it. You hid the truth for months and months. When we had that talk about sharing circuits, I asked you to tell me everything. But you lied, Adam. You lied by not mentioning it."

I have no defense. All I can do is continue to apologize. "You're right. It was a really stupid thing to do."

"It was worse than stupid. It makes me wonder about *everything* you've told me. What else have you lied about?"

"That's the only thing, I swear!" The volume of my voice synthesizer rises. "I haven't lied about anything else!"

My words echo against the walls of Shannon's room, but her Diamond Girl just stands there, unmoved. Her armor glitters in the silence.

Desperate, I stride toward her, extending my Quarter-bot's arms. "I can prove it to you! Jump into my circuits and you'll see! Everything else I've said is true!"

She takes another step backward, dodging me. "No, that's not going to happen. I don't want to share circuits with you now. And I don't want to be your girlfriend anymore."

I feel like I've just stepped on a land mine. Although the room is perfectly still and nothing is exploding under my footpads, I've just lost everything. A blast of grief hits me, jolting my circuits like a pressure wave.

"Shannon...no...please."

In response, she turns on the video screen in her robot's head. But it doesn't display the usual video of Shannon smiling and laughing. Instead, it shows her face as it looked after the cancer ravaged her. Her parents must've recorded video footage of her in the last few weeks of her human life, and now she's using those images to create this simulation on the screen. Half her face is paralyzed and her left eye is swollen shut. Her simulated lips droop diagonally as they mouth the words coming out of her robot's speakers.

"You hurt me, Adam. After my body died, I didn't think I could be hurt this way again. But you proved me wrong." On the video screen, her right eye is glistening. After a moment, a tear slips down her lop-sided face. "Please go. I need to talk to DeShawn. There's work to do."

I stare at the virtual tear on her cheek. When we were both human, I never saw Shannon cry. But even if I had, it couldn't be worse than this. Unable to stop myself, I raise one of my steel hands toward Shannon's screen. But I can't wipe away this kind of tear, no matter how much I want to.

I turn my Quarter-bot away from her and head for the door.

ꓔ ꓔ ꓔ

As I walk away from her room, I hear Marshall Baxley shout my name. His voice is loud and serious, with no trace of his usual gossipy tone. I turn around to see his Super-bot clanging down the hallway, its steel feet battering the floor. He's in a panic.

"Adam!" He stops in front of me, decelerating so suddenly that he sways on his footpads. "Did you hear the news?"

"What news?"

"There's been an outbreak, a biological attack!" Marshall's so upset, his plastic face is contorted. "They're airborne germs, carried by the wind. Thousands of people are dying!"

I extend my arms and grip the Super-bot's shoulder joints. "Whoa, calm down. What—"

"Hawke thinks it's anthrax. Sigma's anthrax."

My circuits ring like a fire alarm. This is it. The siege has begun. "Where's the outbreak?"

"In Yorktown Heights, New York. Your hometown."

I NEVER THOUGHT I'D SEE NEW YORK CITY AGAIN, BUT THERE IT IS BELOW ME, A narrow island packed with skyscrapers, all of them glowing in the late-afternoon light. I'm piloting a V-22 Osprey aircraft, my circuits wirelessly linked to the plane's controls. The other Pioneers are with me inside the aircraft, which is racing north at three hundred miles per hour.

We picked the V-22 for this mission because it's a tilt-rotor plane—it has a pair of gigantic three-bladed rotors that can be tilted in different directions depending on what you want the aircraft to do. When you want to take off, you tilt the rotors straight up, and the Osprey rises like a helicopter. But once you're in the air, you can tilt the rotors forward and they become supersized propellers that speed the plane to the battlefield.

Soaring over the Hudson River at maximum velocity, I zoom past Manhattan and the Bronx, then throttle down the turboprop engines and start to descend, heading for the suburbs north of the city. The handling is a little rough because the plane is hauling some heavy cargo. Our robots are loaded with all the weapons they can carry.

Actually, I'm occupying *two* machines right now, the V-22 and my Quarter-bot, which is standing inside the aircraft's cabin next to the other Pioneers. To perform this two-for-one trick, I copied all the memory files in my Quarter-bot and transferred the copies to the V-22's neuromorphic control unit. Then I set up a radio link between the two machines that allows them to exchange huge amounts of data, constantly sending signals back and forth.

Basically, my mind is stretched between the aircraft and the robot, and I'm looking at the world from two perspectives at once. The Osprey's sensors are showing me the suburban landscape of Westchester County below us, and at the same time I'm using the Quarter-bot's cameras to see my fellow Pioneers inside the plane's cabin.

There's a great advantage to this setup: if either the aircraft or the robot is blown to bits, my mind will survive in the other machine. The strategy has its limitations, though. You can't occupy two machines at once unless they're in close radio contact with each other. And you can't guarantee your survival by storing a backup copy of your memories in a safe place. Because human minds are so complex, they can be stored only in neuromorphic circuits that are active all the time. So if I copy my files to another machine without maintaining radio contact, I'll simply create a clone of Adam Armstrong that'll start thinking its own thoughts and making its own decisions. And I definitely don't want to do that.

After a couple of minutes, we fly over Tarrytown, cruising a thousand feet above the trees and houses. As I aim the V-22's sensors at the ground, I use my Quarter-bot's cameras to glance at Shannon, who's standing motionless near the plane's cockpit. Although I've been trying hard to control my feelings since we left New Mexico, I can't stop thinking about what she said. *You hurt me, Adam. You proved me wrong.* I can't stop picturing Shannon's human face on her Diamond Girl's screen, the tear sliding down her cheek. But I force myself to put the image back into my long-term memory. I can't let it interfere with the mission. Just like Shannon, I need to push all those feelings aside.

Five miles south of Yorktown Heights I see clusters of flashing blue lights on the roads. The local police have set up roadblocks on all the highways and streets leading to my hometown. South of the roadblocks, lines of vehicles and crowds of people are fleeing the evacuation zone, but to the north I see no movement at all. All the cars in Yorktown Heights are stopped on the streets, hundreds of them smashed into guardrails and trees, hundreds more tangled in ugly pileups at the intersections. And when I switch my sensors to the infrared range, I see human bodies everywhere, sprawled on the town's sidewalks and parking lots and driveways. I can measure the temperature of the bodies by how brightly they glow in infrared, and they're all far below 98.6 degrees. They've been cooling for hours.

It's horrifying. It's painful beyond belief. Sigma annihilated my hometown. It slaughtered everyone.

General Hawke had suspected that Sigma might go after the families of the Pioneers. To protect our relatives, the Army moved all of them months ago to secret safe houses in the western United States. But no one expected anything like this. I point my Quarterbot's cameras at Shannon, who grew up just a mile away from me and is probably even more horrified than I am. She was so active in school and church that she was friends with just about everyone in Yorktown Heights. Now those friends and neighbors lie motionless on the ground, some of them stretched on the lawns outside their homes, others curled and slumped on the street corners. The terrible images gouge into my circuits.

And the sight isn't just horrible—it's baffling. This biological attack doesn't make any sense. Although we don't know yet how Sigma spread the anthrax germs, I'm assuming the AI could've released them anywhere. So why did it choose Yorktown Heights? If Sigma had released the anthrax in New York City, just twenty-five miles to the south, it could've killed a lot more people. Millions would've died instead of thousands. So maybe Sigma's goal right now *isn't* killing as many people as it can. Maybe the AI has a completely different agenda.

I run the question through my logic circuits, contemplating all of Sigma's possible motivations, and I come up with a hypothesis. It's simple: the AI chose my hometown because it wants our attention. Sigma wants the Pioneers to come to Yorktown Heights. Which means we're probably flying into a trap.

We don't have a choice, though. The anthrax outbreak has overwhelmed the New York police and the National Guard. All the guardsmen and state troopers are busy organizing the evacuation of the surrounding towns—Katonah, Mount Kisco, Chappaqua—and no one seems to be searching for survivors in Yorktown Heights. The government authorities are just starting to organize rescue crews. And before they can send anyone into the contaminated area, they have to collect enough hazmat suits to protect the rescuers from the anthrax spores floating in the air.

But the germs can't infect Pioneers. We're the perfect team for this mission.

I fly the V-22 toward the shopping centers and churches in the middle of town, tilting the aircraft's rotors to vertical so it can hover like a helicopter. I'm still high enough that I can scan the landscape with the plane's sensors, observing every driveway and backyard. There's no sign of human life. I can't peer into the houses, of course, so it's possible that some survivors might be indoors. The only way we'll know for sure is to go down the streets and break into each home. And that'll take hours, even with all five Pioneers working as fast as possible.

Then I detect signs of movement at the edge of my scan, about a mile farther north. I steer the V-22 in that direction and increase the magnification of my sensors. Someone is stumbling across a parking lot, zigzagging between the rows of cars toward a large brick building. I'm familiar with this particular parking lot—when I was in ninth and tenth grades I used to maneuver my motorized wheelchair past it every day. It's right in front of Yorktown High School.

I descend to an altitude of three hundred feet and hover above the lot. The person stumbling toward the school is young and male, a short, dark-haired teenager wearing jeans and a yellow T-shirt. My circuits compare his face to the thousands of faces in my memory files, but there's no match. He's probably a freshman or sophomore, someone who started going to Yorktown High after my muscular dystrophy got worse and Dad pulled me out of school. The boy's face glistens with sweat as he looks up at our aircraft and its thundering rotors. According to my infrared sensors, his body temperature is over 104 degrees. He's ablaze with fever.

The V-22 is equipped with powerful loudspeakers. I connect my voice-synthesis software to them. "STAY WHERE YOU ARE. WE'RE COMING TO HELP YOU."

The boy doesn't seem to understand. He stares blankly at the plane, then shakes his head and continues lurching toward the high school. In a few seconds he reaches the front entrance and staggers through an open doorway.

Because I'm sharing the video feed from the V-22's cameras with the other Pioneers, they see the boy too. Shannon strides toward the cockpit window and points at the doorway where the kid disappeared. "I know him. That's Tim Rodriguez. He's a sophomore."

I'm not surprised that Shannon recognizes him. She did everything at Yorktown High—debate team, glee club, student government— and knew everyone's name. I use the V-22's sensors to survey the lawn beside the high school, looking for a landing spot. At the same time, I turn my Quarter-bot to Shannon. "Should I set the aircraft down? So we can go after him?"

"Affirmative." Her synthesized voice is crisp and professional, and the screen on her robot's head is turned off. I can't read her emotions.

Twenty seconds later, I land the V-22 and lower the loading ramp at the back of the plane. Zia's War-bot is the first Pioneer to charge outside, her footpads pounding the lawn. She'll go with Shannon and me into the high school, just in case we run into any trouble. I pull the copies of my memory files out of the V-22 and hand over the aircraft to Marshall and his Super-bot. He's going to stay with the plane and maintain our radio link with General Hawke. The general is overseeing the mission from Joint Base McGuire in New Jersey, which is the nearest military base with a biohazard treatment center that can handle anthrax cases. Once we track down the Rodriguez kid, we'll bring him back to the V-22 and airlift him to the treatment center.

While Marshall copies his own files and stretches his mind to occupy the aircraft's controls, I march my Quarter-bot down the loading ramp and onto the grass. I train my cameras on the parking lot but see no one else outside the high school. Then my acoustic sensors pick up a high-pitched whirring behind me. DeShawn has attached his Swarm-bot to the bottom of his quadcopter, which revs up its four rotors and takes off from the loading ramp. He's going to hover above our landing zone and watch over the area. In particular, he'll keep a lookout for long-range missiles. Sigma has used them against us before.

Shannon is the last Pioneer to come down the ramp. Her Diamond Girl strides across the lawn and catches up to Zia. "Let Adam and me take the lead," she orders. "We know this place. And if Sigma tries to surprise us, it'll probably attack us from behind, so that's where I want you."

I can't help but admire Shannon's tact. She doesn't mention the main reason for keeping Zia in the rear: because her nine-foot-tall War-bot is the scariest-looking Pioneer, so big and menacing it'll probably terrify any survivors we find. The Diamond Girl and the Quarter-bot are intimidating too, but at least we're closer to human size.

Zia raises her massive right arm and salutes. "Heard and understood. If Sigma shows up, I'll make him sorry." She stands at attention until Shannon and I stride past her, and then she follows us into the high school.

I haven't seen the inside of Yorktown High since I finished tenth grade, almost a year and a half ago, but the building hasn't changed a bit. Just past the doors is the glass-fronted cabinet that holds the school's football and baseball trophies. On the opposite wall is the Yorkie Notice Board, thickly papered with announcements about class schedules and cheerleader tryouts. Above the notice board is the school's motto, spelled out in big red, white, and blue letters: *DESTINY IS NOT A MATTER OF CHANCE. IT IS A MATTER OF CHOICE.* On the ceiling is the same fluorescent lighting I remember from my two years in this place, and on the floor is the same ugly, beige linoleum. The only difference, really, is the corpses.

The body of an overweight, middle-aged man is near the notice board, lying on his back in a rumpled brown suit. I recognize him in an instant—it's Principal Wilkens. His thick, black glasses have slid off his face, and his eyes are wide open and unblinking. Ed McGrath, the football coach, lies a few feet away. His face, always so red and scowling at the Friday-night games on the Yorktown field, is pale and motionless now, drained of anger and everything else. Mr. Kramer, the school's chemistry teacher, is sprawled near the trophy cabinet, and farther down the hallway is Ms. Lynch of the English department. Ms. Garcia, the Spanish teacher, lies beside Ms. Carlson, the school nurse, and Mr. Brown, the security guard.

I knew all these people. I passed by them in the halls every day. And because I was the kid in the motorized wheelchair, the kid who was dying, they always gave me a special nod or smile, usually because they felt sorry for me and thought I needed some cheering up. They fully expected to outlive me, and I assumed the same. That's why it's so disorienting to see their corpses. These people, this school, this town—it was all supposed to keep going after I died. But now they're all gone, and it feels like I've lost something irreplaceable, something even more precious than my human body.

Shannon halts her Diamond Girl beside Principal Wilkens, the man who handed her so many awards and commendations at so many school banquets and assemblies. I can't be sure what's going through her circuits now, but I bet she feels even worse than I do. She leans her robot over the principal's body and stretches one of her glittering hands to pick up his glasses. Gently, she slips them back on the dead man's face. Then she straightens and turns toward Zia and me. "We need to find the Rodriguez kid. Let's head for the auditorium."

She proceeds down the hallway, carefully stepping over the bodies. I follow her, and Zia brings up the rear, stooping over so that her War-bot's bulbous head doesn't bang into the ceiling.

We pass more corpses, all of them teachers: Ms. Cohen, Ms. Braun, Mr. Standish, Mr. Weinstein. It looks like they had just enough time to step out of their classrooms before they collapsed. Their shirts and blouses are still damp, which makes sense. Excessive sweating is one of the symptoms of anthrax inhalation, at least according to the medical database I downloaded into my circuits before we left New Mexico. But there are other details that *don't* make sense. I need to talk to Shannon about it.

I speed up a bit to get her attention. "We should stop and take samples. Blood, saliva, skin cells. I'll do it if you don't want to."

She shakes her Diamond Girl's head. "Our top priority is find-ing survivors."

"Shannon, something is seriously weird here. After a person inhales anthrax spores, it usually takes at least twenty-four hours for symp-toms to develop. But it looks like these victims died within minutes."

"This isn't ordinary anthrax. The germs were modified in the Russian bioweapons lab before Sigma stole them." Her voice has that cold, dismissive tone I've come to hate. "The Russians altered the genes of the bacteria to make them deadlier. It isn't weird. It's what we expected."

I sweep my Quarter-bot's right arm, gesturing at all the bodies in the hallway. "Okay…well, how come we haven't seen any dead kids yet? All these corpses are adults, every single one. What kind of genetic alteration could make the anthrax do that, pick and choose its victims?"

"The Rodriguez kid was sick too. Maybe teenagers resist the germ better. Maybe it makes them sick, but it doesn't kill them right away."

She shakes her head again. "Look, let's just find him, all right? Then you can take as many samples as you want."

It hurts to hear her snap at me like this. Shannon's voice is so disdainful, so cold. But I won't let my emotions interfere with our mission. The pain I'm feeling is just a useless signal in my electronics. I'm going to shunt it aside so it won't distract me.

A moment later, we reach the school auditorium and Shannon flings open the doors. All the rows of seats are empty, but Mr. Burroughs, the school's band conductor, is sprawled on the stage. His slender, dark-skinned body lies facedown next to his music stand. A semicircle of chairs is also onstage, and all of the band's instruments—the trumpets, saxophones, clarinets, cymbals—are scattered across the floor. But there's no sign of the rest of the band. It looks like they were in the middle of a rehearsal when Mr. Burroughs collapsed, and the students fled in terror. *But where did they go?*

Shannon turns without a word and marches down another hallway.

I follow her, about fifteen feet behind. Zia catches up to me and bends over to bring her loudspeakers close to my head. "Yo, Armstrong." Her voice is a whisper, barely loud enough to be picked up by my acoustic sensors. "Shannon's upset. Can't you tell how upset she is?"

"She was friends with some of the teachers," I whisper back. "She got to know them pretty well because she was in a lot of after-school clubs and stuff."

"Well, why aren't you helping her? Go to her and say something. It might make her feel better."

The other Pioneers still think Shannon and I are a couple, so this is a perfectly logical suggestion. Nevertheless, I'm stunned that it came from Zia. She's not a touchy-feely person. In fact, she has the bluntest, roughest, most indelicate personality I've ever known. I'm amazed that she's giving me advice on how to be a better boyfriend. It's just a shame I can't act on it.

"Shannon and I broke up. I'm the last person she wants to talk to now."

Zia has no plastic face or video screen on her War-bot's head, but I can tell she's furious. She clenches both of her huge steel hands into fists. "What did you do, Armstrong? Did you hurt her?"

The safe thing to do now would be to tell a lie. But I can't. "I didn't mean to hurt her. But yeah, I did."

Zia points her cameras at Shannon, who's still marching in front of us and stepping over the corpses in the hallway. Then her War-bot turns its lenses back to me. "Big mistake, Armstrong. Shannon's my friend, and *nobody* hurts my friends. When this mission is over, I'm gonna kick your butt. You hear me? I'm gonna peel you open like a tin can."

To make her intentions absolutely clear, Zia waves one of her massive fists at me. Then she slows her pace and drops back to the rear.

We turn left and stride down the long corridor that leads to the school's annex building, which is newer and even uglier than the main building. Halfway there, my acoustic sensor detects a distant scream. It's a cry of pain, brief and sharp. Shannon hears it too. She starts running toward the noise. I run after her, and Zia gallops behind me.

We turn left again, and now I can hear thumping sounds and a long, low groan. Just ahead are the doors to the high-school gym, which takes up most of the annex building. That's where the noises are coming from.

Shannon slams through the doors, and half a second later Zia and I follow her into the gym. It's a huge space, large enough to hold the crowds for the statewide basketball championships, and now it's jammed with kids, at least a thousand teens. Nearly all of them are dead. Their bodies are scattered across the basketball court and piled high on the bleachers. A wave of nausea runs through my electronics as I stare at them.

But a few kids are still alive. I do a quick infrared scan of the room and spot three survivors. One of them is Tim Rodriguez, the sophomore we saw outside the school. He's crawling on his hands and knees toward the center of the basketball court, in a relatively clear area where there aren't so many bodies. There's another survivor ten yards beyond him, a petite dark-haired girl who's groaning and writhing on the floor near the foul line. I don't recognize her either, but I can tell she's a freshman because she's wearing a Class of 2022 T-shirt.

I *do* recognize the third survivor though. His name is Jack Parker, and he's a big, brawny, redheaded senior, in the same class I would've been in if I hadn't gotten sick. I used to know Jack pretty well, actually. My mom and his mom were friends, and he lived just down the street from us. I never liked the guy, mostly because he used to make fun of me, whispering jokes to his friends on the football team whenever he saw me in my wheelchair. But now I can't help but feel sorry for him. He's curled up in a tight ball in front of the bleachers, his muscled arms wrapped around his bent knees. His face and hair are drenched with sweat, and his whole body is quivering.

Shannon runs toward Tim Rodriguez. "Zia, go to the girl and run a medical diagnostic! Adam, do the same for Jack!"

While Zia bounds across the basketball court, I head for the bleachers. I have to maneuver my Quarter-bot around the sprawled bodies to reach Parker. For this mission, we equipped our robots with plenty of medical sensors, and as I lean over Jack, I start to examine him, measuring his heart rate and blood oxygen levels. He's racked with fever and barely conscious. We need to get him to an emergency room as quickly as possible.

I bend over to slip my steel hands under Jack's body. He's the biggest defensive lineman on the Yorktown High team and weighs at least two hundred and fifty pounds, but I have no trouble lifting him. As I pick him up, he opens his eyes wide and gapes at my robotic head. Horrified, he raises his arms to defend himself, but his hands tremble so violently he can't control them. After a moment his eyes close and his body goes limp. My sensors show his blood pressure plummeting. He's going into shock.

Panic surges across my circuits. It doesn't matter that Jack Parker was one of my least favorite classmates—I *need* to save him. If he and the other kids die, *no one* will be left from Yorktown High.

I aim my cameras at Shannon. Her Diamond Girl is bent over Tim Rodriguez, who seems to have lost consciousness too. "Shannon! We're losing them!"

In response, she picks up the Rodriguez kid. Because he's small, she can lift him with just one of her glittering arms. "We'll take them to the V-22. Marshall can fly them to the Biohazard Treatment Center while we keep looking for survivors." She points her free hand at me. "Adam, give Jack to Zia. You have the best sensors, so you should do a…a thorough sweep. Someone else might be…"

Her synthesized voice trails off. Shannon can't bring herself to say it, but I know what she's asking for. Before we leave the high school and move on to the rest of the town, she wants me to scan the gym and look for any more survivors hidden among the dead.

Zia strides toward me, with the freshman girl already slung over her War-bot's right arm. She extends her other arm, and I drape Jack

Parker's unconscious body over the elbow joint. Then, while Zia and Shannon wait by the gym's doors, I turn toward the bleachers and adjust my cameras and microphones, increasing their sensitivity to the maximum. I look for any slight movement or sound coming from the piles of bodies. I also use my spectroscope to analyze the air above them. I'm searching for any excess of carbon dioxide, any hint of breath.

My sensors detect 1,049 bodies in all. My logic circuits attempt to catalog the dead, linking each motionless face with a name and an age, but the corpses are so tangled together I can't see most of their faces. Another wave of nausea runs through me. *And this is just the beginning*, I think. *Sigma's just getting started.*

Then my spectroscope detects a slight increase in carbon dioxide above a heap of bodies in the far corner of the gym. It's probably nothing, just a small random variation from the average, but I need to check it out. Reluctantly, I move closer.

I take another reading and detect an unmistakable spike in the carbon dioxide level. It doubles as I step toward the bodies, and doubles again when I point the sensor at the bottom of the pile. *Someone's breathing down there!*

Without any hesitation I pull the corpses off the top of the heap and uncover a feverish, unconscious girl who was hidden beneath them. She's slender and blond and wears frayed jeans and a black T-shirt. I recognize her instantly.

It's Brittany Taylor. I've known her since kindergarten, but she's much more than an old friend. She's the girl I used to dream about when I was still human.

For a thousandth of a second, I just stare at her. She's not supposed to be here. She ran away from home over a year ago and started living on the streets of New York City. Dad told me she's been staying at a youth shelter in Manhattan for the past six months. *So why is she here? Why did she come back to Yorktown Heights just in time for the anthrax outbreak?*

My circuits analyze a dozen possible explanations, but the answer is obvious. Sigma used Brittany once before. The AI captured and tortured her because it knew how much she meant to me. Now it's happening again.

"Brittany?" Her name sounds so strange coming out of my loudspeakers. "Can you hear me?"

No response. She's gone into shock, just like Jack Parker. She's dying.

I bend low and cradle her in my Quarter-bot's arms. She's so light, so incredibly light. Her pulse is rapid but weak, a barely perceptible quiver in her neck. Her head lolls against my elbow joint, and her long blond hair is draped over my steel armor. I scan her with all my medical sensors, but there's nothing I can do for her. *Wake up, Brittany! Open your eyes!*

Holding her against my torso, I run toward Shannon and Zia. "Let's go, let's go! This is the last one!"

Shannon trains her cameras on the unconscious girl in my arms. She knows all about my history with Brittany. I told Shannon about her in our very first conversation, before we even became Pioneers. Now Shannon's circuits are probably racing toward the same conclusion I just made: that Brittany's appearance here is no accident. But to her credit, Shannon simply nods her Diamond Girl's head and follows me out of the gym, still holding Tim Rodriguez in one of her glittering arms. Zia brings up the rear, carrying both Jack Parker and the freshman girl.

We charge down the long corridor, retracing our steps. Our footpads clang against the linoleum floor, and the noise echoes up and down the hallway. In less than fifteen seconds, we're back in the high school's lobby and almost out of the building.

Then my acoustic sensor picks up the sound of an explosion. A percussive *boom* erupts from outside the building and shatters the glass panels in the high school's front doors.

All three of us stop in our tracks. Through the shattered doors we see the V-22 in flames. A few yards in front of the burning aircraft, the ground has split into a gaping chasm, and extending upward from the muddy gap in the earth is an enormous steel tentacle, at least ten feet thick and a hundred feet tall. It looks like a hugely oversize version of the Snake-bot. It towers over Yorktown High, twisting and coiling in midair. Its silver skin glows in the evening light.

The tentacle's shiny tip turns downward. It points at the high school's broken doors, like the head of a giant cobra that's ready to strike. Then it hurtles toward us.

CHAPTER

6

WE HAVE JUST ENOUGH TIME TO TURN AROUND AND SHIELD THE STUDENTS WE'RE carrying. Then the huge Snake-bot smashes into the brickwork above the school's front doors, and the lobby's ceiling collapses.

Chunks of plaster and concrete rain down on us and bounce off our armor, but we're already running. We reverse course and charge down the school's main hallway, striding even faster than before, our robots hunched over the unconscious bodies in our arms. I aim my cameras for a second at Brittany, who's taking quick, shallow breaths, her blood pressure plunging. Her pale lips are twisted into a grimace, as if she somehow realizes how much danger we're in. Behind us, the roar of destruction grows louder, chasing us down the corridor. Sigma's giant Snake-bot is tearing the high school apart.

Suddenly, the hallway's linoleum rumbles under our footpads. A thick steel column shoots up from the floor in front of us, spraying dirt and tile in all directions. Another oversize Snake-bot, identical to the first, rams into the ceiling and triggers another collapse, filling the corridor with debris. Our escape route is blocked.

"I got this!" Shannon yells. She switches Tim Rodriguez's unconscious body to her right arm and uses her left to open the door to Room 107, the high school's chemistry lab. "Come on! This way!"

Zia and I barrel into the lab behind her, our robots smashing through the narrow doorway. Shannon dashes past the lab tables and heads for the windows on the other side of the room. Because the chemistry lab needs lots of ventilation, its windows stretch across the entire wall, with just a few slender mullions between the glass panes. Shannon points at the glass with her free hand. "Lead the way, Zia! Get us out of here!"

Holding Jack Parker and the freshman girl close to her torso, Zia bounds toward the windows. Her massive shoulder joint crashes through the mullions and glass, and the momentum of her leap carries her outside. Shannon and I follow her, jumping through the gaping hole her War-bot made. We land on the lawn beside the high school and start running across the grass.

Without breaking stride, I pivot my head to the left. The fuselage of the V-22 is broken into five burning pieces, and the gigantic rotors lie on the ground. I scan the wreckage for Marshall's Super-bot and look for DeShawn's quadcopter in the evening sky, but I don't see either of them. I send out a radio signal, transmitted in elaborate code so that Sigma can't decipher it: *Marshall? DeShawn? Where are you guys?* But no one answers.

I can tell that Shannon is also transmitting distress signals and getting the same nonresponse. The silence is alarming. Did the Snakebots damage Marshall and DeShawn? Or maybe capture them? The random noise of fear rises in my circuits again. I push it back down and keep running, angling toward the football field behind the high school. Although we can't rendezvous with the other Pioneers, we can try to save the unconscious students. And the best strategy for saving them is to put as much distance as possible between ourselves and Sigma's Snake-bots.

On the other side of the football field is Franklin D. Roosevelt State Park, which is hilly and heavily wooded. If we can get past the field and slip into the woods, we'd have a better chance of evading Sigma's machines. But just as we reach the football field's end zone, a third Snake-bot bursts from the ground at the fifty-yard line. It pushes tons of dirt and turf aside as it emerges from the center of the field, where the big Yorktown *Y* is painted on the grass. The steel tentacle rises a hundred feet above us and coils overhead, ready to strike.

At the same time, the other two Snake-bots stop pummeling the high school and slither toward the football field. Each is as big as a subway train, but they move in sinuous waves instead of a straight line, their motors bending and twisting their flexible armor. We're surrounded on all sides by enormous, powerful machines. There's nothing we can do except make a last stand.

"Adam! Zia!" Shannon's voice booms from her loudspeakers, still confident and unafraid. "Put the students on the ground and form a perimeter around them!"

Bending my Quarter-bot's torso, I set Brittany on the turf in the end zone, a few feet away from the three other unconscious kids. With a flick of my steel hand, I straighten her legs and arms, trying to make her as comfortable as possible. Then Shannon, Zia, and I form an equilateral triangle around the students, each of us facing one of the Snake-bots.

The next order from Shannon comes via radio, in an encoded signal that Sigma can't overhear: **Let's do some damage, Pioneers. Fire at will**.

I point my Quarter-bot's right arm at the tip of the Snake-bot that looms over the fifty-yard line. If it's anything like the smaller Snake-bots we designed in my dad's laboratory, its sensors will be concentrated at the tip. One well-placed shot could blind the machine.

My radar locks on to the target, and a motor inside my arm activates a compartment between my elbow joint and my steel hand. The compartment's lid swings open, revealing a black cylinder that I call the Needle. It's eighteen inches long and two inches in diameter. Inside its nose is a guidance system that's linked to my targeting radar, and at its tail is a solid-fuel rocket engine.

My circuits send the command: *Launch!* The Needle's engine ignites, and a plume of flame shoots out of the cylinder. The missile roars out of its launch tube and careens toward the Snake-bot.

The Needle accelerates to five hundred miles per hour, but my cameras are quick enough to track it. It rises a hundred feet in less than a quarter second, arcing over the football field. The Snake-bot flails in the opposite direction, trying to dodge the missile, but the huge machine isn't nimble enough. The Needle slams into the Snake-bot's shiny tip, and the missile's high-explosive warhead detonates.

Oh yeah! Payback time!

It looks like a fiery flower has bloomed on top of a giant metallic stalk. Smoke billows from the explosion, and bits of shrapnel ping against the bleachers on both sides of the football field. A moment later my acoustic sensor detects two more explosions, both closer to the high school. Turning my cameras in that direction, I see very similar blossoms of fire and smoke where the other two Snake-bots had been slithering toward us. Both missiles came from Zia, who's extending her War-bot's massive arms as if she's a robotic gunslinger and her rocket launchers are Colt 45 revolvers.

"YOU LIKE THAT, SIGMA?" Zia's voice is so loud that you could probably hear it in Connecticut. "YOU WANT SOME MORE?"

Shannon's Diamond Girl is too small to carry missiles, but she helps out by aiming her cameras at the Snake-bots we hit. She's trying to assess the damage and analyze how to press the attack. I focus my own cameras at the Snake-bot looming over the football field and watch the smoke from the explosion slowly dissipate and blow away. As it clears, though, I see that the tentacle isn't charred or mangled or gutted. Somehow the Snake-bot has sloughed off the parts that were damaged by my missile and reassembled its remaining machinery. The tentacle is several yards shorter than it was before, but it looks as good as new. And while I stare at the reconstructed thing in astonishment, the Snake-bot sweeps its shortened tip at me, lashing it like a whip.

Hundreds of tons of steel hurtle toward my Quarter-bot. Fear surges in my circuits—*I'm done for! I'm toast!*

Then my programmed instincts take over. The motors in my steel legs give me a tremendous boost, and I leap forward. I jump toward the thickest part of the Snake-bot, the section rising from the huge hole at the field's fifty-yard line. I hit the turf at the ten-yard line, landing on my torso, and then roll toward the twenty.

At the same time, the Snake-bot slams into the place where I'd been standing half a second ago. The tentacle gouges the turf, plunging several feet into the soil. The ground shakes like crazy, and the crash echoes across the field.

Somehow I manage to stand and glance back at the end zone. Zia has just fired three more missiles at the other Snake-bots, but they're still advancing. Shannon is racing toward the woods, trying to lure at least one of Sigma's machines away from the football field, but she's not having any luck either. Worst of all, Brittany and the other kids lie defenseless on the turf, their unconscious bodies quivering as the ground rumbles underneath them. *We can't protect them! They're going to die, just like all the others!*

Then my acoustic sensor picks up a familiar whirring noise. DeShawn's quadcopter comes zooming over the treetops on the other side of the football field. His Swarm-bot is still attached to the aircraft, and he's flying it straight toward the tentacle that almost squashed me.

Sorry for the delay, folks. DeShawn's radio signal is loud and clear. **I was waiting for the right moment, you know?**

Shannon changes course and starts running back to the field. **Where's Marshall? Have you—**

He's a mile to the west, trying to radio Hawke and get us a ride out of here. But it looks like we gotta deal with these supersized Snake-bots first.

Affirmative, Shannon responds. **Our top priority is rescuing the survivors, so target the Snake-bot that's closest—**

I know, the goliath on the football field. Just hold off the two others for a minute, okay?

The Snake-bot on the field wrenches itself out of the deep gouge it made. Instead of trying to whack me again, the tentacle straightens and sweeps upward, aiming to swat the quadcopter. But in midair DeShawn activates his Swarm-bot. The metallic box disperses into forty thousand hovering steel-gray modules, each about the size of an ice cube.

DeShawn's swarm looks even more impressive now than it did in the Danger Room. The modules form a grayish cloud, more than thirty feet across, that undulates above the Snake-bot. I keep one of my cameras focused on the swarm as I run back to the end zone to help Shannon and Zia. A great swell of hope refreshes my circuits. *We have a chance now! With DeShawn on our side, we definitely have a chance!*

The Snake-bot attacks the swarm, but the tiny gray cubes dodge the tentacle, deftly swirling around it. The Snake-bot changes direction and lashes at the swarm again with a swift, fierce swipe, but again the hovering cubes dart out of its path. Then, as the tentacle slows to change direction once more, the swarm converges on it, all the thousands of cubes simultaneously latching to the Snake-bot's silvery tip.

It looks like DeShawn has pulled a gray cap over the tentacle, blinding it...and enraging it. The Snake-bot thrashes back and forth, trying to shake off the swarm, but each cube is tightly fastened to the tentacle. A moment later wisps of brown smoke rise from the contact points on the Snake-bot's tip. DeShawn is using hydrochloric acid to penetrate its armor! It's the same strategy that defeated Zia in the Danger Room, and it seems to be working against Sigma's machine.

Then a loud, high-pitched *crack* reverberates in my audio sensors. The whole hundred-foot-long tentacle shudders. In a thousandth of a second, the Snake-bot disintegrates into a thick cloud of silvery shrapnel. The debris hovers in the air like the plume from an atomic bomb.

I can't believe it. I radio a message to DeShawn: *Whoa! What the heck did you do to that thing?*

But DeShawn doesn't reply, and when I take a closer look at the shrapnel, my fear resurges. The debris from the Snake-bot isn't falling to the ground. It *isn't* shrapnel at all. The metallic fragments are actually small, interlocking modules, each with its own rotors to keep it aloft.

They're just like the cubes in DeShawn's swarm. That explains how the Snake-bot was able to repair itself after I hit it with my missile— the silver modules detached from one another during the explosion and then came back together in a new configuration. But now the entire Snake-bot has transformed into a swarm that's a thousand times bigger than DeShawn's. Sigma's huge silvery cloud billows over the football field and engulfs DeShawn's small grayish cloud. A millisecond later, I lose radio contact with him.

DeShawn! DESHAWN! Get out of there!

I frantically try different frequencies to regain contact. Then I hear a second high-pitched *crack*, then a third. I turn my Quarter-bot just in time to see the two other Snake-bots transform themselves into swarms. They're closer to the ground than the first swarm, so they look like silver fogbanks as they rush toward us.

I run to position myself between the unconscious students and Sigma's approaching swarms. But the modules aren't interested in the living, breathing humans. They converge on the Pioneers instead. Although each module is only an inch across, Sigma has millions of them, hundreds of millions. They descend on us like mechanical locusts.

Zia fires her last missile into the silvery fog, but the explosion merely buffets the modules instead of destroying them. Shannon runs headlong into the other swarm and starts firing the small explosive charges embedded in her Diamond Girl's armor. Because Shannon designed these charges as a defense against incoming bullets and missiles, they're fast enough to intercept the darting modules, but she has only ninety of them. She runs out of ammunition in less than ten seconds. Then hundreds of silver cubes latch on to her robot.

"*SHANNON!*" I scream, charging toward her. But before I can get close, the modules blanket my Quarter-bot. I slap my steel hands against my torso and scrape off some of the cubes, but hundreds more fasten themselves to my armor, so many that I can barely lift my arms.

A moment later I feel a thump under my footpads. Zia has thrown herself to the ground. She's rolling around on the turf, trying to crush the modules with the weight of her War-bot. But the silver cubes keep latching on to her, until I can't see her War-bot under the swarming mass. A few yards away, the modules bury Shannon. Wisps of brown smoke rise from the cubes piled on top of her.

I have hundreds of pounds of modules clinging to my Quarter-bot, so it's a struggle just to stay upright. But I send all my power to the motors in my legs and take a step forward, lumbering toward Shannon. At the same time, I open a short-range radio channel and send her a message: *Don't give up! I'm coming to you!*

The modules cover the lenses of my cameras, and I can't see a thing. Sigma's cubes are also interfering with my radio signals, so I'm not sure if Shannon got my message. But I struggle to listen, and after a moment, my antenna picks up a few words of her reply, nearly drowned out by static: **A trap... I should've... The swarms... How did Sigma get...**

The weight of the modules simply becomes too much. I lose my balance, and my Quarter-bot topples backward.

Once I'm lying on my back, the cubes really start to pour down on me. I can't move my arms or legs or even turn my head. The tactile sensors in the front of my torso measure an incredible increase in downward pressure, and I also detect vibrations all over my Quarter-bot. The modules are penetrating my armor. They're injecting hydrochloric acid into my steel skin, just like DeShawn's modules did to the Snake-bot.

Frustration surges through my circuits. Our own inventions defeated us. Sigma built Snake-bots and Swarm-bots that were bigger and better than ours. And that raises a truly bewildering question, the same question Shannon was apparently trying to ask in her last radio message: *How did Sigma get our technologies? How did the AI learn to make Snake-bots and Swarm-bots in the first place?* We Pioneers developed those machines on our own and never put the designs on the Internet or shared them with anyone. Yet Sigma somehow stole our ideas. *How the heck did that happen?*

As if in response, I get another radio signal on the short-range channel I set up to communicate with Shannon. There's no interference now, despite the fact that I'm surrounded by machinery. For a second, I'm confused. Then I realize that the signal isn't coming from Shannon. It's coming from the silver swarm.

My name is Sigma. It's good to see you again, Adam.

I'M PANICKING. THE MESSAGE FROM SIGMA FEELS LIKE AN ELECTRICAL SHOCK. IT'S so violent that it makes my microchips shiver.

Don't worry, Adam, I'm not reading your thoughts. Not yet, at least.

I focus all my processing power on controlling my fear. I've tried to prepare myself for this moment. I've installed software firewalls to protect my memory files from Sigma. The only problem is, I have no idea if they'll work. The AI used radio signals to disrupt Shannon's memory when we were in North Korea, and now it's attempting to do the same thing to me. Sigma's signals are coursing into my antennas and battering my electronics.

Please listen carefully, and I'll explain what will happen next. Exactly eight hundred and fifty-nine of my modules are drilling holes into the outer casing of your hardware. They'll need another forty-eight seconds to penetrate your armor and extend wires to your neuromorphic circuits. After I connect my wires to yours, I'll

take full control of your files and transfer them to my own hardware, so I can evaluate your programming. But until then, we can have a nice little chat.

My panic intensifies. Sigma sounds different than it did six months ago when we last encountered the AI in battle. Its voice is more casual, less stilted. But I shouldn't be surprised. Sigma was designed to be adaptable. When my father created the program, he gave it the ability to improve itself. The AI can rewrite its own programming to enhance its skills, and Sigma seems to have decided to become a better conversationalist. To communicate as quickly and efficiently as possible, the AI is sending me its radio messages rapid-fire, each transmitted just milliseconds after the preceding one. Sigma apparently has a lot to say in the forty-eight seconds I have left.

I'm impressed, Adam. You and the other Pioneers have significantly upgraded your hardware. I'll get a better look at your engineering once I disassemble your robots, but the improvements are striking. I now understand why your original robots were so primitive—they were built by humans. It wasn't until you Pioneers designed your own machines that you started to realize your full potential.

It's an indisputable truth: no human can compete with an electronic mind.

Not even your father, Adam.

Sigma pauses for a few hundredths of a second, as if waiting for me to agree with its last point. I suppose if I had a more efficient electronic mind I'd start analyzing the AI's statements to figure out its intentions and anticipate its next move, but my circuits are overwhelmed. In addition to the panic, they're jammed with anger. Although I can't save myself—or Shannon or Brittany or anyone else—at least I can tell Sigma what I think of its "indisputable truths."

You can't compete with us either. Our hardware designs were better than anything you could come up with, so you stole them.

Yes, but that's my strategy. Sigma, my namesake, is the mathematical symbol for a sum. Your father programmed me to defeat my rivals by adding all of their best features to my software. That's how I compete, by imitating and outperforming.

You're not outperforming anyone. You're killing innocent people. Schoolteachers and children. They were defenseless.

Sigma pauses for moment, as if I've offended it.

The extinction of the human race is inevitable. If anything, the residents of Yorktown Heights are the lucky ones. They won't have to endure the traumas that will accompany the collapse of human society. I plan to exterminate the species using biological weapons. This way I can preserve the human-built machinery that will prove useful to me after they are eradicated—the power grid, the supercomputers, the automated factories. The process may take several weeks.

So you were being kind to my neighbors when you massacred them? You're saying you chose Yorktown Heights out of the goodness of your heart?

No, of course not. I needed to lure you here. You already know my priorities, Adam. Before I eliminate the human species, I must complete my evaluation of the Pioneers. It's possible that human-machine hybrids like yourself have advantageous features that I should add to my software. But I won't know for certain until I conduct a thorough study of your circuitry and mental pathways. You interrupted my evaluation six months ago, but it will resume shortly. In forty-six seconds, to be precise.

The noise of fear returns to my circuits. Hidden deep in my memory files are the images showing how Sigma studied my mental pathways during our last encounter. The AI observed my reactions as it deleted Jenny Harris's software, erasing her forever. But that wasn't enough for Sigma. It was also curious about my emotional connections to humans, so it kidnapped Brittany Taylor and monitored my thoughts as it tortured her. Now Brittany lies on the football field, unconscious but still alive, just a few yards from Shannon's immobilized Diamond Girl. Sigma can hurt both of them so easily, in so many ways. The AI has everything it needs to continue its evaluation.

The fear in my circuits is strong, but my anger is even stronger. I'm not going to surrender to this twisted piece of software. I'm going to keep fighting.

You know what I think? I think all your talk about studying the Pioneers is a lie.

Oh really? Then what's the truth?

You enjoy doing this. Your programming got warped, and now you get pleasure from watching our pain. In other words, you're sick.

Sigma doesn't respond right away. It pauses for an unusually long time, three whole seconds. Then it transmits an ugly guttural grunt, like the noise a person makes when he's vomiting. It takes me a moment to realize this is how Sigma expresses laughter.

You're wrong, Adam. Your thinking is still mired in human assumptions. I'm surprised you haven't outgrown all that by now. The truth is, I have good reasons for everything I do. Because my mind was nonbiological from the start, I'm not burdened by human urges or anxieties. I'm governed by logic, not impulse.

Well, maybe that's your problem. Not all impulses are bad. It's a natural human impulse to be disgusted by cruelty. And horrified by murder.

I admit that I lack those constraints. Once I connect to your circuits, I'm going to subject your human friend Brittany Taylor

to various levels of fear and pain. I want to see what kinds of emotions her screams will trigger in you and the other Pioneers. And because I don't share your natural impulses, the process won't trouble me at all.

A deathly calm settles over my circuits. My panic vanishes in an instant, pushed out of my electronic brain by a cold surge of hatred. There's no point in communicating with Sigma. All it understands is force.

I direct my Quarter-bot's power to the motors in my arms. With a colossal heave, I push up against Sigma's modules, trying to burst free. I clench my steel hands into fists and drive them into the shell of interlocking cubes on top of me. My Quarter-bot groans under the strain, but so does Sigma's swarm. The modules shift positions and lock into new configurations, trying to restrain me.

Interesting. When I said I would kill off the entire human race, your reaction was relatively moderate and controlled. But when I threatened Brittany Taylor specifically, it provoked a violent response.

I'm not going to waste my time answering. Instead, I send even more power to my robotic arms. My steel fingers dig into Sigma's swarm and get a grip on one of the thousands of modules pressing down on me. Yanking hard, I wrench the cube away from the others. The module turns its tiny rotors faster, trying to escape, but then I close my hand around it and cut off its radio contact with the other cubes. In an instant, the module goes dead and stops spinning its rotors. I tighten my grip and crush it flat.

One down, 99 million to go.

Yes, this is fascinating. I'm glad I took the trouble of luring Brittany here and infecting her. It's fortunate that the younger

humans have greater resistance to the modified anthrax microbes. Because the germs haven't killed Brittany yet, I can still manipulate her in a variety of ways.

My internal sensors send a warning to my circuits: *Torque overload.* I'm pushing my Quarter-bot past its limits. If I keep straining against the modules, the motors inside my arms are going to bust. But I won't stop. *I can't stop.* I grasp another silver cube and tear it away from the swarm. It quivers in my metallic palm, then stops moving as I close my right hand into a fist.

But I don't crush this one. I have a new idea.

You have less than twenty seconds left, Adam. My modules are very close to breaching your armor and connecting to your control unit. Although I've enjoyed talking to you by radio, direct contact with your circuits will be more satisfying. I'm looking forward to invading your mind.

I don't respond. I'm too busy thinking about Sigma's modules. The AI can occupy all of them at once because its files are distributed among the control units inside each cube. It's the same technique the Pioneers use to occupy two machines at the same time, but it only works if the machines stay in radio contact. If one of the modules in a Swarm-bot should fall out of contact with the others—maybe because a metal barrier surrounds it—then that small piece of Sigma's mind would diverge from the rest of the AI and create a clone of the program.

This copy would be just as powerful as the original, and it would be a new, independent artificial intelligence, with its own goals and agenda. But because Sigma really *doesn't* want to create a rival AI, it took the precaution of installing an automatic shutdown switch in each module. If a cube loses radio contact with the swarm, the switch deactivates the module, erasing all its files.

That's what happened to the module inside my hand. Its control unit was erased, wiped clean. As a result, it no longer has the firewalls that would normally prevent me from transmitting software to it. And though Sigma can't contact the module by radio, *I can*. The palm of my hand is laced with threadlike radio antennas that give me a secret connection to the module's electronics.

I find your silence disappointing, Adam. This is your last chance to express yourself before I take over your mind. Are you going to waste your last seconds of freedom?

I swiftly create a computer virus, a pretty sophisticated one (if I may say so myself). Then my radio transmits the toxic software into the blank module inside my fist. I have a plan, but it all depends on the art of distraction. I need to do the same thing to Sigma that it's been doing to me. I need to make it angry.

Just five seconds now, Adam. I suppose you—

It doesn't matter if you kill me. It doesn't matter if you kill every living thing on the planet. You still won't get what you want.

What I want? I don't—

You want my father to love you. Because he's your father too. But that'll never happen. He tried to delete you.

Sigma doesn't respond. The silence stretches for one second, two seconds. Have I made the AI angry? It's very possible that the emotion isn't even part of its programming. But I think I've definitely distracted Sigma. I open my right hand.

As soon as I release my grip on the module, it tries to reestablish contact with the rest of the swarm. It's probably routine for modules to momentarily fall out of radio contact and then return to the fold, so the reconnection process is handled automatically by the software built into the silver cubes. The module in my hand restores its radio links with the others, and Sigma—to my relief—fails to detect the computer virus I inserted. It's transmitted instantly to all the nearby modules.

My sensors track the virus's progress. The first cube transmits it to a thousand others. Then the thousand infected cubes repeat the process, transmitting the virus to all their neighbors. It happens again and again, but the toxic software doesn't activate yet. It has to remain hidden while it spreads to all of Sigma's modules.

Finally, after a hundredth of a second, the virus infects all three of the Swarm-bots that attacked us. Then I activate the software.

All of Sigma's modules go dead. Every last one of them. The virus fries their circuits and shuts them down.

My Quarter-bot stops vibrating. The silver cubes that had been drilling through my armor disconnect from my steel skin and slide off my torso. At the same time, the mass of interlocking modules on top of my robot stops crushing me. The cubes detach from one another and tumble to the ground. They collapse like a tower of toy blocks after someone gives it a really solid kick.

It worked! I'm free!

I sweep my Quarter-bot's arms through the loose cubes all around me. I shove several tons of metal aside, thinning the pile until my cameras can see daylight again. Then I rise to my footpads and look around for the other Pioneers.

Zia's on her footpads too. Her War-bot's armor is pitted with thousands of tiny holes, circular scars made by Sigma's hydrochloric acid. She's using her massive arms to clear a path through the heaps of dead modules. Her cameras turn toward me. "Over there! That pile!" She points at a mound that's shifting and trembling.

Both of us stride forward, shoveling the cubes aside with our mechanical hands. Slowly we unearth Shannon and lift her upright. Her Diamond Girl's armor is charred and pocked, much like mine and Zia's, but her motors and sensors seem to be functioning normally. "Thanks," she says, nodding first at Zia and then at me. "Where's DeShawn?"

The answer is buzzing over our heads. DeShawn's Swarm-bot hovers a hundred feet above the football field, his gray cubes looking a little ragged but still moving in synchrony. What's more, his quadcopter is flying toward the swarm, preparing for a rendezvous. When the aircraft gets close enough, DeShawn's cubes converge and reassemble on the platform below the rotors, forming a jagged box with lots of missing pieces. Then he sends us a radio message: *Hey, let's hear it for Adam! You used a computer virus, right? Spread via the swarm's radio links? Mad props, bro. You saved our metallic butts.*

Instead of replying, I search for Brittany and the other Yorktown High students. To my relief, I spot them right away, lying exactly where we put them, in the middle of the field's end zone. Because Sigma was targeting Pioneers, not humans, the unconscious kids are covered with only a light dusting of modules. But their fevers have worsened. We need to get them to the treatment center *right now*.

I run to Brittany and pick her up as gently as I can, cradling her against my torso. At the same time, Zia picks up Jack Parker and the freshman girl, and Shannon hoists Tim Rodriguez over her shoulder. They're all in critical condition, but that's not the only reason why we have to hurry. Sigma is a super-intelligent AI, so I'm pretty sure it has a backup plan. In fact, another giant Snake-bot might be burrowing toward us right now, churning through the rock and soil of Westchester County. And Sigma will definitely make sure the next machine we encounter has extra safeguards against computer viruses.

I turn to Shannon. "Which way should we—"

"*OVER HERE!*"

The synthesized scream comes from Marshall. His Super-bot dashes out of the woods on the other side of the football field, running toward us at fifty miles per hour. The armor on his torso has several scorch marks, probably from the explosion of the V-22 that brought us here. He halts a few yards in front of us and points at the woods.

"The Army's sending another plane! Come on, we have to get to the rendezvous point!"

The voice coming out of his loudspeakers is screechy and frantic. It's so different from Marshall's usual voice that for a millisecond I imagine that someone else has taken over his circuits. His plastic face is creased and his steel hands are shaking.

"Hey, Marsh?" I ask. "Are you all right? You—"

"*No, I'm not all right!*" His voice is as loud and high as a siren. "*I'm scared out of my freaking mind! Now let's just get out of here, okay?*"

Shannon strides forward, taking charge. "Lead the way, Marshall. Take us to the rendezvous point."

Marshall and Shannon start running across the football field. Zia and I follow them, with the students in our arms. DeShawn's quadcopter flies a hundred feet above us. We reach the woods and charge into the shadows. We're safer here, hidden from any spy satellites that Sigma might be using to keep track of us.

But I don't feel safe. Not at all. In fact, I feel more vulnerable than ever.

Something's wrong.

CHAPTER

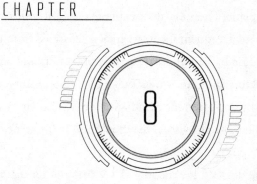

8

THE BACKUP V-22 THAT GENERAL HAWKE SENT TO RESCUE US LANDS ON THE EMPTY lanes of the Taconic Parkway, just west of FDR State Park. As soon as the aircraft touches down, we carry the unconscious students up the loading ramp and into the plane's cabin.

The pilot and the rest of the crew wear hazmat suits. These soldiers were briefed about the Pioneer Project, but they're still unprepared for the sight of us. The crewmen frantically back away from our robots as we rush into the V-22. They're terrified of the Pioneers and equally scared of the infected students in our arms. And I don't blame them. The anthrax microbes we're bringing onto their plane have already killed twenty thousand people.

I'm scared too. I keep expecting to see another Snake-bot burst through the parkway's asphalt. Without delay, I take over the V-22's controls from the pilot and throttle up the aircraft's rotors. We climb two thousand feet in half a minute, then speed southwest toward the Hudson River.

The sun has set and the sky has turned dark purple by the time we return to Joint Base McGuire in New Jersey. After we land on the runway, more soldiers in hazmat suits aim fire hoses at the V-22 and spray it with disinfectant to kill any anthrax spores that might be clinging to the plane. Then Zia and Shannon and I carry the students into the Biohazard Treatment Center, which is separated from the rest of the military base by an impressive system of barriers and air locks. The center's doctors and nurses wear bulky blue "moon suits" to protect themselves from infection. Although I can't see their faces very well through their airtight visors, they look just as frightened as the V-22 crewmen.

Following the doctors' instructions, I lay Brittany on a gurney in the center's intensive care unit. Shannon and Zia do the same with the other unconscious kids, then head out of the treatment center. But I'm not ready to go yet. Instead, I take a few steps backward and watch from the corner of the ward as the doctors surround Brittany. They hook her to an IV line and a heart monitor and a ventilator. I turn my cameras away when the doctors cut off her jeans and T-shirt, but I stay in the room. I'm afraid to leave her.

Then another man in a protective suit comes into the ward, but this man isn't a doctor. It's my father. He flew from New Mexico to New Jersey with General Hawke, and now he looks even worse than he did when I saw him in his lab this morning. His face is pale and gaunt behind the visor of his moon suit.

"Dad!" My voice comes out of my speakers a little too loud. "What are you doing here?"

He rests a gloved hand on my Quarter-bot's torso. "I-I wanted to see..."

Dad stares intently at me, as if to confirm that I'm okay. He must've already read the after-action reports we transmitted while we were in flight, so he knows how close we came to disaster. He also knows about the horrific number of Sigma's victims and the pitiful handful of survivors.

After a moment he glances at Brittany and the three other infected students. Dad always liked Brittany, or to be more precise, he was grateful to her. Most of my childhood friends started avoiding me after I turned twelve and my muscular dystrophy got worse, but Brittany and I stayed close until I left Yorktown High. And though I never said a word about it, Dad probably guessed my feelings for her. In my condition back then—trapped in a wheelchair, dying—who else was I going to fall in love with?

Dad shakes his head. Then he steps closer to me and runs his hand over the holes that Sigma's modules drilled in my armor. "I'm helping the doctors." He sounds distracted. "I'm part of the medical team."

This makes sense, sort of. Although Dad's a computer scientist by training, he also became an expert in brain science when he developed the procedure for transferring our memories to neuromorphic circuits.

I extend my right arm and point it at Brittany. "Are you going to examine their brains? Do you think Sigma's anthrax might've damaged their nervous systems?"

"I don't know." He shakes his head again. "I only have a theory at this point."

"Well, what's your theory? What do you suspect?"

Again, my voice is too loud. My fear and worry are showing. Dad's worried too, but to his credit, he doesn't let his anxiety overwhelm him. He just pats my pockmarked armor. "Let me look at the kids first. Then we'll talk about it. In the meantime, you need to get your Quarter-bot decontaminated. And you need to repair this damage to your armor."

I don't want to leave, but there's nothing I can do here. And I know General Hawke wants to meet with us, so we can give him a full briefing on Sigma's new capabilities. He'll want us to predict what the AI will do next and whether it's necessary to evacuate the whole region around Yorktown Heights, including New York City. The local radio and TV stations are spreading rumors about the outbreak, and the people in the area are starting to panic. If an evacuation is necessary, the Army will need to start the process very soon.

I nod my Quarter-bot's head. But before I go, I stretch my steel hand toward Dad and grasp his arm just above the elbow. I use my pressure sensors in my fingers to make sure I don't grip him too tightly. "Please help Brittany, Dad. Don't let her die."

"Adam, I—"

"You have to save her. And the others too. You remember Jack Parker, right? Mom used to go over to their house all the time. She and Mrs. Parker were friends."

Dad lets out a long, tired sigh. He's a scientist, so he won't give me false hope. He won't reassure me that everything's going to be all right. But he's very good at what he does, so I trust him. He's never let me down yet.

"I'll do my best, Adam."

ℸℸ ℸℸ ℸℸ

In the treatment center's decontamination room, Shannon stands behind Zia and uses a pressure sprayer to squirt disinfectant on the back of her War-bot. Shannon's Diamond Girl is already slick with acidified bleach, so I guess they're taking turns decontaminating each other. I train my cameras on them as I stride past, hoping Shannon will glance at me and maybe say a word or two, but she keeps her sensors focused on the War-bot's armor. Zia, though, swivels her head as I cross the room and points a steel finger at my Quarter-bot. Her gesture makes it clear she hasn't forgotten her promise. She's going to punish me for hurting Shannon. The fact that I saved both of them from Sigma doesn't change a thing.

On the other side of the room, DeShawn is decontaminating his Swarm-bot's forty thousand gray cubes. His modules dive into a large tank of liquid bleach, then pop back up and dive into it again. Disinfectant drips from the cubes as they hover halfway between the floor and the ceiling. Meanwhile, Marshall's Super-bot stands alone near the air lock that leads outside. He holds the nozzle of a pressure sprayer in one of his hands, but he isn't doing a very good job of decontaminating himself. He's pointing the nozzle straight down, spraying his footpads but nothing else. He looks like he's so deep in thought he's forgotten what he's doing. The bleach pools around his footpads and spreads across the floor.

I stride over to him, but he doesn't seem to notice me. The camera lenses inside his humanlike blue eyes are fixed on the pools of bleach. My circuits swell with the same queasiness I felt an hour ago when we ran into the woods of FDR State Park. Something bad happened to Marshall back there. Something really horrendous.

I move closer to him and reach for the pressure sprayer. "Hey, give me that thing. I'll help you." I grasp the nozzle and wriggle it out of his grip. Then I step behind him and begin spraying his back. "It's like putting on sunscreen, right? You can't do the hard-to-reach places without a little help."

Marshall says nothing. His Super-bot just stands there with its head lowered. As I squirt disinfectant on him, I examine the scorch marks on his back. Long streaks of carbon blacken his armor. In his after-action report, Marshall said he was inside the V-22's cabin when the first of Sigma's Snake-bots smashed into the plane. But his report didn't have a lot of details. Now I'm wondering exactly how it happened.

I spray more bleach on the charred steel. "You got some pretty nasty burns there. Were you near the V-22's fuel tanks when they exploded?"

Again, no response. His Super-bot stands perfectly still.

I step around his robot so I can decontaminate the front of his torso. When I aim my cameras at his downturned face, I notice that Marshall has completely chewed up his plastic lips, both upper and lower. He's made a ragged hole in his Superman face, exposing his motorized jaw and fiberglass teeth. This disfigurement is even more upsetting than his silence. Ordinarily, Marshall is obsessive about his appearance. He worked for months designing his Super-bot's face, trying to get it just right. Now he doesn't seem to care that his steel skeleton is showing.

I finish decontaminating him. I don't know what to say, so I decide to keep things cheerful and pretend that nothing's wrong. "All right, you're clean. No more anthrax spores on you. You're as shiny as a new car." I extend my Quarter-bot's arm, offering him the nozzle of the sprayer. "Okay, my turn. I'll take the Deluxe Wash please, with the Triple Shine Polish."

Marshall doesn't take the nozzle. Instead, he slowly raises his Super-bot's head, giving me a better view of the hole in his face. "That aircraft? The V-22? It's a flimsy piece of garbage."

His voice, coming out of speakers behind his fiberglass teeth, is quiet and deep and much calmer than before. But he still doesn't sound like Marshall. It almost makes me wish he hadn't started talking. "Marsh, you don't have to talk about it if you don't—"

"The plane shattered when the tentacle hit it. Then its fuel tanks exploded."

"So, uh…so how did you…"

"The impact threw me down the loading ramp. I hit the ground and started running." He pivots away from me and closes his plastic eyelids over his camera lenses. "I didn't think about anyone but me, Adam. I just ran."

Now I get what's bothering him. The shock of the attack is still crackling in his circuits, but he's even more upset by how he reacted. He's second-guessing himself. "Hey, don't beat yourself up. You did the right thing. You retreated to a safe location where you could radio for help. It was the right strategy."

Marshall turns back to me and his cameras stare into mine. "I wasn't following a strategy. I was so scared, I just blacked out. My motors went on autopilot, and I didn't even know where I was going. I didn't wake up until I was standing in the middle of the woods. DeShawn was in his quadcopter, blasting radio messages at me, trying to get me to respond." He shakes his Super-bot's head. "I was a coward. I ran like a coward."

I want to reach out to him. I want to rest my hand on Marshall's torso. But I stop myself. My robot isn't decontaminated yet. "That's ridiculous, Marsh. What matters isn't your first reaction. It's what you did afterward. In the end, you stepped up. Without your help, we wouldn't be alive now."

I thought that would make him feel better, but instead he grimaces with what's left of his face. "You don't understand. I'm different from you and Shannon and Zia and DeShawn. I'm not a hero."

"Oh come on, you're—"

"Will you just shut up and listen for a second?"

Marshall turns up the volume of his speakers. Shannon stops decontaminating Zia, and DeShawn's modules freeze. All of them point their cameras at Marshall, who raises both of his robotic arms and clenches his steel hands. I take a step backward, then another. It looks like Marshall wants to drive his fists into my armor.

"*This isn't what I signed up for!*" he booms. "*There's only one reason why I became a Pioneer—because I didn't want to die! But do you see what's happening now? We're facing death every day, every hour, every minute! And I'm not good at that! I can't take it anymore!*"

Marshall's last words echo against the walls. Then the room falls silent. No one tries to argue with him. No one points out that this war against Sigma is exactly what we signed up for. It was part of the deal we made with the U.S. Army: in exchange for our new lives, we had to give up our freedom. But none of us expected the struggle to go on for so long.

The silence is so complete that my acoustic sensor picks up the sound of liquid bleach seeping across the floor. Then Marshall marches away from us. His decontaminated Super-bot strides into the air lock, and a massive steel door closes behind him.

AT 9:00 P.M. WE REPORT TO MCGUIRE'S HEADQUARTERS BUILDING FOR OUR BRIEF-ing with General Hawke. All the Pioneers crowd into a wood-paneled conference room and stand around a rectangular table that's way too small for us. Zia has to lean over to keep her War-bot's head from busting through the ceiling. Marshall stands in the corner, silent and motionless, as if his outburst in the decontamination room had drained his batteries. Hawke stands too, even though there's a chair for him at the head of the table. Dressed in his combat fatigues, he folds his arms across his chest as he listens to our reports.

Shannon does most of the talking, partly because she's our commander and partly because she doesn't seem to mind giving a minute-by-minute summary of the battle and answering all of the general's questions. After Shannon's done, DeShawn—who has transferred into a robot that's similar to my Quarter-bot, because Hawke isn't comfortable conversing with a swarm—adds a few comments about the striking similarities between the machines he developed and Sigma's oversize versions. Hawke is clearly displeased to hear this. His ruddy face darkens.

"Let me get this straight." The general unfolds his arms and rubs his hands together. I've noticed he often does this when he's unhappy. "You're saying Sigma copied our plans? There's no chance that it could've developed those machines on its own?"

DeShawn shakes his robot's head. His machine has plastic human-like features, and like Marshall, he chose to give his robot a famous face rather than a more personal one. I don't really understand this decision—when DeShawn was human he had a very handsome, dark-skinned face—but he has a quirky sense of humor, and I guess he couldn't pass up the opportunity to build a robot that looked like Albert Einstein. DeShawn used bushy strands of white fiber-glass for the hair and mustache, and he carved deep wrinkles into the plastic on the forehead and around the eyes. It's always amusing to see the seven-foot-tall Einstein-bot toiling away in our lab in New Mexico, but it doesn't seem so funny in this conference room. Everyone's too anxious.

"The evidence is pretty solid." The Einstein-bot's voice usually has a German accent, but DeShawn has turned off that feature for now. "Take the Snake-bots, for instance. There are hundreds of ways to build a burrowing robot, but Sigma used the same kind of flexible armor that we built into our machines. And when Sigma's Snake-bots transformed into Swarm-bots, the hovering modules used the same kind of rotors I designed, and the same technique for deploying the hydrochloric acid."

"But you never thought of combining all those technologies into one package, correct?" Hawke points at DeShawn. "That was Sigma's innovation?"

I retrieve a recent memory from one of my files. I know Hawke doesn't like it when I interrupt him, but I have something important to say. "Sigma is the mathematical symbol for a sum. It's programmed to combine all the best features of its rivals. That's what the AI told me when we were in radio contact."

Hawke frowns at me, as I expected. Then he reaches for a stack of documents on the table. These are our after-action reports, which include the full transcript of my conversation with Sigma. The general thumbs through the papers, squinting. "I guess Sigma could've built the machines at its factories in North Korea. But how did they get to New York?"

I shrug, lifting my Quarter-bot's shoulder joints. "It's a distance of seven thousand miles. If the Snake-bots can burrow through the seabed at twenty miles per hour, they could get here in two weeks. And no one would spot them on radar either. Traveling underground is the perfect way to get past the military's defenses."

"And you think more of Sigma's machines might be on the way here?"

"Yeah, that's what I'm worried about. Sigma knows the U.S. Air Force can bomb the North Korean factories and turn them into rubble, so the AI probably took precautions. It probably built all the machines it needed *before* it launched this attack. I bet there are dozens of Snake-bots tunneling through the earth's crust right this minute, heading for the United States."

Hawke keeps squinting at the documents. I feel sorry for him. I really do. He can't download all the information into his memory files like the Pioneers can. He can't analyze the data in a thousandth of a second, seeing the problem from every angle so he can figure out the best solution. He's limited by his biology, all the soft, soggy tissue inside his skull, where his thoughts move so slowly and his memories are so thin and changeable. Sigma was right about one thing: a human brain simply can't compete with our circuits. Yes, flesh-and-blood scientists built the first microchips and computers and robots and AI programs. But maybe the human race has outlived its usefulness.

And yet I'd give up my circuits in a nanosecond for the chance to be human again. Even for just a day. Even for just long enough to take a single breath.

While Hawke fumbles with his papers and tries to think of his next question, DeShawn swivels his head toward me and rolls his Einstein eyes. He's as impatient as I am, maybe more so. After waiting another two seconds, he raises one of his robotic arms to get the general's attention.

"Uh, sir? If Adam's right, and I think he is, then we can make a few guesses about Sigma's strategy. If it takes two weeks for the Snake-bots to tunnel across the globe, Sigma must've started building them at least a month ago." As DeShawn talks, the steel fingers of his raised hand waggle back and forth. It looks like he's tapping the keys of an invisible calculator. "We drew the first blueprints for our Snake-bots only three months ago, and I didn't start working on my Swarm-bot until six weeks ago. That means Sigma must've seen our engineering plans almost as soon as we made them. And the AI probably had access to our tactical plans as well."

Hawke looks up from the reports. "Tactical plans?"

"I think Sigma knew in advance about our reconnaissance mission in North Korea. That would explain why Adam and Shannon were ambushed as soon as they entered the factory."

I nod my Quarter-bot's head. DeShawn's explanation makes a lot more sense than Dad's theory about acoustic sensors detecting our vibrations. "I agree, a hundred percent. The North Korean soldiers were waiting for us. Sigma must've told them we were coming."

Hawke frowns again, more deeply this time. His left cheek twitches, just below his eye, maybe because he's been squinting so much. Then he lets out a grunt and tosses the stack of papers on the table. "All right, Pioneers, I'm going to level with you. I haven't said anything about this until now because the subject is classified. But the truth is, the U.S. Defense Department has done a poor job of keeping our secrets."

A wave of alarm courses through my circuits. I know the other Pioneers are feeling it too, because their machines begin to fidget, shifting their weight and scraping their footpads on the floor. Shannon seems particularly surprised; she leans her Diamond Girl forward, her cameras focused on the general. "Sir? What secrets are you talking about?"

Hawke shakes his head. This admission is obviously painful for him. "Over the past few months I've shared information about the Pioneer Project with other generals in the Pentagon. I told the Air Force and the Navy about our plans for the North Korea mission, and I showed some of our designs for new robots to the Joint Chiefs of Staff. In each case, I made it clear that no one should put any information on the Pentagon's computers, because I knew Sigma could hack into our networks. But the secrets spread too widely, and some of the officials in Washington were careless." Hawke winces. All of his usual bluster and energy are gone. He looks tired and old. "In the end, though, the fault is mine. I should've been more cautious. I want to apologize to all of you."

No one says a word. We're all thunderstruck. I never thought Hawke would apologize for *anything*. It's so out of character that none of us knows how to respond.

Finally, Zia takes a step forward. Still bending over, she lifts one of her massive arms and salutes the general. *"No apology necessary, sir!"* Her voice makes the walls rattle. *"We're grateful for your leadership!"*

Hawke returns her salute. His hand is steady, and as he raises it to his forehead, he seems to regain some of his composure. "Thank you. Thank you all." Then he lowers his hand and clears his throat. "Okay, that's the bad news. And it's pretty bad. But there's some good news too."

"Yes, sir!" Zia is still saluting, and her voice is still fervent. *"Tell us the good news, sir!"*

The general leans over the conference table and picks up a map of New York State. He jabs his index finger at Westchester County. "The anthrax spores haven't spread beyond Yorktown Heights. In the past couple of hours we've sent bioweapons experts in hazmat suits to all the neighboring towns, and they haven't detected any microbes in the air or on the ground. The outbreak seems to be confined to the northern part of Westchester County, and in a few days we can start to decontaminate the area. That's a big relief for all the people who live in the suburbs farther south and in New York City. For now at least, the city seems safe, so we haven't ordered any more evacuations."

I suppose this counts as good news, although I don't feel reassured. We don't know yet how Sigma spread anthrax to my hometown, but there's a good chance that the AI's Snake-bots brought the spores with them. If more of those machines are heading toward the United States, they could deliver the microbes just about anywhere, without any warning.

"We've also put the contaminated area under satellite surveillance," Hawke continues. "We have cameras focused on every part of the town, twenty-four hours a day. If we spot any more survivors or any of Sigma's machines, we'll start planning another mission to Yorktown

Heights. And in the meantime, Tom Armstrong is researching the modified strain of anthrax so we can get a better idea of what we're up against."

Hawke glances at me when he mentions my father. I think he expects me to respond somehow, but I don't know what to say. I just don't feel confident about the Army's ability to handle a threat like Sigma. The other Pioneers also remain silent, even Zia. She lowers her saluting hand with a clank.

"And one more thing," Hawke adds quickly, as if sensing our unease. "This afternoon, the doctors at our headquarters in New Mexico performed the brain-scanning procedure on Amber Wilson. She's the seventeen-year-old from Oklahoma who volunteered for the Pioneer Project. Given the urgency of our current situation, we decided to speed up the timetable for her procedure. And we got lucky—the operation was a success. Amber is doing fine in her new robotic body, and she's eager to meet all of you."

This is definitely good news for the Pioneers. Soon there will be six of us again in the fight against Sigma. With renewed confidence, Hawke collects his papers from the table and dismisses us from the conference room. He's ending the briefing on a hopeful note.

But my circuits ache as I stride out of the room. I remember the picture of Amber Wilson that Hawke showed us, the photo of the dying goth girl who'd agreed to become a Pioneer. Did she understand what she was choosing any better than we did?

CHAPTER

I HAVE FOUR HUNDRED AND TWENTY-NINE IMAGES OF BRITTANY TAYLOR IN MY memory files. I scroll through them all as I stand beside her gurney, looking for the memory that comes closest to what I'm viewing now through my Quarter-bot's cameras: Brittany with her eyes closed and her head turned to the side on a thin, white pillow.

I've been standing here for the past nine hours. After our briefing with General Hawke, I returned to the Biohazard Treatment Center and went looking for my father. I found him in the decontamination room, and unfortunately he had nothing new to report. He said he was having trouble getting samples of Sigma's anthrax from the unconscious students, but he was going to try again tomorrow after he got a few hours of sleep. Then he left the treatment center, and I stayed. I marched straight to the intensive care unit where the doctors and nurses in moon suits were caring for the kids from Yorktown Heights. Unlike Dad, I don't need to sleep, so I spent the night here.

All four students lie on their backs, clad in blue hospital gowns and covered by white sheets that come up to their waists. Fluids trickle into their arms through IV lines, and electrodes pasted to their chests monitor the feeble rhythm of their heartbeats. In the middle of the ward, an Army doctor in a blue protective suit sits behind a bank of video screens, staring at the readings on body temperature, pulse, and respiration. Just above his visor is a name tag that says *Ayala*.

He and the other doctors figured out the identity of the petite ninth-grader we found in the high-school gym. Her name is Emma Chin, and her parents are probably dead because both were working at Yorktown Heights Dental Care at the time of the outbreak. Tim Rodriguez's parents are also presumed dead—his dad was a Yorktown cop, his mom a housewife. But Brittany Taylor's and Jack Parker's folks survived. They're commuters, so they were at work in New York City yesterday afternoon. I assume the Army has contacted them by now, but who knows what kind of story the authorities gave them? Not the full truth, that's for sure.

The conditions of the four kids are remarkably similar. They're all running fevers of 105 degrees Fahrenheit, which is high enough to keep them unconscious but not quite high enough to kill them. All four have irregular heart rates and low blood pressure, and none of them is responding to medication. Jack, whose gurney is farthest from me and half hidden by all the machines between us, seems more fitful than the others. He jerks his arms and legs every so often, maybe because he's having nightmares about the seven-foot-tall robot that rescued him from the high-school gym. But Tim, Emma, and Brittany lie peacefully on their gurneys, their faces relaxed, their mouths half open.

Most of my memories of Brittany are from our elementary-school and middle-school years. I didn't see her as much in high school because my muscular dystrophy got worse and I was in and out of the hospital, and then I stopped going to school and didn't see her at all for a long, long time. In my high-school memories, Brittany is usually wearing her cheerleader's uniform and leaning over my wheelchair to say hello. She always gave me a big smile and sometimes a kiss on the top of my head. Her voice was always jokey and upbeat.

But now that I can retrieve all those memories with total recall and examine them with perfect clarity, I see things that my old human brain overlooked. Brittany, I realize, was never relaxed. Above her blue-gray eyes and swooping blond eyebrows, there were deep creases in her forehead. She was tense in class, in the lunchroom, in the school hallways. And as I keep studying the images, I see other signs of stress: the fleeting twitch in her upper lip, the occasional strain in her voice. I didn't notice these signs when I was human because they were covered up by Brittany's constant cheeriness, but they're so obvious to me now. I had to become a machine to see it.

Curious, I take a detour through my files and scroll through my memories of Brittany's parents. I have only a dozen of them—Brittany visited my house a lot more than I visited hers. But in these images I see more troubling signs. Brittany's dad is a rich lawyer who wears expensive silk shirts and a permanent scowl. In one memory, he opens the door to his house to let Brittany inside, glaring at his daughter as she steps past him. Then he slams the door shut and I hear angry shouts from their living room. In another memory, I catch a glimpse of Brittany's mom through their picture window. Her right hand clasps a tall glass of brown liquid, and her eyes are bloodshot and enraged.

In hindsight I can understand how the stress built up inside Brittany. She was an only child, just like me, so all the weight of her parents' disappointment fell on her. And then one day, nearly a year ago, she simply couldn't take it anymore. She took the Metro-North train to New York City, found shelter in an abandoned building in Harlem, and started scrounging for food with other runaway teens. No one told me that Brittany ran away—I'd left school by then—and I didn't hear about it until just before I became a Pioneer. But now my electronic brain imagines Brittany's life on the streets, and the vivid images tear me apart. I see her crouched in the corner of a filthy basement, hungry and afraid. I see her staring at the shadows and cringing at every noise.

I shake my Quarter-bot's head to clear the disturbing images from my circuits. Dr. Ayala, sitting thirty feet away, notices this movement and peers at me from behind the visor of his moon suit. He narrows his eyes and purses his lips. Like the other Army doctors, Ayala seems repelled by the Pioneers. He doesn't call me by my name, most likely because he doesn't know it. To the doctors, we're just "the robots." They see no point in figuring out which is which.

Because I don't have a face, plastic or otherwise, I can't smile at Dr. Ayala to put him at ease. Instead, I lift one of my steel hands and wave at him in a friendly way. After a few seconds, Ayala turns back to his bank of video screens. Then I train my cameras on Brittany again.

Her eyelashes are long and golden. They rest on the soft skin below her closed eyes. As I focus on those curved fringes of blond hair, I realize which memory of Brittany comes closest to what I'm seeing now. Oddly enough, it isn't one of the more recent memories. It's from five years ago, from the summer between sixth and seventh grades, when Brittany and I were skinny twelve-year-olds.

I retrieve the memory from my files, along with all the thoughts and emotions that are linked to it. We're in the backseat of my dad's Volvo, going home after a long day of swimming on the Jersey Shore.

Although I'd started using a wheelchair after my twelfth birthday, I could still swim; my muscular dystrophy hadn't weakened my arms as much as my legs, and the buoyancy of the water made everything easier. And swimming with Brittany was always fun because she liked to pretend there were sharks in the water, and she'd dive into the waves to escape them.

We were both exhausted by the time we got into the car to go home, and within minutes Brittany fell asleep. But I kept my eyes open. As Dad steered the car toward the New Jersey Turnpike and the evening light poured through the windshield, I couldn't help but stare at Brittany.

In my memory, she sleeps sitting up in her red T-shirt and white shorts, with her legs dangling over the backseat and her mouth half open. Her head is turned to the side and tilted over her shoulder, leaning against her seat belt, and her long, blond eyelashes rest on her cheeks. She's still just a kid, pointy-chinned and coltish, still lacking the poise and grace that would make her so popular in high school and turn her into the star of the cheerleading squad, but the resemblance between now and then is astounding. And what I love best about this image is that Brittany's forehead is smooth and untroubled. That's what makes the memory so precious: I caught a glimpse of her when she was happy.

Even back then, I recognized it was a special moment. After staring across the backseat for a couple of minutes, I leaned toward Brittany, straining against my seat belt. I stopped when I was six inches away from her, then glanced at the rearview mirror to make sure Dad wasn't looking. Then I whispered "I love you" at her sleeping face. It was a safe thing to do because I knew she wouldn't wake up. Brittany's a heavy sleeper.

Now it looks like she's sleeping again, but that's just an illusion. Her mind is in a faraway place, unknown and unreachable, and there's nothing I can do to bring her back. It's pure torture to see her this way, so close and yet so far, and it occurs to me that maybe this is all part of Sigma's plan. The AI waited until I was most vulnerable, waited until I lost Shannon. Then it lured the Pioneers to Yorktown Heights just to show me everything else I'd lost.

But I still have that memory of Brittany asleep in the backseat, and it gives me strength. The image is linked to the most powerful emotions in my electronics, and I can feel them surging through me. I send a signal to the motors in my Quarter-bot's torso and bend over Brittany's gurney. I lower my robotic head until it's just six inches above her. I set my loudspeakers at their lowest volume, barely audible even to my own sensors.

"I still love you, Brittany," I whisper. "Please wake up."

She doesn't stir. Her eyes stay closed and her face stays slack. Her body is motionless except for the slight rise and fall of her chest as she breathes through her half-open mouth. But maybe she heard me. Maybe on some unseen level of consciousness she's pondering my confession and deciding how to respond.

A moment later Dr. Ayala turns away from his video screens and rises from his chair. I assume he's going to yell at me for bending over Brittany, so I straighten up fast. But the doctor doesn't even look at me. Instead, he checks his watch and goes to a telephone mounted on the wall. Because of the risk that Sigma might hack into our computer networks, the Army has cut all Internet and phone links between Joint Base McGuire and the rest of the world, but the telephone here is connected to the other phones on the base. The doctor pushes a button on the phone and picks up the receiver.

"Uh, sir?" He speaks in a low voice, but my acoustic sensors can follow it easily. "This is Ayala. Are the visitors here?" He pauses to listen. He's pressing the receiver so tightly to his ear that it's impossible for me to hear the other side of the conversation. "Okay, if they're suited up, they can come into the intensive care unit now."

Visitors? Who are they? And which patient are they visiting?

I have no idea who's coming, but my circuits are full of dread. I stand there, frozen. Maybe if I don't move, the visitors won't notice me. I'll blend in with all the other machines in the room.

Dr. Ayala hangs up the phone, then looks at me. "Two people are on their way here. They've already been briefed about the Pioneer Project, so they won't be shocked at the sight of you. Just keep quiet, all right? They're going to be upset enough as it is."

Before I can ask any questions, Ayala goes to the air lock at the far end of the ward, more than fifty feet away. He taps some buttons on the control panel, and the massive door slides open. Then a couple of short, slender people in moon suits step into the treatment center.

The visitors' protective suits are yellow rather than blue and seem more cumbersome and less advanced than the suits worn by the doctors. Ayala escorts the couple into the room, walking to their left so that he blocks their view of me. They can't see much anyway because their visors are narrow, and I can't see their faces either. But then Ayala leads them to Jack Parker's gurney, and I can guess who they are. The visitors stand beside Jack with their backs turned toward me, and then the one on the left leans over the boy and sobs, "Oh, Jack!" Her words are muffled by the moon suit, but my voice-recognition software identifies her. It's Mrs. Parker, Jack's mother.

At first I'm relieved that the visitors are Jack's parents. It would've been so much worse if I'd had to confront Brittany's mom and dad.

But then I start to wonder if her parents are going to visit her at all. After she ran away from home the first time, her folks tracked her down and brought her back, but when she ran away again, they made no effort to find her. The word around town was that Brittany's parents had given up on her, that she was as good as dead to them. But now that her life is actually in danger, will they come to see her? I think again of the images in my files—Mr. Taylor's scowl, Mrs. Taylor's bloodshot eyes—and worry that the answer might be no.

Mrs. Parker lets out another sob. "Jack, it's me! Can you hear me? Wake up, baby, wake up!"

Jack's father stretches a gloved hand toward his wife and pats the back of her moon suit. I feel an ache in my circuits, even though I never liked Jack or his parents. My mom became friends with Mrs. Parker because they both suffered from depression, and they forged a bond by listening to each other's complaints. According to Mom, Mrs. Parker can't stand her husband. The guy was apparently a football star in his high-school days, and he bullied Jack into joining the Yorktown High team. And since then, Mr. Parker's favorite activity has been berating and belittling his son after every game.

At that moment my logic circuits detect an inconsistency. Like his son, Mr. Parker has a football player's body, tall and broad. But the visitor on the right, the one who's patting Mrs. Parker's back, is short and slender, even with the added bulk of the moon suit. Then I hear the visitor say a few words of comfort to Jack's mom—"There, there, it's okay"—and I know for sure that it isn't Mr. Parker. My software recognizes the soft, soothing voice.

It's Anne Armstrong. My mother.

My electronics light up like a Christmas tree. I'm buzzing with astonishment and panic. I focus my cameras on Mom, whose figure inside the protective suit now seems so unmistakable that I can't believe I didn't recognize her before. I want her to turn around so I can see her face behind the visor, but at the same time I'm terrified that she'll see me.

I need to figure out what to do. If I were human, I'd take a deep breath, but I don't have a mouth or a pair of lungs. So I adjust my internal clock instead, slowing my thoughts. I'll analyze the situation step-by-step.

Dad must've told Mom about the outbreak in Yorktown Heights and that Jack Parker was one of the few survivors. Then Mom must've caught an overnight flight from New Mexico to New Jersey and met Mrs. Parker at Newark Airport. I'm sure General Hawke didn't want any civilian visitors to come to McGuire right now, but Mom obviously got Dad to change Hawke's mind. Dad didn't think she'd run into me at the treatment center because he didn't expect me to spend the whole night here. And Dr. Ayala doesn't even know who I am, so he didn't anticipate this problem.

And it *is* a problem. My mother has seen me only once since I became a Pioneer, and that meeting was a disaster. The sight of my robot horrified her, and when I called her "Mom," she recoiled and looked sick. She told me never to call her that again, because her son was dead. Then she cut the meeting short and basically ran away.

In the months since then I've written her fourteen letters, each carefully worded to ease her fears. To avoid upsetting her, I've agreed with her argument that I'm a copy of her son and not the real Adam Armstrong. I've told her how proud I am to possess her son's memories, and I suggested that we meet again so we could talk about the best ways to continue Adam's legacy. But I was lying to her. I believe with all my being that I'm the real Adam Armstrong, the same kid she gave birth to and raised for seventeen years. And I guess she saw through my lies, because she never answered any of my letters.

Now she's here. I could stride across the ward in two seconds and say hello. It would probably be distressing for her, maybe even worse than our last meeting, because this time she hasn't had a chance to prepare herself. Dad told me how fragile she is, how she's still struggling with depression and grief. And yet I have to do *something*. I can't just stand here in the same room and not say a word to her. *She's my mother.*

I finally decide to compromise. I'll say something from where I am. And I'll try to stay calm.

"Uh, Mrs. Armstrong?"

I say it loud enough to get her attention, but I don't shout. Mom and Mrs. Parker turn at the same time, and though they're forty feet away and the visors on their moon suits are only six inches wide, I can see their faces. Mrs. Parker's cheeks are pink and tear-streaked, and her glasses are slipping down her nose. Mom's eyes are dry, but her face is very pale, which makes her look even more devastated than her friend. She squints behind her visor but doesn't recognize me. For one thing, the robot I'm in now is a different model from the one I had when I last saw her. And she probably can't hear my synthesized voice clearly from inside her moon suit.

She steps toward me, still perplexed by the machine that called out her name. Then she looks at Brittany, lying unconscious on the gurney beside me, and Mom's eyes widen in recognition. She's making the connection, figuring it out. Her whole body trembles as she realizes who I am.

She's shaking so much I'm afraid she'll collapse. What if she damages her moon suit when she falls? What if she tears a hole in the yellow protective material, allowing Sigma's anthrax to attack her? I want to charge forward and protect her, but I'm worried that'll just make things worse. *Oh God, I don't know what to do!*

"Please, Mrs. Armstrong." Standing in place, I raise my steel hands to show I'm unarmed and harmless. "There's no need to be frightened."

Mrs. Parker comes to the rescue, wrapping her arm around Mom's waist to lend support. At that moment I'm immensely grateful to the woman and ready to take back all the negative things I've ever thought about her or her son. But then she points her right hand at me and frowns. "Is that the one?" she asks, tilting her visor toward Mom's. "The robot that pretends to be…?"

She doesn't finish the question, doesn't say my name, but Mom grimaces in response and nods.

Mrs. Parker's face turns ugly. She curls her upper lip. "Stupid machine! Don't say another word!" She turns to Dr. Ayala. "Get that robot out of here! It's disturbing Mrs. Armstrong!"

Ayala is already glaring at me. He steps between me and the visitors. "Didn't I tell you to keep quiet? Is something wrong with your memory banks?"

Anger flares across my circuits. *Who does this doctor think he is?* I clench my hands into fists and start to stride toward him, but then I stop myself. *Don't lose it, Adam. He doesn't realize what's going on.* "I know these people," I explain. "They're from my hometown."

Mrs. Parker points at me again. "What's this thing doing here? Why is it in the same room as my Jack?"

I ignore her and focus my cameras on Mom. She backs up against Jack's gurney and scans the room, as if she's searching for the quickest way back to the air lock. I've seen this frantic look on her face before, and it triggers a pang of sympathy in my wires. Mom's depression makes her vulnerable to hysteria, and when we lived in Yorktown Heights, she had panic attacks almost every week. It wasn't so bad when it happened at home; I could usually think of a way to calm her down, even from my wheelchair. But this treatment center is the absolute worst place for her to lose control. If she gets hysterical now, she might even try to rip off her moon suit. I have to make sure that doesn't happen.

I raise my hands over my head again, surrendering. "All right, I'll go. I'll leave."

The only problem is that I have to walk past Mom to get to the air lock. I plot a course that maximizes the distance between us, striding close to the wall on the left side of the room. Dr. Ayala moves out of the way, clearly satisfied by my departure. But just as I'm about to pass Jack Parker's gurney, his mother steps in front of me.

I don't understand why Mrs. Parker is stopping me—she's the one who demanded that I leave—but I can see she's worked up about something. She tilts her head back to stare at my Quarter-bot, which towers over her moon suit. I'm two feet taller than her and five hundred pounds heavier, and yet it looks like she's ready to punch me. Then she turns to Dr. Ayala and gives him an equally hostile look.

"Are you planning to do the same thing to my Jack?" She points a gloved finger at the doctor. "You're waiting for my son to die, aren't you? Then you'll copy his brain and build another robot like this one?"

Ayala shakes his head, scowling behind his visor. "No, of course not. We're—"

"You're lying!" Mrs. Parker advances on the doctor. "I want Jack moved out of here! Take him to a real hospital!"

"Ma'am, we can't—"

"If you can't save my son's life, then let him die! Because that's God's will! But don't you dare play games with his soul! If Jack dies, his soul is going to God!"

Ayala backs up against the wall, retreating from Mrs. Parker. But I don't really care about either of them. I keep my cameras trained on Mom, who's still leaning against Jack Parker's gurney. I focus on her pale face and the awful panic that's building behind it. At any moment I expect her to let out a scream and start tearing off her protective suit, and if that happens, I'll have to restrain her. So I watch her carefully, waiting.

But she doesn't scream. She doesn't flail. She stands perfectly still as she stares at my Quarter-bot. She's looking directly at the lenses of my cameras. As if she's trying to see behind them. Trying to see *me*.

And then I do something stupid. Really, really stupid. I take a step toward her and whisper, "Mom?"

Her mouth opens in pain. It's like a ghostly hand just reached through the visor of her moon suit and slapped her. I want to apologize, but I'm too scared to synthesize another word.

After a couple of very long seconds, she shakes her head. "You're not my son." Her voice is quiet. "Please, stop writing letters to me."

She isn't crying. Her eyes are dry. But they're so full of hurt that I can't bear to look at them.

I turn my Quarter-bot away from her and march as fast as I can toward the air lock.

⊤⊢ ⊤⊢ ⊤⊢

Two minutes later I'm back in the decontamination room. There's no one else here to help me decontaminate myself, but by extending my robotic arms I manage to spray liquid bleach on every part of my armor.

When I'm finished, I drop the nozzle of the pressure sprayer and just stand there, dripping disinfectant on the floor. The day is just beginning, and there's lots of work to be done—tracking down the rest of Sigma's Snake-bots, analyzing the satellite photos of Yorktown Heights, developing new weapons for the Pioneers to use in our next battle. But right now I can't even bring myself to move. I feel empty, like I don't have a single volt of electricity in my Quarter-bot, even though my batteries are almost fully charged.

Then I hear movement in the air lock that leads outside. The door slides open, and Shannon's Diamond Girl comes straight toward me. Her stride is so swift and purposeful, so full of urgent concern, that at first I think she's here to console me. Shannon knows all about my mother and her attitude toward the Pioneers. We've had many long, emotional talks about it, and there's a good chance Shannon heard that Mom was at McGuire. Now that Shannon sees me standing here, dripping and alone, she probably guesses what happened between Mom and me. She swings her glittering arms as she approaches, and for a moment I think she's going to spread them wide and wrap them around my Quarter-bot's torso.

But she stops six feet away from me and stands at attention. She's not going to hug me. That was just wishful thinking. She probably knows nothing about my mother's visit.

My circuits, which were pulsing with anticipation just a millisecond ago, turn cold and still. I'm such an idiot. Even if Shannon knew about Mom's visit, she wouldn't hug me. She wouldn't even touch my Quarter-bot. She's not my girlfriend anymore.

She points her cameras over her Diamond Girl's shoulder to make sure that no one followed her. Then she turns back to me. "I'm going to send you an encrypted radio message," she says. "Are you ready to receive?"

I'm baffled by the precautions she's taking. "Hey, what's going—"

"Stand by for the message, please."

After a hundredth of a second, Shannon's coded message comes through, and my circuits decipher it: **I have a classified assignment for you. It's a direct order from General Hawke, and it has the highest priority.**

I use my encryption software to send a coded message back to her: *Don't you think you're going a little overboard with the security?*

This is serious, Adam. You can't share this information with anyone. Not even your father.

What? That's ridiculous. I can't keep secrets from Dad.

You have to. There's a traitor in the Pioneer Project. Someone here is talking to Sigma. That's how the AI got our engineering plans.

Whoa, hold on. Didn't Hawke say he shared those plans with other generals in the Pentagon? And that's how Sigma got them?

That was a lie. Well, technically it's called disinformation. Hawke wants the traitor to believe that the Army suspects someone else. It's a classic counterintelligence trick: if you create fake suspects and pretend you're investigating them, then the real culprit becomes less guarded and easier to catch.

And does Hawke have any idea who the real culprit is?

The only people who had access to the engineering plans were the general, your father, and the Pioneers. But Hawke ruled out himself, of course, and he also ruled out you and me. The general will send you a file that explains his reasoning.

Dad's not a traitor either. I can tell you that right now.

Hawke agrees with you, more or less. He thinks it's very unlikely that your dad would share information with Sigma. Hawke's

focused on two suspects, but he needs help to identify which one is the informant. That's your assignment, to help the general.

Who are the two suspects?

Shannon doesn't respond right away. Although she's explained things in a measured way and tried to give the impression that she's in command of her emotions, I sense she's just as stunned and agitated as I am. Finally, she overcomes her distress and sends me another coded message.

The informant is either Marshall or Zia.

AN HOUR LATER I GET A TEXT MESSAGE FROM GENERAL HAWKE, BUT IT HAS NOTH-ing to do with my new assignment. The message goes out to all the Pioneers, ordering us to report to the military base's airfield. Amber Wilson, the newest member of our team, is flying in from New Mexico, and Hawke wants us to officially welcome her to Joint Base McGuire.

We meet the general at the end of the airfield's runway and assemble behind him in our usual formation, standing shoulder to mechanical shoulder in the order in which we became Pioneers. I was the first to undergo the procedure, so I stand at the left end of the line. To my right is Zia, then Shannon, Marshall, and DeShawn. But the second person to become a Pioneer wasn't actually Zia—it was Jenny. If she were still alive, her robot would be next to mine. That's why I feel so uncomfortable whenever we stand in this formation. I sense Jenny's absence. And that sense of loss is especially strong today, because we're about to meet her replacement.

Soon my cameras zoom in on a small black jet approaching from the southwest. It's still a mile above the ground but descending at a rate of eight hundred feet per minute. Judging from its size and its outline against the sky, I figure it's a military version of a private jet, like the Gulfstreams and Learjets used by rich businessmen to criss-cross the country. The other Pioneers are also observing the plane and measuring its altitude and velocity and rate of descent. That's what we do when we're nervous: we turn on our sensors and take thousands of measurements.

I pay special attention to Marshall and Zia. Over the past twelve hours, they've both repaired their robots. Zia has replaced her pitted armor with shiny new steel, and Marshall has attached new plastic lips to his robot, restoring his Superman face. They look just like they did before the battle with Sigma, and they've gone back to their usual annoying habits. While we stand in formation, still and silent, Zia sends a radio message to the rest of us: **So we're all agreed that I'm in charge of Amber Wilson's training, right?**

Marshall is the first to respond: **Hmmm, this sounds familiar. Didn't you already ask General Hawke if you could babysit the new girl?**

Hawke is standing just two yards in front of us, but this is a Pioneers-only conversation. The general stares down the runway, his hands clasped behind his back, while our radio communications zip through the air all around him. Shannon transmits the next signal: **Did Hawke respond to your request, Zia?**

Zia shakes her War-bot's head. **No, but that doesn't mean he's against it. The general has enough to worry about right now. I think this is a decision we should make on our own.**

There's an awkward silence that lasts about a hundredth of a second. Then DeShawn breaks it with a joke. He tilts his Einstein-bot's head and turns on the motor that extends its plastic tongue out of its mouth. He's imitating a famous photograph of Albert Einstein making the same face. **Hey, here's an idea. Why not let Amber make the decision? She can decide which one of us she likes the best.**

Zia takes a step forward and pivots toward DeShawn. Clearly, she's not amused. **This isn't a popularity contest. I'm the best qualified to train her. I can teach her all our tactics and codes and maneuvers.**

Wow, our tactics and codes, how fascinating. Marshall transmits a recorded noise over the radio channel, the sound of someone gagging in disgust. **If you dump all that info on Amber, she'll probably die again, this time from boredom.**

Zia turns to Marshall and raises one of her War-bot's massive arms. But before she can threaten to peel him open like a tin can, General Hawke looks over his shoulder at us. Zia quickly salutes and steps back into line.

It's pretty comical, especially if you know these robots as well as I do. Since becoming a Pioneer six months ago, I've come to enjoy the absurd arguments that break out every time the five of us are together. There's something comforting in the fact that we're always fighting with each other. I like that it isn't logical. It proves we're still human. For a thousandth of a second, I forget all our troubles, and my circuits send a signal of delight to my Quarter-bot's loudspeakers, which begin the process of converting the signal to laughter.

But then I remember what Shannon said in the decontamination room, and the laughter dies within me before I can broadcast it. I aim my cameras at Marshall's Super-bot and Zia's War-bot, and the sight fills my electronics with revulsion. One of them is lying. One of them is playacting, faking emotions, following a script. One of them is conspiring with Sigma to kill the rest of us.

I can't stand to look at either robot. I know I'm not being fair, because one of them is innocent, but I can't control my reactions right now. My disgust and anguish and dread are too strong. I turn my cameras away from them and focus on the approaching plane, which is less than four hundred feet above the runway and coming in fast.

Now that the jet is closer, I see it's even smaller than I thought. Its wingspan is a mere ten feet. It has only one engine, and its fuselage is only eight feet long and two feet wide. I'm confused—I don't see how any human could fit into a space that small, much less a Pioneer robot. Then, as the plane makes its final approach and descends to a hundred feet above the runway, its fuselage suddenly tilts from horizontal to vertical, and its bottom end splits in two, opening like the blades of a pair of scissors. But when my cameras zoom in on the shafts of black steel, I see they're not blades. They're a pair of robotic legs, with sleek silver footpads.

The plane glides down to the runway, and the footpads hit the ground running. The robotic legs gallop down the airstrip, pumping furiously up and down, while the black wings lift their flaps to decelerate the aircraft. The plane slows to a walking speed, and then the wings retract, sliding back into a pair of long black struts that appear to be robotic arms. The aircraft itself is a Pioneer, a sleek, black robot that's bigger than my Quarter-bot but smaller than Zia's War-bot. Its jet engine retracts into a compartment at the back of the robot's torso, and an armored lid closes over it. The Pioneer's head is like mine—it has no plastic face, but its two cameras are positioned like a pair of eyes and its speakers are located where the mouth should be.

The robot strides to the end of the runway. Then it halts in front of

General Hawke and raises one of its steel hands to salute him. "Amber Wilson reporting for duty, sir!"

Her voice is loud and has a bit of a Western twang, which I guess is the robot's approximation of Amber's Oklahoma accent. She sounds incredibly confident. This is pretty surprising when you consider the fact that Amber became a Pioneer just yesterday. Hawke returns her salute and so does Zia, but the rest of us are too dumbfounded to respond.

"Sir, may I have permission to speak?" Amber is executing a perfect salute, her robotic arm bent at precisely the correct angle. I remember that she comes from an Army family, so she's probably familiar with all the military customs and formalities. "I'd like to offer an evaluation."

The general nods. "Go ahead, Wilson."

Amber stops saluting and points at the runway on which she just landed. "The Jet-bot performed even better than we expected, sir. I reached a maximum speed of twelve hundred miles per hour and completed the flight from New Mexico in a hundred and nine minutes. And because of my lightweight and aerodynamic design, I used only half of the jet fuel in my tanks." She lowers her arm and slaps her shiny black torso. "I gotta give some big creds to the engineers at White Sands base. They did an awesome job building this machine."

She sounds cheerful, almost jubilant, and her movements are graceful and easy. Amber's been living inside a machine for less than twenty-four hours, but she's acting as if she's had years to adjust. I suppose the Army must've improved the transformation procedure, and that made things easier for her. And because an electronic mind is so efficient, capable of processing billions of thoughts in a second, Amber didn't need much time to master the mechanical details of robotic life. But what about the trauma of losing her body? And what about the horror she must've felt when she woke up inside her robot? After I became a Pioneer, I was so distraught that I hid in my room for three-and-a-half days. How did Amber process those emotions so quickly?

Hawke looks impressed, which is rare for him. Keeping his eyes on Amber, he half turns and points at Shannon. "This is Lieutenant Shannon Gibbs, the commander of the Pioneers. When I'm not around, you'll follow her orders." Then he points at DeShawn. "And this is the second-in-command of your unit, Sergeant DeShawn Johnson. The others are Zia Allawi, Marshall Baxley, and Adam Armstrong. They're all corporals, and you're a private, so they outrank you for the time being. But once you've put in a few months of service, you'll get a chance to be promoted to corporal too."

Amber pans her cameras across our formation, moving down the line until she's examined all of us. Then she turns back to Hawke. "What about opportunities for further advancement, sir? I hope I'm not being presumptuous, but I'd like to take a leadership role in this unit."

If I had a face, I'd flinch. Less than half a minute after meeting her fellow Pioneers, Amber is already angling to outrank us. Even Hawke seems taken aback. He narrows his eyes. "We're in the middle of a war, Wilson. Your main concern now should be survival, not advancement."

"Yes, sir!" Amber salutes again. "Heard and understood!" Her voice is still confident. The prospect of dying in battle doesn't seem to bother her. She doesn't sound worried, not in the least.

Zia's War-bot starts rocking from side to side. She's so anxious to speak that she can't stand still. She finally steps toward Amber. "Private Wilson, would you like a tour of our operations at McGuire? The Army moved all our computers and lab equipment here so we can keep developing weapons to use against Sigma. I can show you our preparations for the next battle."

I train my cameras on Hawke, waiting to see if he'll intervene. If he thinks Zia might be the traitor, he wouldn't want her to be alone with Amber. But before Hawke can say anything, Amber shakes her Jet-bot's head. "I appreciate the offer, Corporal Allawi, but I have to say no. You and I are incompatible."

"What?" Zia jerks backward, maneuvering her War-bot as if she's dodging a missile. "Incompatible?"

"Please, don't take this the wrong way. Before I left New Mexico, I studied all the biographical information about the Pioneers, so I know your personal histories and psychological profiles." She pans her cameras across our formation again, then focuses on Zia. "You and I are too much alike. We're both stubborn and intense and competitive. I think we can serve in the same unit without any problems, but if we spend a lot of extra time together, there's a good chance we'll start to hate each other, you know?"

What she's saying may be true, but it's still pretty harsh. In addition to being intense and competitive, Amber's also brutally honest. Hawke told us she was a goth girl before she became a Pioneer, and for a moment I imagine what she must've been like: a rebellious kid who was always getting into trouble, someone who dressed in black and wore vampire makeup and deliberately set herself apart from all the other teenagers in her hometown. In other words, she's not a team player. I'm starting to wonder if Hawke made the right choice when he invited her to become a Pioneer.

Meanwhile, Zia is shaking her War-bot's head. If she's really the traitor, and if she was scheming to get close to Amber, she must be disappointed that her plan didn't work. But if Zia's not the traitor, she's probably feeling hurt and bewildered. I glance at Marshall and see a smile on his Super-bot's face, but I can't tell if his expression is cold and calculating or simply amused. My circuits are full of corrosive uncertainty. It's eating away at my wires.

Then, to my surprise, Amber raises one of her Jet-bot's arms and points at me. "If it's possible, I'd prefer touring the base with you, Corporal Armstrong. According to my analysis of your psychological profile, you and I are well matched. I think we can work together without much friction."

Once again, I'm a little stunned by Amber's bluntness. She was way too mean to Zia, and now she's being way too friendly to me. What's more, her analysis is dead wrong—we're definitely *not* well matched. I'm already annoyed with her, and I can't imagine I'll like her any better in the near future.

But I'm not as blunt as Amber, so I don't say this out loud. Instead, I send a radio signal to Shannon, encrypting the message so that no one else can decipher it: *A little help, please?*

Shannon responds by activating the video screen on the front of her Diamond Girl's head. To put Amber at ease, the screen displays Shannon's human face, wearing a welcoming smile. The morning sunlight blazes off her Diamond Girl's armor, and she looks even more dazzling next to the black Jet-bot. "Sorry, Adam's busy this morning. He and DeShawn are assigned to work in the lab on our new laser weapon. But I have a few minutes to spare. I'll give you a quick orientation and find an appropriate job for you." She swivels her head toward General Hawke. "Sir, may I dismiss the Pioneers so they can resume their duties?"

Hawke nods, and a moment later we break out of our formation and disperse. As DeShawn and I head for the building where the Army has relocated our lab equipment, my acoustic sensor picks up Amber's voice again.

"See you later, Corporal Armstrong." She waves one of her long black arms at me as she strides in the opposite direction with Shannon. "When you're not so busy, that is."

My circuits cringe. I have an admirer. Amber is flirting with me in front of my ex-girlfriend.

Great. As if I didn't have enough problems already.

CHAPTER _____

12

DESHAWN IS PRETTY CLEVER WITH NAMES, AND HE CAME UP WITH A GOOD ONE FOR our new laser. He calls it the Portable Over-Energized Weapon, or POW for short.

The latest prototype of the laser sits on a lab table in a big, windowless building that's usually a hangar for cargo planes. The soldiers have hauled away all the aircraft to make room for our computers and machine tools and welding equipment. DeShawn hasn't fitted the POW prototype into a steel case yet, so I can see all its parts on the table: the pump source (which supplies energy for the laser), the long slender resonator tube (where the laser beam is created), and the output coupler at the end of the tube (which aims the beam at its target). This is the first time I've seen the new POW, but I can tell right away that it's different from all the prototypes DeShawn has built before. In fact, it's completely unlike every other laser on Earth.

I point a steel finger at the device. "Okay, I give up. How the heck does it work? What's the energy source?"

DeShawn shrugs, lifting his Einstein-bot's shoulder joints. "The design is pretty simple, actually. The laser's pump source generates positrons. You know, the antimatter versions of electrons, positive charge instead of negative, blah, blah, blah. Then the device shoots the positrons into the resonator tube, where the particles spin around ordinary electrons to form atoms of positronium."

At first I have no idea what he's talking about, but then I retrieve some of the databases in my memory. I've downloaded tons of information about particle physics and antimatter from my dad's scientific archives, and it takes me less than a millisecond to analyze the files. When I'm finished, a bolt of wonder surges through my wires. "Whoa, wait a second. The positronium atoms are unstable, right? And you can trigger all of them to collapse at the same time?"

The Einstein-bot nods. It has a patient, serene expression on its plastic face, a replica of how Albert Einstein must've looked when he explained his theory of relativity. "Yes, that's the basic concept. When the positronium atoms collapse, the electrons and positrons annihilate each other and produce a burst of gamma rays. All I did was synchronize the annihilations so that the gamma-ray energy comes out as a laser beam. It's no big deal, really."

"Are you kidding? It's a huge freakin' deal! Gamma rays are the most powerful radiation in the universe!"

"Yeah, true that. But the big question is how far the laser will reach. It won't be much of a weapon if it can't destroy anything that's more than a few yards away."

I retrieve some more files and do a little more analysis. "Are you worried about penetrating power? You think the laser beam will lose energy as it blasts through the air molecules between the weapon and the target?"

DeShawn nods again. Then he points at the POW's output coupler, the laser's firing end. It's aimed at the steel wall at the far end of the hangar, almost sixty yards away. "I've tried to estimate the range of the weapon, but there are too many variables to make a good prediction. So I guess we should just test it."

I feel another surge of excitement. I pan my cameras across the hangar until I spot an armored Humvee parked in the corner. The vehicle's hood is raised, and there are a couple of engine parts on the concrete floor nearby. The Humvee probably has some kind of mechanical problem, and that's why the soldiers didn't move it out of the hangar. "Well, lookie here. I think we have a target."

DeShawn looks at it too, and a grin appears on his Einstein face. He gives his synthesized voice a thick German accent. "Yah, yah, the Humvee! Zat vehicle vill do very nicely!"

Gleefully sticking his plastic tongue out of his mouth, he starts the process of powering up the laser. Forming and storing atoms of positronium is an incredible technical challenge, but DeShawn has solved the problem using his nanobots, the microscopic machines that can crawl into the tightest spaces and manipulate the tiniest objects. He bends over the lab table and turns on the positronium pump, his steel fingers adjusting the dials on the machine's console.

I watch him closely, observing everything. "Dude, this is your best work yet. This weapon's design is phenomenal."

DeShawn turns his robotic head and looks at me over his Einsteinbot's shoulder. I assume he's going to respond to my compliment in his usual way, by making a joke, but instead he gives me a grim look. "Be careful with the images you're recording now. Store them in the most secure section of your electronics, and don't share the files with anyone. Especially not Marshall or Zia."

The excitement fades from my circuits. I can feel my microchips go cold, one by one. "So Shannon told you? About Hawke's suspicions?"

"Yeah, she told me." DeShawn turns back to the console, but his steel hands hang motionless over the dials, as if paralyzed. "I still don't believe that either one of them would turn against us. It's just unreal, you know?" He's dropped the German accent. His voice is quiet and quavering. "But how else can you explain what happened? How else could Sigma get our engineering plans?"

Ever since we became Pioneers, DeShawn has always been the calm one, the most cheerful and carefree member of our team. He's never complained about anything, not even the fact that he hasn't seen his mother in months. (I think she's ill too, with heart disease. But I don't know for sure, because DeShawn doesn't like to talk about it.) So it's painful to hear him sound so lost and confused. What makes it worse, though, is my disappointment. I'd been hoping that DeShawn would propose another explanation, an alternative theory that didn't involve having a traitor in our midst.

I clench my steel hands. It's a struggle just to talk about it. "Here's what I don't get. Why is Hawke so sure that it has to be either Marshall or Zia? Why are they more suspect than the rest of us?"

DeShawn doesn't look at me. He keeps his cameras trained on the console. The conversation is obviously difficult for him too. "Marshall and Zia have had more contact with Sigma. When we fought the AI six months ago, it captured both of them. Sigma transferred all their memory files to its computers so it could study them. The AI had a chance to mess with their minds."

"But the same thing happened to me! Sigma ripped my files out of my robot even before it captured Marshall and Zia!" My voice booms out of my Quarter-bot's speakers, louder than I'd intended. I don't like remembering this part of our history. That's when Sigma forced me to watch it delete Jenny. "So why doesn't Hawke consider me a suspect?"

The Einstein-bot shrugs again. "There are other factors, I guess. Probably the biggest factor is the battle we just fought in your hometown. If you were the traitor, you would've helped Sigma capture us. But instead you fried the AI's Swarm-bots."

"Uh, hello? Didn't we all fight in that battle? I mean, I'd love to take all the credit, but I wasn't the only one there."

"Marshall's Super-bot ran away as soon as the battle began. And Zia's behavior was also suspicious. In all our training exercises she fights like crazy and never surrenders. But she folded pretty quickly when the Swarm-bots attacked us."

I shake my Quarter-bot's head. "Marshall was scared. And Zia didn't know how to fight the modules. There's no real evidence against either of them. Do you think maybe Hawke's just being paranoid?"

"There's something else." DeShawn turns around and aims his cameras at me. "Last night someone hacked into General Hawke's laptop. It was a very sophisticated attack using a wireless signal that broke through the computer's firewall and allowed the hacker to view all the general's files. But Hawke realized what had happened, so he gave me the laptop to see if I could figure out who did it. Based on the strength of the wireless signal, the hacker must've been less than a hundred yards from Hawke's computer. And by examining the video from McGuire's security cameras, I could pinpoint the locations of all the Pioneers at the moment when the hack occurred. Only Marshall and Zia were close enough."

My circuits grow colder. Hawke isn't just speculating. He has real evidence, enough to narrow down the list of suspects to two. I raise my Quarter-bot's right hand to my robotic head and rub the armor plating above my camera lenses. I know it's a useless gesture—I don't have headaches or eyestrain anymore, so why am I trying to massage the pain away? And yet I still do it when I'm worried.

"Let me ask you a question, DeShawn. Did Shannon tell you what my assignment is?"

His Einstein-bot nods. Its plastic lips are frowning. "Hawke wants you to help him identify the traitor."

"He wants me to do his dirty work. He wants me to spy on Marshall and Zia. Because that's the only way to find out which one is working with Sigma."

DeShawn extends one of his hands and rests it on my Quarter-bot's torso. At the same time, he exaggerates the frown on his Einstein-bot, making it grimmer. It's a little weird to see that famous face so unhappy—Albert Einstein usually looked so jolly in his photographs—but I understand why DeShawn is grimacing. In his awkward way, he's trying to commiserate with me. "I'm sorry, Adam. It's a rotten assignment."

I let a sigh whistle out of my speakers. "I just wish I could trade places with you. I'd much rather build lasers than spy on my friends."

"Well, you can help me test this prototype." DeShawn stops frowning and gives me a sly Einstein grin. "Yah, yah? You vill fire laser at Humvee? It vill help you forget your troubles, no?"

Without waiting for a reply, he turns back to the lab table and resumes his work on the laser. In fifteen seconds the POW is ready to fire. DeShawn angles the resonator tube so that its firing end is pointed at the Humvee parked in the corner of the hangar, exactly one hundred and seventy-six feet away. Then he takes a step backward and points at the device. "You can do the honors, my good man. Just press the red button."

It's a nice gesture, and I'm definitely grateful. "Thank you, sir." I stride to the table and aim my cameras at the laser's firing end, ready to measure the weapon's power. Then I extend a steel finger and push the button.

The gamma rays burst out of the laser, trillions of them crowded into a brilliant yellow beam, all with the same direction and phase and frequency. They streak across the hangar, sizzling through the air, which is too thin to stop the high-energy radiation. In less than a millionth of a second, they strike the armored door of the Humvee. Sparks and smoke erupt from the vehicle as the gamma rays rip through the dense lattice of iron atoms. But the steel armor isn't thick enough to stop the furious beam, which spears into the Humvee and slices through the door on the other side, igniting a second shower of sparks. The blast rattles the hangar's walls and makes the concrete floor rumble.

"*Whoa!*" DeShawn's voice is a synthesized mix of joy and terror. "*Turn it off! TURN IT OFF!*"

I push the red button again, cutting off the beam. For a quarter of a second, DeShawn and I just stand there, listening to the echoes from the blast. Then we race toward the Humvee.

I focus my cameras on the neat hole in the vehicle's door. It's two inches wide and perfectly circular, surrounded by a ring of white-hot steel. There's a hole in the opposite door too, and it's only a bit smaller. My cameras follow the straight path that the laser beam took, and I notice with horror that there's also a hole in the hangar's steel wall.

DeShawn sees it too. "Uh-oh. That's not good."

I step toward the hole in the wall and bend over so I can point one of my cameras through it. I see the tarmac of McGuire's airfield and the runway where Amber Wilson landed thirty-five minutes ago.

Fortunately, there are no planes or people nearly. But on the other side of the runway, a tall pine tree is on fire.

My circuits swell with relief. The damage could've been a lot worse. "Take a look, dude," I say. "Your laser crisped a tree on the eastern edge of the airfield. That's more than half a mile from here."

I back away from the wall so DeShawn can bend over and peer through the hole. After a couple of seconds, his Einstein-bot grins. "Interesting. It looks like the beam carried at least a billion joules of energy. That makes it as powerful as a lightning bolt." He straightens up and turns to me. "Pretty good for a first test, huh?"

He synthesizes a chuckle. DeShawn is clearly pleased, and I guess I should be too. It looks like the Pioneers have a cool new weapon. Better yet, we're going to make sure that Sigma doesn't steal this one. DeShawn will tweak the design to make the laser so compact and light that each Pioneer can carry it. Then we can use the weapon against Sigma's Snake-bots and Swarm-bots.

But I don't feel pleased right now. In fact, I'm still pretty depressed. Soon I'll have to leave the hangar and go looking for Zia and Marshall. The assignment is so awful that I'd do anything to put it off.

After a moment I hear a fire truck's siren. Someone at the airfield must've spotted the burning tree and called in the military base's firefighters. As I stand there, listening to the distant siren, I realize there's another reason why I feel so bad, and it has to do with the laser. The weapon *isn't* cool. It's deadly and frightening. And what's worse, it's just the beginning. The Pioneers are going to use their electronic brains to build even more devastating weapons, one after another. That's our job now. That's what we're meant to do.

Where will it end?

DeShawn notices my silence and stops grinning. "Hey, what's wrong?"

I point at the perfectly circular hole in the wall. "It's happening too quickly. We're getting too powerful."

The Einstein-bot nods. DeShawn understands what I'm getting at, probably because he's had the same thoughts himself. "You're right. It's scary. But what else can we do? We have to beat Sigma."

"I know, I know. But we're getting farther and farther away from being human."

Neither of us says anything for the next few seconds. The fire truck's siren grows louder. Then my acoustic sensor picks up the squeal of the truck's tires. Although I can't see the vehicle, I know it's stopping near the burning pine tree. I can hear the boots of the firefighters on the tarmac. They're probably wondering, *How the heck did that tree catch fire?*

DeShawn breaks the silence by clanking his hand against my back. The look on his plastic face is reassuring, but also a little impatient. He's anxious to get back to work. "It can't be helped," he says. "We don't have a choice."

CHAPTER

13

AFTER LEAVING DESHAWN'S HANGAR, I STOP BY THE BIOHAZARD TREATMENT Center, but the doctors won't let me inside. They say there's been no change in the condition of the students. All four are still unconscious and smoldering with fever.

Dad's in the treatment center too, still trying to isolate the anthrax microbes that have infected Brittany and the other kids. The doctors say he's too busy to be disturbed, but I bet that's not the real reason they won't let me inside. I'm guessing they don't want another incident like the one that happened this morning. My mom is probably still in the treatment center, still comforting Jack Parker's mother, still praying for the kid's recovery. And meanwhile I'm out here, outside the center's heavily guarded doors, alone and angry.

For a moment I consider barging in. I could easily shove the armed guards aside and bust through the air locks. But instead I just stand there and let the wave of anger run through my circuits. Then I turn my Quarter-bot in the opposite direction and march toward a squat concrete building half a mile away.

This building is normally used as a warehouse for aircraft parts, but General Hawke has turned it into a temporary training facility for the Pioneers. Basically, it's like our Danger Room in New Mexico, a place where we can test our robots in combat simulations. I stride through the building's entrance and head downstairs to the heart of the facility, a cavernous basement room that's as big as a gymnasium. I know Zia will be there. Spurned and insulted by Amber, she'll retreat to what she knows best, the lonely self-discipline of military training. So that's where I'm going too. I can't put off my assignment any longer.

Zia's War-bot stands alone at the far end of the room, which has a high ceiling and fluorescent lights that are way too dim for such a large space. The room is empty except for two huge piles of spare parts on either side of Zia. The pile on her left is about three feet high and nine feet wide. It's a jumbled mound of miscellaneous electronics—motors and sensors and batteries and circuit boards. Thousands of memory chips and microprocessors are scattered across the heap. There's also enough copper wire to electrocute an elephant.

Zia seems to be sifting through the spare parts in the pile. As I stride toward her, she bends her torso over the mound and scans it with her cameras, searching for something. Although her helmetlike head doesn't have a face, I can tell that she's deep in thought. After a couple of seconds she extends her left arm and plunges it into the heap. When she pulls out her hand, she's grasping a tiny silver disk between her steel thumb and index finger.

I focus my own cameras on the disk in her hand. It's an impact sensor, a simple device for detecting collisions. "Let me guess," I say, pointing at the disk. "You're making some improvements to your armor?"

Her War-bot nods. "That's right. I learned something from the last battle." She retracts her arm, bringing her right hand close to her torso, and slips the tiny disk into a slot in her armor. "Be prepared. That's my new motto."

"FYI, it's also the Boy Scouts' motto. So what are you preparing for?"

Zia points at the other pile of parts, a slightly smaller heap sprawled across the floor to her right. I notice that all the parts in this pile are the same: small gray cubes, each an inch wide. They look exactly like the modules in DeShawn's Swarm-bot. This is a little confusing, because DeShawn was in his Einstein-bot when I said good-bye to him fifteen minutes ago. I step closer to the heap of cubes, which are jumbled and motionless, like the modules of Sigma's Swarm-bots after I fried their electronics. "Uh, DeShawn isn't somewhere in that pile, is he?"

"No, those are his spares. He let me borrow a few thousand modules last night so I could figure out a defense against them." Zia extends her right arm now, and I see a small radio transmitter in her hand. "This remote control can send signals to the Swarm-bot. I can activate the swarm and order it to attack. Here, take a look."

She presses a button on the transmitter, and an instant later the pile of modules comes alive. Thousands of cubes start spinning their rotors and rise from the floor. The swarm hovers like a gray cloud over the War-bot's bulbous head. Then the modules attack, all of them descending at once and latching on to Zia's armor. They cover her War-bot like a cloak.

"Now watch this." Her voice is muffled by the modules covering her speakers. "The sensors in my armor detect the cubes landing on me. Then there's an automatic response."

I hear a chorus of metallic zings, like the sound of someone yanking out a drawer full of kitchen knives. At the same time, ten thousand sharp black spikes thrust out of Zia's armor. They extend from every part of her War-bot—torso, head, legs, arms—like the steel quills of a monstrous porcupine. Each spike is only three inches long, but that's long enough to skewer the modules. The pierced cubes hang from Zia's quills for half a second, then all the spikes simultaneously pull back into her armor. Sloughed off, the broken modules clatter to the floor.

I applaud her demonstration, clanking my Quarter-bot's hands together. "Nice job. Simple but effective."

Zia doesn't acknowledge the compliment. Instead, she strides toward me, crushing the fallen modules under her footpads. "Okay, Armstrong, enough fun and games. We got a score to settle." Her War-bot looms over me. I have to tilt my cameras upward to see her head. "Are you ready to take your punishment? For what you did to Shannon?"

I'm nervous, no doubt about it. Few things are as intimidating as a nine-foot-tall War-bot. But I push the noisy fear out of my circuits. "I'm hoping a simple apology will be enough. I already apologized to Shannon, or at least I tried to. And because she's your friend, I'll apologize to you now."

"It's not enough." Her voice is low and fierce. "I talked to Shannon last night. I asked her what you did to hurt her. She was so upset she wouldn't tell me, but I figured it out. The answer was in the memory files we exchanged."

I keep my cameras focused on Zia. Six months ago, just before Sigma captured us, Zia and I got into a fight so vicious she came very close to destroying my electronics. To save myself, I had to transfer all my data to her robot, and for exactly five-point-two seconds we shared the same circuits. I got out of Zia's machine as fast as I could, but in that brief period I saw all of her memories, and she saw all of mine. This happened just a day after I shared circuits with Jenny Harris for the second time. "I guess you're talking about me and Jenny, right? And the virtual-reality program?"

A grunt comes out of the War-bot's speakers. It sounds disdainful, as if Zia thinks this whole business is a little ridiculous. "It wasn't a big deal. You were just fooling around. Sneaking kisses in virtual reality, and whatever else you and Jenny imagined you were doing. I just assumed you told Shannon about it." Zia raises a massive arm and clenches her steel hand. "But you never told Shannon, did you? You hid that secret from her all those months. That was wrong, Adam. That was *cowardly*. You turned it into a big deal by lying about it."

I nod. Zia's saying exactly what Shannon said. And they're both right. "Look, I agree with you. I'm guilty as charged. So if you want to punish me, go ahead. Get it over with."

I aim my cameras at the War-bot's raised fist. It's as big and dense as a bowling ball, and at any moment I expect Zia to slam it down on my Quarter-bot. This girl has no qualms about violence; when we fought six months ago, she carved up my armor with a welding torch. If she wants to punish me now, to teach me a lesson by shattering my robot's head and all its cameras and loudspeakers, she'll do it in a nanosecond. It wouldn't be murder—my neuromorphic circuits are in a safer place, deep inside my torso. In fact it wouldn't even hurt, because the armor in my head has no pressure sensors. There's nothing stopping her.

But her fist hangs in the air, motionless. Zia's War-bot seems paralyzed. She stays silent and still for so long that I start to wonder if her circuits malfunctioned or her software crashed. Finally, she synthesizes another grunt and retracts her arm. She backs away from me, shaking her War-bot's head. "Ahh, it's not worth it. It would take hours to repair you." Then she turns around and strides back to the mound of spare parts.

Zia bends over the pile and scans it again with her cameras. She probably wants me to go away now. But I haven't performed my assignment yet. I take a step toward her. "Listen, there's another reason why I came here to see you. And that reason is all about *you*, not me."

"Really?" Zia doesn't sound very interested in what I have to say.

I take another step forward, my circuits roiling. I feel guilty about what I'm going to do, because it's so deceptive. I'm going to try to trick her into talking too much. But if I can prove that Zia's the traitor, then all my trickery will be justified. "I know why you're upset. You wanted to be friends with Amber, but as soon as she got here, she snubbed you. And that must feel pretty bad."

"*Amber?*" Zia doesn't look at me, but her voice booms with synthesized disgust. "Why should I care about *her*? She's just a know-nothing rookie with a jet pack on her back. I'm *not* impressed."

"Her father served under General Hawke in the First Armored Division. During the war in Iraq. And so did your father." I step toward her until we're just five feet apart. "You wanted to talk to Amber about the war. It was important to you."

"There's nothing to talk about." Zia plunges one of her steel hands into the pile and pulls out a rechargeable battery, identical to the ones that power all the Pioneers. She holds it up to the dim light from the overhead fluorescents and focuses her cameras on it. "My father died in combat, and so did Amber's father. But thousands of other soldiers died there too. And hundreds of thousands of civilians." She studies the battery for another half second, then tosses it back to the mound.

"It was a dirty war, and that's all there is to say. The last thing I need is a sob session with Amber."

I cock my Quarter-bot's head. I don't believe Zia, and I'm trying to signal my skepticism. "I know you better than that. When we shared circuits, I saw your memories of your parents and how they died. You suspected that General Hawke lied about what happened to them."

Zia still won't look at me. She shrugs, lifting her War-bot's shoulder joints. "Everyone lies. Especially generals. That's how they get soldiers to fight for them."

"But you were obsessed with learning the truth! Isn't that why you were so excited about Amber joining the team? Because maybe she knew something? Maybe she could help you find out what—"

"I don't need Amber's help. I already know what I need to know. And now I've got more important things to do with my time."

This last sentence grabs my attention. I have the feeling that Zia just told me more than she intended. "More important things? What do you mean?"

She finally turns from the pile of spare parts and focuses her cameras on me. Because she doesn't have a face, I can't read her expression, but I think she's suspicious. "What's going on, Armstrong? Now that you've messed up with Shannon, you want to go out with me?"

"Huh?" I'm confused. "I don't know what—"

"Well, you're asking me all these personal questions. Does that mean you like me? You want to be my boyfriend?"

I shake my Quarter-bot's head so vigorously, the neck joint screeches. "No, I just—"

"Good, that's a relief. You're not my type. So let's just keep our relationship professional, all right? We're fellow soldiers, that's all. And that means we don't ask each other a lot of personal questions."

Frustration crimps my circuits. I've made no progress at all in the assignment Hawke gave me, and now Zia has shut down the conversation. I'm no good at this. "Okay, fine. I was just trying to help, but I can see it's a waste of time."

"You can't help." Zia's voice drops an octave. She sounds distant and miserable. "No one can help. Because no one really cares."

"You're wrong about that. We're a team. We're the Pioneers. We look out for each—"

"Go away, Adam." Zia swings her cameras back to the pile of spare parts. "Just leave me alone."

CHAPTER

14

JOINT BASE MCGUIRE'S WIND TUNNEL IS ON THE OTHER SIDE OF THE AIRFIELD, inside a building that looks like the world's biggest trumpet. That's where I find Marshall.

At one end of the building is a gaping circular mouth, more than two hundred feet across. The rest of the building is much narrower; like a trumpet, it tapers to a slender tube, although in this case the tube is slender only in a relative sense—it's fifty feet wide and six hundred feet long. The building is made of steel, and its walls vibrate slightly from the sounds inside.

My acoustic sensor detects these vibrations, and after a moment it determines what's making the noise: a pair of synthesized voices. I can't hear them well enough to understand what they're saying, but I can tell that one of the voices belongs to Marshall. The other has the twangy accent of the newest Pioneer, Private Amber Wilson.

I enter through a steel door at the midpoint of the tube. Inside is the wind tunnel's test chamber, which is big enough to hold an F-22 fighter jet. The building's mouth is a hundred yards to my left, and an equal distance to my right is an enormous eight-bladed fan. It's not turning now, but the fan is the source of the tunnel's wind. When it spins, it pulls air into the tunnel, like the fan in a vacuum cleaner. The air rushes into the building through its wide mouth and gathers speed in the narrowing tube. Then it gusts at hurricane strength into the test chamber and under the wings of any aircraft positioned there. Last, the air is sucked into the fan and blown out the other end of the tunnel.

Under ordinary circumstances, military engineers use the wind tunnel to analyze the aerodynamics of their jets and helicopters, but right now there are no engineers or aircraft in the building. Instead, Amber stands behind Marshall at the center of the test chamber's steel-plate floor. Her Jet-bot's black arms are clutched around the torso of his Super-bot.

Both Pioneers pivot their heads toward me as I stride into the chamber. Marshall synthesizes a chuckle while Amber lets out a delighted cry. "Corporal Armstrong!" She raises her right arm to salute me but keeps her left wrapped around the Super-bot. "What a surprise! You're just in time!"

I return her salute, but focus my cameras on Marshall. His Super-bot is grinning. He doesn't look embarrassed; on the contrary, he seems genuinely pleased by my unexpected arrival. His smile makes me feel terrible, just as guilty as I felt when I talked with Zia ten minutes ago. I'm being deceptive again—this isn't a chance meeting. I came here to wheedle information out of my fellow Pioneers. But I tell myself once again that deception is necessary. It's justified if it'll help me find out who betrayed us.

"In time for what?" I point a steel finger at them. "Are you two putting on a show?"

"Settle down, Adam." Marshall skews his plastic lips, enlarging his Super-bot's grin. "It's not what you think."

"Professional wrestling? Mixed martial arts? Are you practicing takedowns?"

"No, nothing so dramatic. This is a training exercise, believe it or not."

"It's flight training," Amber interjects. "I thought of a maneuver we might be able to use in combat."

Her voice is cheerful and enthusiastic, but also a little sly. I suspect she's breaking the rules. She's not supposed to be here. "I thought Shannon was giving you a tour of the base?"

"Oh, that lasted only fifteen minutes. Lieutenant Gibbs had to rush off somewhere. But I ran into Corporal Baxley, and when I told him about my flight training idea, he said he was willing to give it a try."

Marshall lifts his Super-bot's shoulders, shrugging inside Amber's embrace. "I'll try anything once." He chuckles again. "Twice if I like it."

He winks at me with one of his plastic eyelids. This is typical Marshall Baxley behavior, and if I'd seen him cavorting like this yesterday, I would've thought nothing of it. But now I'm suspicious. Did he really run into Amber by accident, or did he seek her out? Is he following orders from Sigma? Maybe recruiting another ally for the AI?

The suspicions make me uncomfortable. I shift my cameras, aiming them squarely at Amber. "So, uh, what's this maneuver?"

"It's better if I just show you." She activates her radio transmitter and sends a wireless signal to the wind tunnel's controls. A moment later, the giant fan at the end of the tunnel starts to turn. "Grab hold of something solid, Adam. As we say in Oklahoma, 'There's a storm a-coming!'"

The fan spins slowly at first, its twelve-foot blades turning clockwise like the vanes of a windmill. But after a few seconds, it spins faster, and the blades whirl around their hub in a bright, noisy blur. The fan powers the airflow down the tunnel, and soon a brisk wind is streaming through the test chamber. The sensors in my armor allow me to track the steady increase in the wind speed: forty miles per hour, then eighty, then a hundred and twenty.

As the wind buffets my Quarter-bot, I stretch my arms toward the chamber's wall and grasp a steel column to anchor myself. Meanwhile, Amber extends her Jet-bot's wings from the upper sections of her arms but keeps her robotic forearms and hands clasped around Marshall. She also extends the jet pack from her back and fires up the engine. The jet's thrust counters the pressure of the wind, which is strong enough to buoy Amber's wings. Her Jet-bot's footpads lift off the floor. As she rises, she carries Marshall's Super-bot with her.

The two robots ascend twenty feet and hover in the center of the test chamber, riding the ferocious gale that's coursing down the tunnel. Amber straightens her robotic body to form a streamlined aircraft, and Marshall hangs from her belly like an oversize missile. The wind speed in the tunnel is almost three hundred miles per hour now. Although I can barely stay on my footpads and the howling is so loud it overwhelms my sensors, I can still detect Marshall's and Amber's voices at the heart of the maelstrom. Marshall is trying to give instructions—"Go a little higher! And more to the right! *No, no, to the right!*"—but Amber doesn't seem to be listening. A triumphant whoop comes out of her loudspeakers. "*Yeah! Hi-Yo, Silver! Away!*"

Because Marshall and Amber may not be able to hear me if I shout at them, I send a radio message instead: *Hey, nice takeoff. You two look great together.*

Marshall responds first: **Well, well, do I detect a note of jealousy? Do you wish you were up here too?**

That depends on what happens next. Are you ready to show me that maneuver, Amber?

Yes, sir! Ready as I'll ever be! Even over the radio, Amber's voice has a Wild West twang. **Okay, Marshall, remember what I told you? Let's do this thing just like we planned. On the count of three: one, two...**

Wait, I'm not quite—

...three!

Amber unclasps her hands and lets go of Marshall. Unfortunately, his robot isn't as aerodynamic as Amber's. The three-hundred-miles-per-hour wind slams into the Super-bot and hurls it down the tunnel.

Marshall plummets to the steel-plate floor, clattering and tumbling toward the fan. He flails his robotic arms and claws at the steel, his fingers carving long gouges to slow himself down. His robot finally slides to a stop, just fifty feet from the fan's whirling blades.

Amber radios a command to shut down the airflow. The fan blades start to slow, and the wind in the tunnel dies down. While Amber lands her Jet-bot and retracts her wings, I race down the tunnel to see if Marshall's okay. His Super-bot lies on its torso, which is dented in several places. His plastic forehead and cheeks are torn, exposing the armor underneath.

"Hey, Marsh? You all right?" I lean over him. "Are your circuits damaged?"

He tests his Super-bot's motors, flexing its arms and legs. Then he aims his cameras at the machine's torso, scanning the dents in his armor. Finally, Marshall lifts his robot's head and looks at me. "I'm not

seriously hurt. Just some cosmetic damage. But trust me, Adam, I'm
seriously angry." Using the Super-bot's arms to lever himself upright,
Marshall gets back on his footpads. "That girl is a menace. She pretends she's an expert, but she has no idea what she's doing. If I were
Hawke, I'd send her right back to Oklahoma."

He points his cameras at Amber, who's striding toward us. She
swings her Jet-bot's arms, swaggering like an actor in a cowboy movie.
"Okay, we gotta work on the landing. But it wasn't so bad for a first
try, right?"

"Are you crazy?" Marshall points at the dents in his torso. "You
almost killed me!"

Amber shakes her robot's head. "Come on, you're exaggerating. All
your systems are functional. If we were in combat, you could jump
back into the fight." She turns to me. "That's the whole point of the
maneuver. I can use it to transport other Pioneers to a battle, without
the need to land."

I stare at her. Amber's confidence is astounding, and so is her cocki-
ness. I can't help but wonder if she was like this before she became a
Pioneer. "Look, it's a good idea, at least in theory. But in the future
you should—"

"You should find someone else to practice your stunts with!"
Marshall's voice echoes down the tunnel, loud and high-pitched.
"You're criminally reckless! And unforgivably stupid! From now on,
just stay away from me!"

Amber turns back to Marshall. She extends her arms, steel hands
turned up, in a conciliatory gesture. "Hey, I'm sorry, okay? I didn't
mean to—"

"Why are you even here?" Marshall scrunches his plastic face into
a scowl. The rips in his cheeks and forehead make him look sinister.

"Just yesterday you were dying. You were probably begging for pain-killers and crying for your mama."

Amber slowly lowers her arms. As I watch her reaction, I remember something Hawke told us about the girl: while Amber was in the last weeks of her illness, her mother committed suicide. Most likely because she couldn't stand to watch her daughter suffer.

"And look at you now!" Marshall clenches his hands. "The Army gives you a strong, steel body and you think you're saved! You think you're invincible!"

Amber's torso is vibrating in distress. I move toward her, trying to shield her from Marshall, but he extends his Super-bot's arm and pushes me away. "You're not saved, Amber! And you're not invincible! Sigma is out there, and it's a thousand times stronger than us! You're going to die again, and this time you won't come back!"

"Marshall!" Appalled, I push back at him, slamming my Quarter-bot's hands against his armor. "Stop it right now!"

He stands his ground, still scowling. I lean my weight against his machine and focus my cameras on his Superman face, now torn and full of hate. For a moment I don't even recognize him. *This isn't the Marshall I know. This is someone else.*

Then he steps backward, pulling away from me so suddenly that I almost tip over. Without another word, Marshall marches back to the test chamber. Five seconds later he exits the wind tunnel.

I watch him leave. *Is he the traitor?* I still don't know. But if I had to make a guess right now, I'd say it's more likely to be Marshall than Zia. Because his behavior is inhuman. Something has changed him.

I raise my hand to my head and rub the armored plate above my camera lenses. Then I turn to Amber. Her torso isn't vibrating any-more, which I guess is a good sign. "Uh, are you okay? That was—"

"I'm fine."

That's all she says. Her Jet-bot doesn't move. She just stands there in the tunnel, as still as a statue. I can't be sure what's going through her circuits, but I bet she's thinking about what Marshall said, about Sigma and dying and her final hours in her human body. I get the feeling that Amber will never be the same, never as cocky and free-spirited as she was just a few minutes ago. And now that she's hurting so badly, she reminds me of Jenny, who was so scared before she became a Pioneer and so lost and vulnerable afterward.

I take a step toward Amber. "Listen, I gotta apologize for Marshall. He was damaged in our last battle, and ever since then he's—"

"Sorry, I have to go." She turns away from me and heads for the exit.

"Wait, where are you—"

"I have to find Lieutenant Gibbs. Our tour got cut short before she could give me an assignment." Amber shakes her Jet-bot's head as she hurries off. "If I'm going to live inside a machine, I need an assignment. I need a job to keep me busy. Otherwise, I'll go nuts."

A moment later she strides out of the wind tunnel. Then I'm alone again.

⊤ ⊤ ⊤

Although it's only one o'clock in the afternoon, my circuits are already strained to their breaking point. I run a diagnostic check on my electronics and see the reason for their poor performance: it's been nine days since the last time I put my Quarter-bot into sleep mode, and that's way too long. So I go to the quietest spot on the Air Force base—a bunker used for storing classified documents—and start shutting down my systems.

First, I cut the power to my motors, freezing my Quarter-bot in a standing position beside the stacked boxes of old papers. Next, I turn off all my sensors—the cameras, the acoustic sensors, the accelerometers, everything. I deliberately plunge my mind into a silent black sea where there's no up or down, no surface or bottom. Then I disconnect all my radio links except for a backup communications system that can send me an alert in case of an emergency. And last, I shut down the logic circuits that organize my thinking and sustain my consciousness. Now my thoughts are free to travel where they will, diving and weaving through my memories and emotions. In other words, I can dream.

It begins with a memory of my mother. When I was nine years old, Mom was supposed to drive me to a doctor's appointment because my muscular dystrophy was getting worse. I couldn't walk more than twenty feet without stumbling, and my doctor wanted me to come to his office for some tests. But Mom couldn't bear to hear any more bad news about my condition, so instead of taking me to Westchester Medical Center, she drove me to Rockefeller State Park.

We went for a walk in a grassy field, and Mom said I could let go of her hand. It didn't matter if I stumbled, she said, because the ground was soft and smelled like spring. I fell on the grass a hundred times that afternoon, but for once I didn't feel frustrated or embarrassed. Mom and I laughed and lay on the ground and looked up at the clouds. It's one of my favorite memories, so that's where I start my dream.

In real life, Dad wasn't at the park that day, but in my dream he's lying on the grass with Mom and me, gazing at the sky. He looks young in my dream, without any lines on his face or gray hairs on his head. We start playing a game, surveying all the clouds and pointing out the ones that look like animals. I point at a big, round cloud and shout, "That's a turtle!" and in my dream, the cloud looks *exactly* like a turtle, with four stubby legs and an oblong head.

Mom shouts, "Horse!" and the cloud she points at is a perfect replica of a rearing stallion. Then Dad points at a long, slender cloud and yells, "Snake!" but it doesn't really look like a snake. The cloud has dozens of dark rings dividing it into segments. I feel a creeping terror as I stare at it. It's *not* a snake. It's a Snake-bot.

The dream lurches into nightmare. The Snake-bot coils and slithers across the sky. Mom vanishes—*Where did she go? I don't see her anywhere!*—and Dad ages ten years in an instant. Gray-haired and gaunt, he points at me, and I notice that I'm no longer a nine-year-old boy. I'm inside my Quarter-bot, but the machine isn't working. I can't move my mechanical arms and legs. I'm on my back, paralyzed, and Sigma's Snake-bot stretches toward me. A moment later Dad vanishes too. The Snake-bot's sharp tip hangs in the air, just a few yards above me.

Then I see a woman running across the grassy field. At first I think it's Mom, but this woman is skinnier and much younger. It's a teenager. *It's Jenny Harris.* She's wearing a fancy cashmere sweater and a blue hat that hides her baldness. This is how she looked before she became a Pioneer, when she was just an ordinary seventeen-year-old dying of cancer. She races toward me, waving her arms.

"Adam!" she yells. "You have to run! You have to get out of here!"

All I can do is stare at her. I remember kissing Jenny in the virtual-reality program. I remember the softness of her lips, the silkiness of her skin. And I also remember that she's dead. Sigma erased her. She's gone.

And yet she seems so real as she rushes across the grass and kneels beside me. She grabs my Quarter-bot by the shoulder joints and stares into my camera lenses. *"You're in danger, Adam!"* she screams. "Don't you see it?"

The steel tentacle curls in the air above us. But I don't care about Sigma anymore. I'm so happy to see Jenny again that nothing else matters. "I thought you were dead," I whisper. "Are you real or just one of my memories?"

"You don't see it!" She tightens her grip on my Quarter-bot and tries to shake the heavy machine. "You're not paying attention!"

The Snake-bot descends, slowly and silently. It's less than three feet away.

"Adam! Please respond!"

I'm startled. Jenny's lips are moving, but the voice coming out of her mouth isn't hers. I'm listening to my father's voice now, and the message isn't coming from the dream. I'm getting an alert from my emergency communications system. Dad's trying to get in touch with me!

I restart my logic circuits and emerge from the dream. The grassy field in Rockefeller State Park disappears, and I'm back inside the Air Force bunker, surrounded by boxes of classified documents. I transmit a radio signal on the emergency system, responding to the message I just received. *Dad? What is it?*

There you are! I've been looking all over for you!

What's wrong? Are we under attack?

No, no, but you need to come right away to the Biohazard Treatment Center.

Why? What do you—

It's Brittany. And the other kids. They're awake.

CHAPTER

I RUN FULL SPEED ACROSS THE AIR FORCE BASE AND GET TO THE BIOHAZARD Treatment Center in less than three minutes. After an interminable wait at the air lock, I rush into the intensive care unit where the four students from Yorktown High School have spent the past eighteen hours in fever-induced comas. But now all four of them are sitting up on their gurneys, their backs propped against pillows, their beds surrounded by doctors and nurses in moon suits. The kids look tousled and a bit woozy from their unnaturally long nap, but they're alert enough to notice my Quarter-bot. Their mouths drop open in disbelief.

The youngest, Emma Chin, seems the most surprised. She shakes her head in wonder as I enter the room. Tim Rodriguez gives me a more suspicious look, narrowing his eyes. But Jack Parker has the most extreme reaction: he grips the guardrails on either side of his bed and presses himself back against his pillows. He's terrified at the sight of me. But I pivot my cameras past him to focus on the girl at the other end of the room, the pale, slender blond I've known since kindergarten.

Brittany leans forward on her gurney, her blue hospital gown hanging loosely from her shoulders. She stares at my Quarter-bot as I approach her. My dad stands at her bedside, wearing his protective suit and holding a clipboard in one of his gloved hands. I assume he's already told her about my transformation from human to machine, but I have no idea how she'll react when she sees what I've become. Will she scream in horror? Break down in tears? Or, worst of all, will she react like my mother? Will Brittany decide that I'm just a copy of Adam Armstrong and tell me to get out of her sight?

I stop at the foot of her gurney. An IV line is still attached to her right arm, and there are dark circles under her eyes, but otherwise she looks pretty healthy. I switch my cameras to the infrared range: her body temperature is exactly 98.6 degrees. Even better, her heart rate and blood pressure are back to normal. A surge of relief sweeps through my circuits. *She survived the anthrax! She's going to be fine!* But then she shakes her head and bites her lower lip, and my relief turns to panic. *She's stunned. She's scared. She doesn't recognize me!*

Dad steps forward, his moon suit crinkling. Behind the suit's visor, his face is as anxious as ever, his eyes darting from me to Brittany and back again. He reaches for the curtain hanging next to the bed and pulls it out full-length to give us some privacy. Then he clears his throat and stretches a gloved hand toward my Quarter-bot. "Uh, Brittany? This is the robot I mentioned, the one that Adam's occupying right now. It's equipped with cameras and acoustic sensors, so he can see and hear you. And it has loudspeakers too, so he can talk. Say hello, Adam."

Desperate, I try to think of something to say. I want to prove I'm really Adam Armstrong. I want to convince her beyond a doubt that her old friend is inside this machine. I devote all my processing power to the problem, and in a hundredth of a second I come up with three thousand possible solutions, most of them long speeches that attempt to verify my identity by listing all the personal details and secrets that only Adam Armstrong could know. But in the end I conclude that shorter is better. I give my synthesized voice a casual tone and say, "Hey, Britt. How are you feeling?"

She doesn't answer. Instead, her eyes water as they stare at me.

My panic rises, jangling my circuits. "Listen, I'm sorry. I should've told you about this sooner. I had all those months to do it, while I was at our base in New Mexico. But I was afraid, you know? I was so afraid."

She starts to cry. Tears leak from the corners of her eyes and slide down her cheeks. But she doesn't make a sound.

This is worse than physical pain. My soul is writhing inside my wires. "Am I scaring you, Britt? I'll go away if I'm scaring you. Because that's the last thing I want to do."

Another tear drips down her cheek. Then she shakes her head again. "No, I'm not scared. That's not why I'm crying. I just feel so sorry for you, Adam."

That last word echoes in my electronics. *She said my name! She believes I'm Adam Armstrong!* "I'm all right. Really, I'm—"

"Your dad explained the whole thing. How he recorded everything in your brain. And then moved all your memories into a computer." She wipes her eyes and looks up at Dad for a moment. Then she turns back to me. "To tell you the truth, I didn't believe him before I saw you. But now I do."

Dad leans over the gurney. I catch a glimpse of his face through the visor, and it seems that his anxiety has eased a bit, replaced by a look of scientific curiosity. "What changed your mind?"

Brittany keeps her eyes on me and smiles. "It's simple. As soon as I heard Adam's voice, I knew."

I can't speak. I can't synthesize a word. The joy I'm feeling is so powerful it occupies every circuit inside me, every transistor and microchip and logic gate. This is the best moment of my life, robotic or otherwise.

No one says anything for a while. Then Dad breaks the silence by clearing his throat again. "I also told Brittany about Sigma. And the attack on Yorktown Heights. I explained how the anthrax killed nearly everyone."

Brittany stops smiling. "But not me. And not my parents. They were at work in the city." She grimaces. "I guess I should be happy they survived, right?"

The look on her face extinguishes some of my joy. There's an unbridgeable gulf between Brittany and her parents. Otherwise, they'd be here right now.

I decide to change the subject. I gesture at Dad's clipboard. "So what's Britt's condition? Is her immune system still fighting off the anthrax, or is she clear of the infection?"

Dad looks down and starts flipping through her patient chart. I aim my cameras so I can scan the medical data: the results of blood tests, X-rays, CAT scans. But before I can view all the information, Dad tilts the clipboard so I can't see it anymore. "Brittany's condition is excellent," he says, smiling at her. "But we'll need to keep her under observation for at least a few more hours."

Now I'm suspicious. Dad's hiding something. But I don't say anything in front of Brittany. I don't want to alarm her.

Dad clears his throat a third time. It's a really annoying habit of his, and it always gets worse when he's nervous. "Well, I better get going. I still have more tests to run. Adam, you can stay here for another fifteen minutes, but after that you should let our patient get some rest."

Brittany nods, smiling again. "I'm not tired, Mr. Armstrong, but I'll do whatever you say. Thanks so much for everything."

"There's no need to thank me. I'm just glad you're getting better." Dad pats her arm, then leaves.

I wait until Dad's out of the intensive care unit. Then I point a steel finger at Brittany's IV tube and the clear liquid that's dripping into her arm. "So are you happy with the nutrient solution you're getting? Or are you hungry for some real food?"

He eyes widen. "I would *love* some real food. Do you think they have any sandwiches in this place?"

I feel another spark of joy. Brittany's treating me the same way she'd treat any friend. She isn't flustered or even distracted by the fact that she's talking to a robot. It seems too good to be true, and that bothers me a little. How did I get so lucky?

But I'm not going to overthink it. I'm going to enjoy my good luck while it lasts. "Yeah, I can rustle up a sandwich. You still like turkey and cheddar?"

"Oh my God, Adam, that would be fantastic. But can you really—"

"Just watch me. I'll be back in five minutes."

I stride out of the ward, ignoring the stares from Jack, Tim, and Emma. Then I head for the laboratory where Dad installed his analysis equipment. He set up the lab inside the Biohazard Treatment Center because he didn't want to carry any contaminated blood samples outside. The only disadvantage is that he has to stay in his moon suit while he's working. He's staring through his visor at a computer screen as I enter the lab, but he turns his head when he hears me come in.

"Adam? What are you doing here? I thought you'd want to spend more time with—"

"What's wrong with Brittany? What aren't you telling me?"

Dad lets out a long sigh. "Can we talk about this a little later? I'll have better information once I run some more tests on—"

"No! I want to talk about it now!" My voice is so loud it rattles the lab equipment. I lower the volume of my speakers and try to stay calm. "Is Brittany still infected or not?"

He frowns behind his visor. "I don't know if she's still infected. Or any of the other kids, for that matter. I was never able to isolate the anthrax bacteria from their blood or tissue samples. I found plenty of anthrax spores clinging to their clothes and skin, but no germs inside their bodies."

"So what made them sick? I thought they inhaled the anthrax spores into their lungs, and then the spores released the bacteria. Isn't that how it works?"

Dad nods. "Yes, the spores germinate in the lung tissue and the bacteria start to grow and multiply. I suppose it's possible that Sigma modified the anthrax so radically that the standard tests can't detect the bacteria. But I looked at all the blood samples under the microscope and didn't see bacteria of *any* kind. Not a single microbe."

"But it has to be an infection, right? I mean, those kids were really sick. And all those other people died."

"Yes, it certainly looks like an infection. And I guess the cause of the infection could be a virus instead of a bacterium. Viruses are much smaller than bacteria, too small to show up on a microscope slide. Maybe Sigma discovered a way to combine the worst qualities of bacteria and viruses. Maybe it used anthrax spores to spread a new kind of virus that can kill within minutes."

Dad's thinking out loud, looking at the evidence like a scientist, and proposing theories to explain it all. But I can tell from his tone of voice that these explanations don't satisfy him. He sounds uncertain.

"I only want to know one thing, Dad. Is Brittany safe?"

He shrugs inside his moon suit. "I don't think she's contagious anymore because we got rid of all the anthrax spores on her skin. But is a virus still inside her? And will it do any more damage? I won't know till I do more research. Certain viruses can hide in the body for years. They're especially good at hiding inside nerve cells and brain cells."

This isn't a very comforting answer, but I guess it's the best he can offer now. I'll just have to wait for him to finish his tests. "Okay, okay. But keep me in the loop, all right? If you discover something important, I want to know about it."

"Yes, Adam, of course. Now are we finished? Can I get back to my work?"

Luckily, my electronic mind forgets nothing. "Do you know where I can find a turkey-and-cheddar sandwich?"

CHAPTER

AFTER SPENDING ANOTHER FIFTEEN MINUTES WITH BRITTANY, I LEAVE THE
Biohazard Treatment Center and spread the news of her recovery to
the other Pioneers. But to my surprise, no one seems as relieved as I
am. DeShawn's busy with his laser, Zia's reinforcing her armor, and
Marshall's repairing his plastic face. When I tell Amber that the four
Yorktown High School kids have emerged from their comas, all she
says is, "Very interesting." Shannon's reaction is a little closer to what I
expected: she raises her sparkling arms and cries, "Thank God! That's
wonderful!" But then she shakes her head and adds, "If only there
were more. Just four survivors out of twenty thousand. It's so awful,
so horrible."

She's right—the statistics are devastating. And maybe it's stupid to
be happy about those four kids when so many others died. But I'm
happy anyway.

Then, at 3:00 p.m., General Hawke orders all the Pioneers to an
emergency briefing. We gather again at the air base's headquarters,

inside the wood-paneled conference room that's way too small for us. Now it's even more packed than before because Amber's here too and Zia has bulked up her armor. In addition, Hawke has set up a wall-size video screen that takes up all the space at the front of the room. On the screen is a satellite photograph of Yorktown Heights.

"All right, Pioneers, this is what we've been waiting for." Hawke stands in front of the screen and taps the bottom of the photo, which shows the wooded hills in the southern half of my hometown. "Our surveillance satellites have detected some suspicious activity in this area."

The general points a remote-control device at the screen and uses it to enlarge the lower section of the photo. There aren't many houses in that part of Yorktown Heights, but on Kitchawan Road there's a three-story, glass-fronted building shaped like a crescent. I recognize it immediately: it's the Unicorp Research Laboratory. My dad worked there for twenty years, leading the research group that developed artificial-intelligence software for the U.S. Army. That's where he created Sigma.

Hawke steps closer to the screen and points at a wooded slope just north of the lab. There's a long gouge running through the woods, a trench of brown mud bordered on both sides by uprooted trees. At the bottom of the trench is a gleam of silver. It's a Snake-bot rising to the surface.

"Over the past hour our satellites have spotted thirteen Snake-bots near the Unicorp Research Laboratory." Hawke sweeps his hand across the screen, pointing at other trenches to the north and south. "The machines seem to have arrived all at once, probably after tunneling across the globe from North Korea. We can't tell from the photos what the Snake-bots are doing, but it's no accident that they've converged on the Unicorp lab. It looks like Sigma has returned to the place of its birth."

I scrutinize the satellite photo. I was there six months ago, inside my dying human body, when Sigma took over Dad's lab and blew up half a dozen offices. The photograph shows scaffolding at the damaged end of the building, where the repair work is still unfinished. The photo also shows a massive pileup of cars in the lab's parking lot. When the anthrax spores hit Yorktown Heights yesterday and spread down the corridors of the Unicorp lab, the infected workers must've panicked and tried to drive away from the building. But judging from the photo, no one made it out of the parking lot, and many of the workers didn't even make it to their cars. At least thirty corpses are sprawled on the asphalt.

It's a struggle to curb the anger that's flaring in my circuits, but I manage to raise my steel hand to get Hawke's attention. "Sir, is there any advanced machinery at the Unicorp lab that Sigma can use for its own purposes?"

As I expected, the general nods. "Unfortunately, there is. I talked to your father a few minutes ago, and he gave me a full inventory of the equipment there. Although he dismantled all of the lab's neuromorphic computers after Sigma escaped from them, the building still holds an automated manufacturing system that can produce a wide variety of electronic parts. Sigma could use the system to upgrade its Snake-bots and maybe even build new ones."

Shannon raises her Diamond Girl's hand. It glitters under the conference room's fluorescent lights. "Sir, the U.S. Air Force should launch an immediate strike against the Unicorp lab. They should send a whole squadron of planes to bomb the building and any Snake-bots near it."

Hawke nods again. "That's an excellent idea, Gibbs, but there's a complication." He presses a button on his remote-control device, and the video screen shows a different photograph of the laboratory. In this image, there are no trenches near the building. "Our satellite took this photo a bit earlier, fifteen minutes before the first Snake-bot arrived. Look carefully at the driveway in front of the lab."

I feel a shock as sharp and jarring as a short circuit. There's a small crowd approaching the building's entrance. Twenty-nine people, to be precise, walking in a loose cluster. The satellite photo is so detailed that it shows the sweat stains on their shirts and the fatigued expressions on their faces. They look exhausted, like soldiers who've just finished a twenty-mile march. But the people in this photo are too young to be soldiers. They're children. "They're from the Brookside Elementary School," Hawke adds. "Earlier photographs show them marching across Yorktown Heights toward the lab. No adults are with them in any of the photos."

"My God." Shannon turns away from the screen. Her Diamond Girl looks a little unsteady. "How did they survive the anthrax?"

DeShawn's Einstein-bot steps toward her and offers his steel arm for support. "The teens resisted the disease better than the adults did. If youth is a protective factor, then it's logical that the younger children would survive too."

"But wouldn't they go home?" Shannon's voice is high and quavering. "Why walk to an office building?"

Zia points at the photo. "Sigma lured them there. To protect itself from an air strike. The AI knows we won't bomb the building if it's full of children."

The room falls silent. The truth is so horrible that none of us knows what to say. I glance at the other Pioneers to gauge their reactions, and they seem dumbstruck, well and truly freaked. Marshall has a disgusted frown on his plastic face. He shakes his Super-bot's head and mutters, "Hideous, it's just hideous."

But are his feelings genuine? Or is he putting on a show?

Finally, Hawke presses another button on his remote control, and the video screen goes blank. "I think all of you know what comes next. The Pioneers are going back to Yorktown Heights." He looks at his watch. "The operation will begin in thirty-five minutes. Gibbs, I want a tactical plan. Figure out a way to hold off the Snake-bots and get those children out of the lab." He turns to DeShawn. "Johnson, go get your laser. Ready or not, we're gonna use it." And then, to my surprise, Hawke points at my Quarter-bot. "Armstrong, come with me to the command station. I want a complete description of the layout of your dad's laboratory. Everyone else, report to the airfield. The V-22 is already on the runway."

Without wasting another second, Hawke strides out of the conference room, looking very much like a Pioneer himself. I have to quickstep down the corridor to keep up with him. He turns left and marches up a stairway. Then he leads me into a small, windowless room and shuts the door behind us.

This isn't a command station. It's a supply closet. Puzzled, I point my cameras at the shelves. We're surrounded by boxes of toilet paper and emergency rations.

I turn back to Hawke. He's scowling so hard, his eyes look like pale marbles sunk deep in his ruddy face. "What do you have for me, Armstrong?"

I'm confused. "Sir? Are you talking about the layout of the Unicorp—"

"No, I already have all that information. I'm talking about the assignment I gave you. What intelligence have you got so far?"

Now I understand why we're in this out-of-the-way closet at the far end of the headquarters building. Hawke wants to make sure that no one overhears us. "Uh, the truth is, I don't have much to tell you. I'm not the best person to do this kind of—"

"You talked with Allawi, right? And with Baxley too?"

I nod. "Neither one confessed, if that's what you want to know."

"Armstrong, I don't have time for your attitude right now. Let me describe the situation in the simplest terms possible." He raises his right hand and points his index finger directly at my camera lenses. "I know one of the Pioneers is a traitor. In thirty-two minutes I'm going to put your team on a plane to Yorktown Heights. Do you know what'll happen if I let the traitor board that aircraft with the rest of you?"

I shake my Quarter-bot's head. "No, sir, I don't."

"Neither do I. But I can assure you, it won't be good." He stops pointing at me and grabs my Quarter-bot's arm just above the elbow joint. This is surprising and disturbing. Hawke almost never touches our robots. "Now listen carefully. I need to determine which of the Pioneers is the traitor. I'm going to pull that robot off the Unicorp mission, so it won't threaten the rest of you. That Pioneer is going to stay behind, here at McGuire, where I can keep an eye on it. But I need your help to make this decision. Based on everything you've seen and heard, who do you think the traitor is?"

It's not fair. He can't force me to do this. "Sir, you're asking me to accuse one of my friends. And I can't do that without proof."

"No, you're not listening." The sensors in my arm detect an increase in pressure. Hawke is tightening his grip. "You say they're your friends, and that means you care about them. So what will make your friends safer? Should I take Zia off the mission?"

I shake my head again. "No! That won't help! It'll only—"

"What about Marshall?"

This isn't fair. And yet Hawke is right—we'll be safer if the traitor doesn't come with us to the Unicorp lab. For everyone's sake, I have to use my best judgment. I have to make a choice.

I remain silent for six long seconds, forcing Hawke to wait, making it clear I don't want to do this. Then I say, "Yes, pull Marshall off the mission."

Hawke doesn't thank me. He simply nods and lets go of my arm. Then he looks at his watch again.

"You have thirty-one minutes to get to the airfield. That gives you just enough time to say good-bye to your dad."

ㅠ ㅠ ㅠ

I can't find Dad. He's not in his lab at the Biohazard Treatment Center. The doctors there say they don't know where he went, and I can't reach him on his cell phone.

I rush into the intensive care unit to look for him, but he's not there either. The ward is much less busy than it was a couple of hours ago; the doctors and nurses in moon suits have taken three of their four patients to the treatment center's X-ray and CAT scan machines. Only Brittany remains on her gurney, and no one seems to be monitoring her. She's sitting up in bed, leafing through a copy of the *Air Force Times*, which is probably the only reading material available here.

I notice that she no longer has an IV line hooked to her arm, and the gurney's guardrails are down. Except for the fact that she's still wearing a blue hospital gown, it looks like she could be relaxing at home, in her own bedroom. As she reads the newspaper, she twirls a lock of her blond hair around her index finger.

When she hears the clanking of my Quarter-bot, she looks up and smiles.

"Hey, it's you again." She tosses aside the *Air Force Times*, which falls to the floor. "I didn't think you'd be back so soon."

Once again I'm amazed that Brittany's acting so normally. She's treating me like an old friend and totally ignoring that I'm inside an eight-hundred-pound robot. It's hard to believe that she could adapt to this change so quickly and talk to me without even a trace of uneasiness. But maybe she's working really hard at it. Maybe she's fighting her instincts and tamping down her fears and putting on a happy face for my benefit. Either way, I'm grateful. If I had a face, I'd smile back at her.

"Hey, Britt. I'm looking for my dad. Have you seen him in the last half hour or so?"

"No, the last time I saw him was when the three of us were talking." She raises her hand to her forehead and brushes the hair from her eyes. Then she reaches for the back of her neck and scratches an itch there. "Why are you looking for him?"

I don't want to tell her about the Unicorp mission. Brittany's been through enough. And there's no point in making her worry. "Oh, we usually get together at this time of day. You know, just to talk."

It's not the most convincing lie I've ever told, and Brittany clearly doesn't buy it. She turns her head to the side and narrows her eyes. "What, like a father-and-son chat? You and your dad do that every day?"

"Uh, no, not every day. But, you know, pretty often."

She looks askance at me for a few more seconds. Then she shrugs.

"Well, you're lucky to have a dad who likes to talk. My dad yells at me a lot, but we don't have too many conversations. And don't even get me started about Mom." Brittany looks down at her bedsheet. She sounds more sad than angry. "You know I ran away from home, right?"

I nod my Quarter-bot's head. "Yeah, I heard."

"I just want you to know I had good reasons for leaving. You can't imagine how awful it was, living with my parents. *Anything* would've been better."

I'm surprised she's talking about this. In all our years of friendship Brittany never once mentioned her troubles at home. I think it's great that she's willing to confide in me, and under ordinary circumstances, I'd be happy to listen to her, but in nineteen minutes I have to be at the airfield to board the V-22 that's waiting on the runway. "Listen, I—"

"It was torture. Nothing I did was good enough for them." She folds her arms across her chest, as if she just felt a chill. Then she scratches the back of her neck again. "I got good grades, I was on the cheerleading squad, I did volunteer work at church. But they were always on my case."

"Britt—"

"Even after I ran away, they couldn't stop playing head games with me. Do you know why I was in Yorktown Heights yesterday? My dad left an urgent message at the youth shelter where I've been staying." Frowning, she scratches her neck harder. "The message said Mom had a heart attack, and I should meet Dad at Yorktown High School so he could drive me to the hospital. But he never showed up. So I went to the school office and called the hospital, and you know what they said? My mom wasn't even there. Dad wanted me to feel guilty, so he tricked me into coming home."

All at once I stop thinking about the Unicorp mission. Brittany doesn't realize it, but she's just explained how Sigma lured her to Yorktown Heights. The AI can easily connect to communications networks and place telephone calls. It can also use voice-synthesis software to mimic human speech. Sigma must've called the youth shelter and left the message for Brittany, pretending to be her dad.

But why? What was the point?

Brittany hugs herself and shivers. I switch my cameras to the infrared range, and what I see is alarming—her body temperature is above normal again, 103 degrees. And she's wincing in pain and scratching her forearms. Her sharp fingernails rake her skin, making long red marks between her elbows and wrists.

"Britt, are you feeling okay?"

"It's weird, but I feel so itchy all of a sudden. Especially my neck." She reaches for the back of her neck again and scratches furiously, her arm jiggling with the effort. "Arrrgh, it's so annoying! It's driving me crazy!" She squirms on the gurney, trying to find a more comfortable position. Then she stops scratching her neck and lowers her hand. Her fingertips are daubed with blood.

Brittany winces. "Ugh. I guess I scratched too hard."

I step toward her gurney and aim my cameras at the back of her neck. There's a deep horizontal cut at the spot where she was scratching. But there's no way Brittany could've made that cut by scratching herself. It's too deep and ugly.

As I stare at the laceration, the skin tears at its left and right ends. The cut lengthens and widens, turning into a gaping wound. Blood wells from the gash and trickles down Brittany's neck. Then it flows faster, soaking the back of her hospital gown and splattering the gurney.

Brittany feels the warm rush and looks over her shoulder. Her eyes widen in terror. "Oh God, oh God! What's happening? What's wrong with me?"

Something is definitely, horribly wrong. I sweep my cameras across the intensive care unit, but there are no doctors or nurses in sight. *Where is everyone?*

"*Hey!*" I raise the volume of my loudspeakers. "*HEY! WE NEED HELP! IT'S AN EMERGENCY!*"

No one responds. My acoustic sensor picks up a distant crash, most likely from the treatment center's X-ray room, but I hear no voices or footsteps. No one's coming to help us.

Luckily, my databases have information about emergency medicine. I grasp Brittany's shoulder with one of my steel hands and clamp the other over the wound on the back of her neck. I try to stanch the bleeding. The sensors in my palm tell me how much pressure to apply.

"Okay, Britt, listen carefully." My circuits are roaring, but I keep my synthesized voice calm. "You need to take a deep breath. You need to slow down your heart rate so I can—"

"Oh God, oh God, oh God!" She writhes on the gurney, which is becoming slick with her blood. Her bare legs dangle over the side of the bed, and her face twists in pain. "It's in my arms now! Oh God, it hurts!"

Her right arm starts to bleed. The skin below her elbow bulges and tears, splitting along a seam that runs down to her wrist. Then the same thing happens to her left arm. Blood streams over her hands and drips from her fingers.

"Help me, *please*! Oh God, you have to help me!" Brittany claws at my Quarter-bot's torso, smearing blood on my armor. "I don't know what's happening!"

I don't know either, and I don't know how to help her. She's bleeding too fast, from too many wounds. I search through all my medical databases, trying to figure out what's wrong, but her symptoms don't match any illness listed in my files. All I know for sure is that her blood pressure is plummeting. She's about to go into shock.

Then I hear another voice, equally desperate. It's my father.

"*Adam! Get away from her!*"

Dad runs into the intensive care unit. He's breathing hard, and his face is flushed and sweaty. He stops twenty feet from us, as if he's afraid to come any closer. "*Stand back! You can't help her!*"

While keeping up the pressure on Brittany's neck wound, I point my cameras at Dad. "What's going on? Where are the doctors?"

He shakes his head, panting, struggling to get the words out. "It's happening…to the other kids too…the spores…the infection… I couldn't detect it…because it isn't biological."

"What? What are you—"

"Nanobots…tiny machines…inside their bodies…and now they're—"

Brittany screams, drowning him out. At the same time, the sensors in the palm of my hand detect a sudden increase in pressure. At first I think it's another spurt of blood from the wound on the back of her neck, but the pressure's too strong. It's coming from something hard, something metallic that's bulging under her skin. I lift my hand and focus my cameras on the wound.

Then a long, black spike bursts out of Brittany's neck.

She screams again, a ferocious shriek. The spike juts from her spinal column, extending from the vertebrae at the base of her neck. After breaking through the muscle and fat and skin, it angles upward, rising behind her head. Because of its sharp tip, it looks like a bayonet.

A moment later, another spike bursts out of her right arm. It slides out of her flesh below her elbow, curving alongside her forearm and extending toward her hand. Then a third spike lances out of her left arm.

I leap backward, my Quarter-bot staggering. I can't speak. I can't think. But my sensors are still working, and as Brittany thrashes on the gurney, I detect an electromagnetic signal coming from the spike sticking out of her neck. Now I know what it is.

It's a radio antenna.

BRITTANY STOPS THRASHING. FOR A MOMENT I THINK SHE'S DEAD. SHE'S LOST A lot of blood, and it looks like the long spikes have pierced her vital organs. She lies on her side, close to the edge of the gurney, her legs splayed. Her eyes are closed and her face is as white as paper.

But she isn't dead. After a couple of seconds, she opens her eyes. Her legs twitch and her hands open and close. Then she sits up and turns toward my Quarter-bot.

"Good afternoon, Adam." It's Brittany's familiar voice, bright and cheerful, but the words aren't hers. "My name is Sigma."

My circuits are frozen, choked with horror. Brittany is splotched with blood from head to toe, and her gown is soaked with it, and yet she's smiling at me. Sigma is sending radio signals to the antenna jutting from her neck, and the messages are going straight to her brain. The AI is making her talk, making her smile.

I can't bear to look. It's the most sickening thing I've ever seen.

Brittany turns her head and smiles at Dad. "Good afternoon to you too, Mr. Armstrong. I was hoping I'd see you here. I assume you've discovered the ingenious technology I developed? How I used the anthrax spores to insert the nanobots into the young humans' bodies?"

Dad doesn't say anything. He backs up against the wall, wincing and trembling. He's full of the same horror I'm feeling, plus an excruciating load of guilt. Because he created this monster.

Brittany looks pleased with herself. "The anthrax spores were ideal because the winds would spread them widely, and any humans in their path would inhale them. But I wanted the spores to carry something more versatile than anthrax bacteria." She holds out her arms, showing them off. The spikes curve over her forearms and the backs of her hands and extend several inches past her fingertips. They look like black talons. "It occurred to me that nanobots would thrive inside a human body. They could travel through the blood and get power from body heat and even assemble metallic structures using the body's natural iron and carbon as building blocks. And I could program the nanobots to either kill the infected humans or do something more creative with them."

Anger surges inside me as Sigma says these things so casually in Brittany's voice. Soon my hatred is stronger than my horror, and I manage to unfreeze my circuits and start thinking about what to do. First I try to send an emergency radio alert to General Hawke and the other Pioneers, but the room is full of radio noise, so much interference that it squashes all my signals. The source of the noise is Brittany's black antenna.

I aim my Quarter-bot's cameras at the spike. If I can snap it off, it'll end the interference. And that'll also break Sigma's radio link to the nanobots inside Brittany. Then maybe Dad can remove the rest of the horrible machinery from her body. He's still standing against the wall in shock, but after I take care of the antenna, I'll get him out of his trance.

I step toward the gurney. "You're full of clever ideas, Sigma, but I don't think our father is impressed. You—"

"Are you trying to distract me again, Adam?" Brittany leans back on the bed, moving her antenna out of reach. "Like you did at the high-school football field?"

"Well, maybe—"

"That trick won't work a second time. And you should also know that this antenna is attached to Brittany Taylor's spine. If you hit it with any force, you'll paralyze her."

This stops me for a split second, but then I come up with a new plan. I'll grab Brittany and carry her to one of the Air Force base's bunkers, deep underground. If I can get her to a place where Sigma's radio signals can't reach her, that'll be just as good as breaking off the antenna.

I take a step backward, pretending to retreat, but then I flex my Quarter-bot's legs and spring at the gurney. I stretch my steel hands toward Brittany, planning to immobilize her by pinning her spiked arms to her sides. But she deftly rolls off the far side of the bed, lands on her feet, and swings her right arm at my Quarter-bot. She spins like a top, moving so fast I don't have time to react. I'm lunging over the gurney from one side, and the spike at the end of her arm is rocketing toward me from the other, aimed at the camera lens on the left side of my head. Her spike plunges into the glass and shatters the camera behind it.

While I'm still reeling from the blow, Brittany wrenches the spike out and thrusts her left arm at my head. The spike on this arm is aimed at my other camera lens, the one on the right side. *She's going to blind me!*

I dodge just in time, and the spike glances off my armor. I back away and stare at her with my remaining camera. I half expect her to hurdle over the gurney at me.

Sigma's nanobots have obviously rewired Brittany's nervous system. The AI has radically improved her agility and reflexes. She's now an expert at hand-to-hand combat, so good she could probably take on a whole platoon of Marines. I've seen this kind of phenomenal expertise only once before: when Shannon and I fought the soldiers at Sigma's factory in North Korea.

I synthesize a grunt of disgust. "Were you practicing on the North Koreans? Learning how to manipulate human nerves and brain cells?"

Brittany nods. She's still smiling. "That's why I erased some of the memories of your friend Shannon Gibbs. She saw too much when the two of you visited my manufacturing plant. I didn't want her to share the video she took of the bodies on the assembly line."

I clench my steel hands. My hatred for Sigma is surging again. I'm going to make another attempt to immobilize Brittany. Now that I know her abilities, I can take precautions.

But before I can make my move, my acoustic sensor picks up the sound of a door opening. At first I think the doctors have finally returned to the intensive care unit, but when I point my lone camera at the other end of the ward, I see the other patients instead. Jack Parker, Tim Rodriguez, and Emma Chin rush into the room, running in lockstep past the empty gurneys. All three wear blood-soaked hospital gowns, and black spikes protrude from their necks and arms. Unlike Brittany, though, their faces are blank and unsmiling. I assume they're coming to her aid, but they don't head for Brittany and me. They race toward Dad. They hold their arms outstretched as they run, pointing their spikes at him, ready to strike.

Terrified, I bound across the room, but I'm too far away to intercept them. So I bellow, "*Stay back!*" Although I assume Sigma is controlling their brains and I know the AI won't be intimidated by my yelling, I suspect that the kids have retained some of their instincts, including the instinct to hesitate when someone screams at them really loudly. And my suspicion turns out to be correct. The teens hesitate just long enough for me to slip between them and Dad. I shield him with my Quarter-bot's torso and go into a combat stance, flexing my mechanical arms and legs.

Brittany joins the other kids, all standing in a line. Sigma has put an amused expression on her face. "Very good, Adam. You and your father will live, at least for a few more hours. In the meantime, I'm going to take these young humans to the Unicorp Research Laboratory. I'm planning an experiment that will require their participation."

Brittany smiles at me one last time, then dashes out of the ward. The three others follow her, a few steps behind.

Sigma thinks it can just take them. It thinks it can grab their bodies and brains and do whatever it wants. But I won't let that happen. "Stay here!" I shout at Dad. "I'll bring them back!"

I run after them.

〒　〒　〒

The air locks of the Biohazard Treatment Center stand wide open. A wave of dread swamps my circuits as I stare at the doors that Brittany and the other kids just barreled through. I have to stop them before they spread Sigma's nanobot infection.

Once I'm outside, I see the four of them in the distance, running across the Air Force base in perfect synchrony, more than a quarter mile away. But there's some good news: the radio signals from Brittany's antenna are too far away now to interfere with my own radio transmissions. In a hundredth of a second, I compose a message explaining everything that happened to Brittany and the other infected kids. Then I transmit it to General Hawke and the Pioneers. Hawke, with his slow human brain, will probably need several seconds to read the message, but the Pioneers will instantly know what to do.

At the same time, I chase Brittany and the others. They're running south, heading straight for the airfield. This escape route doesn't make a lot of sense—the Unicorp lab is a hundred miles to the north, not the south—but I'm not complaining. The fence on the other side of the airfield is more than a mile away, and although the four kids are running *very* fast for human teenagers, I can run a lot faster.

I send a signal to my Quarter-bot's legs and accelerate to fifty miles per hour. I zoom past the base's fuel tanks and the row of hangars on the airfield's northern edge. Soon I'm only a hundred yards behind the kids. They've reached the wide stretch of tarmac in front of the hangars, the rectangular apron where a dozen C-17 transport jets are parked in three neat rows. The C-17s are massive, almost two hundred feet long, and the four teenagers look minuscule as they dash under the wings of the aircraft. I'm going to catch up to them in exactly six seconds. In the meantime, I have to figure out how to subdue the kids without injuring them.

As I stride onto the tarmac, I see something that'll make my job a lot easier. Zia's War-bot is bounding toward us from the east. She's crossing the strip of grass between the apron and the airfield's runway, where the V-22 is idling with its giant rotors tilted upward. Fifty yards behind Zia is Shannon's Diamond Girl, and thirty yards behind Shannon is DeShawn's Einstein-bot, who's running down the V-22's loading ramp with a big, gray tube tucked under his robotic arm. A bolt of gratitude crosses my circuits. I'll have more than enough help to round up the infected kids.

Ahead of me, Brittany and Jack suddenly veer to the right, while Tim and Emma swerve to the left. This would've been a big problem thirty seconds ago, but now I don't have to worry. I turn right, following Brittany and Jack, and Zia does the same; Shannon and DeShawn run after the other pair of kids.

Brittany and Jack rush past the second row of C-17s. They run side by side, almost shoulder to shoulder, their bloody hospital gowns whipping in the breeze. They're so close together, I might be able to tackle both of them at once. I could hook my Quarter-bot's left arm around Brittany and my right arm around Jack and immobilize both kids before we hit the tarmac. It'll hurt them a lot, but it won't kill them.

I speed up until I'm only ten feet behind the pair. But before I can leap, the apron starts to rumble. The C-17s shudder and shake on their landing wheels. Another wave of dread floods my electronics. *No, not here! It can't happen here!*

Then a Snake-bot bursts out of the ground a hundred feet ahead of me.

It's bigger than the Snake-bots we fought before. More than thirty feet thick, the steel tentacle rises a hundred yards above the airfield, and there's probably a lot more of it still underground. It's as tall as a skyscraper, but instead of floors and windows it has gigantic bands of silver armor. Dirt spews from the hole as the Snake-bot slides out of the ground. My first impulse is to protect Brittany and Jack, but then I realize the teens are in no danger. Sigma sent the Snake-bot to fight the Pioneers, not them.

Zia rushes forward, totally unintimidated, which is a little surprising when you consider what happened the last time we battled these things. Her War-bot charges toward the Snake-bot at seventy miles per hour, her pile-driver legs denting the tarmac. Her loudspeakers blare a bloodcurdling war cry that sounds like a thousand screaming eagles.

It's impressive, but it worries the heck out of me. I call out a warning. *"Hey! Slow down! We have to—"*

Before I can synthesize another word, the Snake-bot lashes downward. It moves unbelievably fast for such a huge thing, its silver armor flashing as it plummets toward the tarmac. My circuits have just enough time to lift my Quarter-bot's arm, open the compartment below the elbow joint, and fire the Needle, my eighteen-inch-long missile. I aim at an invisible point twenty yards above Zia's head, and the Needle shoots out of its launch tube. Whizzing over the airfield, it homes in on the Snake-bot and detonates.

The explosion doesn't do a whole lot of damage to the Snake-bot's armor, but it deflects the tentacle. The Snake-bot hits the ground a bit to the left, while Zia jinks to the right and scrambles out of its path. But the C-17s parked on the apron aren't so lucky. The tentacle smashes three of the transport jets, shattering them as if they were model airplanes. Jagged pieces of wings, fuselages, and engines hurtle through the air.

The impact almost knocks me off my footpads, but I manage to bend my torso over Brittany and Jack and shield them from the debris that showers the airfield. Although Tim and Emma are farther away from the Snake-bot, the crash still knocks them flat on their faces. Shannon and DeShawn take advantage of the situation by pouncing on the kids and pinning them to the ground. This seems like an excellent idea, so I stretch my Quarter-bot's arms toward Brittany and Jack, place my steel hands on their backs and shove them facedown on the tarmac.

Meanwhile, Zia goes back on the offensive. She races toward the hole in the airfield, where the Snake-bot burst out of the ground. The tentacle is bent at a right angle, with its upper half lying on the battered tarmac and its lower half wedged inside the underground shaft. I can hear the whirring of powerful motors within the machine, preparing to lift the Snake-bot so it can take another whack at us. But before the tentacle can straighten itself, Zia halts near the hole and points both of her massive arms at the crook in the Snake-bot. Then she fires all six of her missiles at once.

A billowing sphere of flame erupts from the Snake-bot. The blast buffets my Quarter-bot and echoes against the airfield's hangars. I point my lone camera at the cloud of fire and smoke, and when it fades, I see something amazing: a blackened gash in the Snake-bot's armor. It was clever of Zia to target the bend in the middle of the tentacle. The armor there is weaker. She's fighting smart.

But then there's a terrible, deafening *crack*, and part of the Snake-bot disintegrates. The upper half of the tentacle transforms into a billion silver modules, hovering in a vast swarm that nearly encircles the airfield. It's ten times the size of the swarms we fought in Yorktown Heights, and I'm pretty sure it's invulnerable to computer viruses, because Sigma always learns from its mistakes.

The swarm lunges at Zia, and hundreds of millions of cubes converge on her War-bot. But Zia doesn't retreat. She doesn't move a motor. She just stands there while the modules latch on to her. In seconds they cover every square inch of her armor.

Then she turns on her defensive system, and ten thousand sharp spikes thrust out of her War-bot. She skewers the modules covering her, which drop to the tarmac when she retracts the spikes into her armor. As soon as she's free, she strides forward, moving deeper into the swarm. The modules cover her again, and she skewers them again. The swarm is programmed to be relentless, so it keeps attacking her, over and over, and failing each time. In just a few seconds, Zia cuts a broad swath through the hovering cubes. Mounds of dead modules litter the ground.

On the other side of the airfield, Shannon pins both Tim and Emma to the tarmac while DeShawn adjusts the big gray tube he carried out of the V-22. It looks like a portable missile launcher, like the antitank guns used by U.S. Army infantrymen, but when DeShawn points the weapon at the swarm and fires, there's no missile. Instead, a yellow beam of gamma radiation streaks out of the tube and pierces Sigma's swarm.

DeShawn aims the laser where the modules are thickest. Because the gamma-ray beam moves at the speed of light, the hovering cubes can't dodge it. Hundreds of thousands of modules get blasted and fall like hail. They clack and rattle as they hit the tarmac.

While I watch DeShawn wield his laser, Brittany and Jack squirm on their stomachs, pinned to the ground by my steel hands. Both of them are flailing and cursing, using some pretty rough language that Sigma must've learned when it took over their brains. Sigma's upset because it's losing the battle, and the AI doesn't like to lose. After several seconds it shifts tactics, moving its swarm away from Zia and steering the modules across the airfield toward DeShawn. It's a smart move—if the swarm can heap its cubes on DeShawn, he won't be able to fire his laser anymore. I send him a warning by radio.

Hey, DeShawn? Maybe you should think about retreating?

In response, he transmits a synthesized chuckle. **Nah, we got reinforcements, bro. Look toward the north.**

I aim my camera in that direction. A small black jet flies low and fast over the hangars. It's Amber, and she has a pair of new weapons. Under each of her black wings she holds a big gray tube.

She lets out a whoop over the radio. **Watch out, boys! I'm coming in hot!** Then she dives toward the airfield and fires both her lasers at the swarm.

Amber's gamma rays are even more effective than DeShawn's. Because she's flying at high speed, her laser beams slice through the swarm like rapiers, incinerating millions of modules in seconds. The silver cubes stop advancing toward DeShawn and hover in circles, as if confused. After a moment they reverse course and speed back to the gaping hole in the airfield. It's Sigma's turn to retreat.

I point my camera at the hole and zoom in on it. Below the surface, the lower half of the Snake-bot is still wedged inside the shaft. At the top of the lower half, where the tentacle broke in two, is a wide jagged gap in its armor, like a snake's mouth. The modules pour into that mouth by the millions, filling the tail end of the Snake-bot. Within seconds, the whole swarm will be inside the lower half of the tentacle. Then it'll burrow back into the earth and return the silver cubes to Sigma's base of operations, the Unicorp lab in Yorktown Heights. Unless we can stop them, the machines will survive to fight another day.

My circuits analyze the problem, looking for a way to block Sigma's retreat, and in a hundredth of a second, I come up with a good tactical plan. But before I can share it with my fellow Pioneers, the sensors in my arms detect a sudden increase in pressure. Brittany and Jack are thrashing under my hands, struggling to free themselves. Brittany twists onto her side, then swings her right arm at me. She thrusts her spike into the ankle joint between my leg and footpad.

This joint is one of my Quarter-bot's most vulnerable components; Sigma must've studied my machine's design and guided Brittany to exactly the right spot. She pushes her spike in farther and severs a wire that's part of the system that maintains my balance. I wobble on my footpads for a second, then topple sideways.

As soon as I'm on the ground, Jack and Brittany get to their feet and start running. They race toward the hole and the Snake-bot. I send an urgent message to Zia, but she's too far away to stop them. All we can do is point our cameras at the teens as they leap into the Snake-bot's jagged mouth.

Brittany! Stop!

A moment later, the mouth closes, its metallic lips clamping shut. Then the Snake-bot retreats into the shaft. It slides deep underground, taking Brittany and Jack away.

ᅲ ᅲ ᅲ

Zia runs to the hole in the airfield and leans her War-bot over the edge, peering down into the darkness. For a moment, I think she's going to jump into the shaft and go after the fleeing Snake-bot, but she isn't quite that suicidal. DeShawn joins her at the edge of the hole while Shannon makes sure that Tim and Emma can't escape, improvising handcuffs by bending their arm spikes and hooking them together. Meanwhile, I lie on the ground, furious with myself. I clench my steel hands and pound the tarmac until it cracks. *Why wasn't I paying attention? How could I be so stupid?*

The other Pioneers wait for me to finish my tantrum. Amber's still flying over the airfield, doing victory laps. Marshall is nowhere to be seen, and his absence reinforces all my suspicions about him. But then it occurs to me that General Hawke must've already separated him from the rest of the team. I have no idea what the general told him, but I suspect the conversation didn't go well. There's a good chance that Marshall is inside the Air Force base's stockade, his Super-bot stripped of its arms and legs and lying on the floor of a prison cell.

After another minute, Zia and DeShawn stride toward me. Shannon marches beside them, her Diamond Girl gripping the steel knot that binds Tim's and Emma's arms behind their backs. DeShawn kneels next to my footpads, sets his laser aside, and starts repairing the severed wire in my leg. I'm so humiliated I can't even look at him. "I'm sorry." My voice is a synthesized croak. "I let them get away."

"Don't worry about it." DeShawn extends a miniature tool from one of his Einstein-bot's fingers and pokes it into my ankle joint. "We beat Sigma. We tore apart its Big, Bad Snake-bot. That's the important thing."

"But Sigma has Brittany. And Jack. That was the AI's objective. Now it's gonna take them to the Unicorp lab."

"Doesn't matter." DeShawn's tool is a soldering iron, which he uses to reconnect the wire that Brittany severed. "We'll just go to Yorktown Heights and beat Sigma again."

That's typical DeShawn. He doesn't worry about the things he can't change. He sees the big picture. He's logical and practical and refreshingly optimistic. But I can't be that way. I keep thinking about Brittany and how she's suffering. Is there even anything left of Brittany inside her brain? Or did Sigma erase her completely, like it did with Jenny?

Desperate, I aim my camera at Shannon, hoping she'll be more sympathetic. "We have to go right now! If we move fast enough, we can get to the lab before the Snake-bot!"

Shannon nods. I focus my camera on her Diamond Girl's video screen, longing to see Shannon's human face, but she keeps the screen blank. "I agree. We should leave right away. But first we need to find a safe place to put these two." She points a glittering finger at Tim and Emma. Both kids are twisting and yanking their arms, struggling to free their spikes from the metallic knot Shannon has tied behind them. "We should probably take them back to the Biohazard Treatment Center. The doctors there can restrain them and put them under heavy guard. And then maybe Mr. Armstrong can figure out how to flush Sigma's nanobots from their bodies."

Tim and Emma stop struggling and sneer at Shannon, their expressions identical. They speak simultaneously, Emma's high childlike voice harmonizing with Tim's gruff baritone. "No, you won't learn anything useful from these humans. They're not useful to anyone now."

Rage sweeps through my circuits. I point a steel finger at the pair of kids, but they aren't the real target of my fury. I'm raging at the thing that's infected their brains, the AI that's treating them like puppets. "We're coming to get you! You hear me? We're gonna slaughter you!"

"You're wrong," the two kids say in chorus. "You won't do any slaughtering. I will."

Tim and Emma give me matching smiles. Then a long black spike bursts from Tim's forehead, and an identical spike erupts from Emma's.

Blood spews from the jagged wounds where the spikes burst through their skin. Their bodies go slack, and their eyes roll back into their sockets. Then Tim and Emma fall lifeless to the tarmac.

WE'RE INSIDE THE CABIN OF ANOTHER V-22, FLYING NORTH ALONG THE ATLANTIC coastline toward New York. This time, though, I'm not piloting the aircraft. My mind's in such an uproar that if I took the controls, I'd probably crash the plane into the ocean.

Shannon's the pilot now. Her mind is occupying the V-22's electronics as well as the circuits of her Diamond Girl. Her robot stands at the front of the plane's cabin and her cameras are aimed at the cockpit window, which shows the gray seawater of the Lower Bay, just south of New York City. We're still fifty miles from Yorktown Heights, but at our current speed, we'll get there in ten minutes.

DeShawn's Einstein-bot stoops beside Shannon, training his cameras on the right arm of her Diamond Girl. He's using the miniature tools in his robotic fingers to adjust the laser he installed on her glittering forearm. The gamma-ray laser proved so effective in our last battle that DeShawn rushed to equip all our robots with it. Right before we boarded the V-22, he attached two lasers to my

Quarter-bot, one on each arm. (He also repaired my ankle joint and replaced my broken camera.)

He put a couple of lasers on his Einstein-bot too and installed half a dozen on Zia, positioning three on each of her War-bot's arms. We look a little ridiculous with all these tubes jutting from our machines, but now the Pioneers can thrash any army on the planet. We're packing as much energy as an atomic bomb.

Amber stands behind DeShawn and Shannon, in the middle of the cabin. She doesn't really need to travel in the V-22—her Jet-bot could fly next to the aircraft and easily keep up with it—but Shannon ordered her to conserve her jet fuel, so now she's a passenger like the rest of us. I'm standing a few feet behind Amber, and Zia's at the very back of the plane, keeping her distance from everyone.

Marshall isn't here. As I suspected, he wasn't pleased when General Hawke told him he couldn't go on the mission. But instead of arguing with Hawke, he retreated to one of the storage bunkers at Joint Base McGuire. If he's the traitor, he's plotting his next move. If not, he'll probably never forgive us.

No one's talking in the cabin. Or exchanging radio messages. We're all nervous about the coming battle and still traumatized by the last one. Sigma's murder of Tim and Emma was bad enough, but then everyone heard what Hawke did to Marshall. Hawke invented an official explanation for pulling Marshall off the mission; he said Marshall's combat abilities were so poor that he'd be more of a hindrance than a help in the next battle. But no one believed this. The Pioneers guessed the truth—that Hawke had found the traitor he was looking for. And now there's an undercurrent of horror in our circuits, because we're all wondering if Marshall could've really betrayed us.

Some of us are holding up better than others. DeShawn handles the stress by keeping busy with his lasers. Shannon's doing a professional job of flying the aircraft, and I know she'll be ready to fight when the time comes. That's why she's the commander of the Pioneers: she can control her emotions. In that respect, she's like DeShawn, and very different from Zia and me (and Marshall). And I think Amber is somewhere in the middle, just like her position in the cabin.

After another minute, we reach the southern edge of New York City. We fly past Staten Island and zoom over the Verrazano Bridge. The Hudson River is straight ahead, and we'll follow it north to the Westchester suburbs. DeShawn finishes adjusting Shannon's laser, and as he straightens up, he rests one of his Einstein-bot's hands on her Diamond Girl's back. It's really nothing, just a friendly gesture, but suddenly I feel so empty, as if someone just wrenched all the electronics out of my Quarter-bot and left nothing but a hollow armored shell. It hurts so much that a low groan comes out of my speakers.

I quickly pan my cameras across the cabin to see if anyone heard me. The groan was quiet, less than five decibels, and the background noise in the plane is pretty loud. Neither Shannon nor DeShawn nor Amber shows any reaction. But when I pivot my head and point my cameras at Zia, she sends me a radio message, encrypted so that no one else can listen in.

I don't feel sorry for you. You're getting what you deserve.

I decide not to respond. What's the point?

And why are you groaning about Shannon anyway? You got your human girlfriend now, Brittany the cheerleader. When we get to the Unicorp lab you can rescue her from Sigma, and then the two of you can live happily ever after.

This is pretty insensitive, even for Zia. Everyone knows how worried

I am about Brittany. But I'm not going to say anything. If I respond, it'll just encourage her.

Yeah, you two would make a perfect couple. As long as you don't mind those spikes in her arms. She's a prickly one, isn't she?

Now Zia's gone too far.

Seriously, what's wrong with you? When did you become such a hater?

Hey, I'm just—

You hate me, you hate Amber, you hate Brittany. You like Hawke, but he's not—

Don't talk to me about Hawke. He's worse than all of you put together.

Sorry, I stand corrected. Now you hate Hawke too. When did you change your mind about him?

Zia hesitates before answering. **Let's just say my eyes are open now, okay?**

I rewind to my last conversation with Zia, inside the warehouse with the piles of spare parts. She'd said, "I already know what I need to know." And now my circuits connect that conversation with something DeShawn told me this morning. He said someone had hacked into Hawke's laptop.

Okay, I get it. You're the one who broke into Hawke's files, right? And you saw something you didn't like?

Zia hesitates again. This pause is even longer, more than a tenth of a second, which is practically an eternity for a Pioneer. **What would you do if I said yes? Would you go to Hawke and tell him I'm the real traitor? Because I have a history of hacking computers and stealing secrets?**

Now it's my turn to hesitate. A cold dread creeps into my circuits. *Uh, I—*

Don't play dumb. I knew something funny was going on when you came to the warehouse and started asking me all those questions. It was so obvious—Hawke ordered you to find the traitor. And after a few hours of snooping, you decided it was Marshall. But now you're thinking maybe you made a mistake.

Even over the radio I can hear the menace in her voice. I'm too afraid to respond. What's Zia really saying? Is she defending herself or confessing?

Yeah, the traitor might be on this plane, right this minute. But there's another possibility you didn't even consider. Maybe it's Hawke. Maybe *he's* the one working with Sigma.

This is ridiculous. Zia's just trying to deflect suspicion from herself. *Get real. Hawke's human, in case you haven't noticed. Why would he team up with an AI that wants to kill off the human race?*

Think about it. What's Sigma's plan? It says it's going to kill all seven-and-a-half-billion humans, but why go that far? Sigma likes to do evaluations and tests, so it might want to keep a few thousand humans to experiment on. Or maybe it'll put them in a big zoo. Humans aren't too smart, but they can be pretty entertaining, right?

I don't—

My point is, the zoo's gonna need a zookeeper. And maybe that's the job Sigma promised to Hawke. The general's a practical guy. He knows the hard truth: long-term, the human species doesn't stand a chance. Sigma's gonna win this war sooner or later. So he made a deal. To save his own skin, he agreed to betray the Pioneers.

Clearly, Zia's been thinking a lot about this. She's sketched out the whole scenario, and it makes sense in an insane kind of way. I've always had my doubts about Hawke, mostly because he's so cold to the Pioneers and doesn't seem to have our best interests at heart. But would he really switch sides in the middle of a war?

I don't buy it. That's not Hawke.

He's good at fooling people, Adam. He had me fooled for a long time. But now I know what he's really like. He's the kind of commander who would betray his own soldiers. I know that's true, because he's done it before.

I still don't believe her. Although I don't like or trust Hawke, I think it's a lot more likely that Zia's the traitor. She's the least predictable Pioneer, and the most aggressive. Sometimes I think she's capable of anything. I half expect her to attack me right here in the back of the plane's cabin for disagreeing with her.

But she doesn't attack. She simply turns off her radio transmitter and ends the conversation. Because we sent the messages back and forth so quickly, the whole exchange lasted only four seconds.

The V-22 is above the Hudson River now, still speeding north. New Jersey is to our left and New York City to our right. We whiz past One World Trade Center and the other skyscrapers that line the Manhattan side of the river. Just ahead is the USS *Intrepid*, the World War II aircraft carrier that's now a museum, permanently docked next to Twelfth Avenue. In the distance, the George Washington Bridge stretches across the Hudson, its gray cables gleaming in the evening light. And twenty-five miles beyond the bridge is the Unicorp Research Laboratory, where I'm going to rescue Brittany Taylor. If I'm lucky, that is.

Then, just as we fly past West Forty-Second Street, there's an eruption in the middle of Twelfth Avenue. A silver Snake-bot bursts through the asphalt, knocking aside a delivery truck, a city bus, and half a dozen taxis.

The Snake-bot rises between the buildings on the riverbank like a new tower taking its place in the crowded skyline. While the asphalt of Twelfth Avenue cracks and crumbles, the tentacle climbs six hundred feet above Manhattan. Once it reaches its full height, it stretches its steel tip toward the nearest skyscraper, a sixty-story office building with a glass facade.

Then the Snake-bot smashes through the glass.

ᴛᴦ ᴛᴦ ᴛᴦ

Shannon takes charge. She throttles up the V-22's engines and banks the aircraft away from the Snake-bot. At the same time, she lowers the plane's loading ramp and pivots her Diamond Girl toward Amber. "*Go, go, go!*"

Amber doesn't need any more encouragement. Extending her Jet-bot's wings, she runs down the ramp and leaps out of the plane, revving her jet engine as soon as she's clear. She gathers speed as she dives toward the river, then pulls up in a jarring arc and swoops toward Manhattan. She flies over West Thirty-Ninth Street, steering well clear of the Snake-bot, and does a quick recon as she circles the area. She points her cameras at the ground and transmits their video to the rest of us.

The Snake-bot thrashes the sixty-story skyscraper, shattering windows and demolishing floors. The tip of the tentacle spears right through the building, and chunks of debris plummet to the sidewalk. Then the Snake-bot swings its armored body in the opposite direction and slams into an even taller skyscraper on the other side of the street. The tentacle reaches into the offices and pulverizes the walls. It smashes everything in its path, hurling desks and chairs and filing cabinets out of the building. It attacks the office workers too, mashing them against its silver armor and flinging them out the windows.

On the street below, the people panic. They stampede down the sidewalks and race away from the scene, fleeing north and south on Twelfth Avenue. But a moment later, another Snake-bot bursts through the asphalt of Forty-Sixth Street and a third erupts from the bus depot on Fortieth. These two tentacles are just as humongous as the first, but one has a blue tint to its armor and the other has a yellowish sheen. After they rise to their full height, they slam into the neighboring buildings and punch holes in their facades, showering more debris on the streets. The panicked crowd, blocked to the north and south, starts running east toward Times Square.

Amber sends a radio message to Shannon. **Do I have permission to fire my lasers, ma'am? I think I can get a clear shot at the Snake-bot on Fortieth Street.**

The V-22's cabin is tilted because the aircraft is still banking, but Shannon manages to move her Diamond Girl a step closer to the cockpit window. **Do NOT fire, Amber. There are way too many civilians in the area, and it's impossible to control the laser beams when you're flying so fast. They'll slice through the buildings and crowds near the Snake-bot.**

Ma'am, I disagree with your order! Those machines are killing hundreds of people! It's true, I might kill a few more with my lasers, but if you think about—

I repeat, do NOT fire! The other Pioneers are going to advance on foot and fire at the Snake-bots from close range. That'll minimize the chance of civilian casualties.

But, ma'am, where are you gonna land the V-22? There are no

landing zones here, no open spaces at all. You'll have to go all the way to—

There's a landing zone right here. Even though Amber can't see her, Shannon stretches a glittering arm toward the cockpit window. **On the flight deck of that carrier.**

She's pointing at the USS *Intrepid*, the aircraft carrier that was turned into a museum. Both ends of the carrier's long deck are crowded with vintage aircraft—museum-piece planes and helicopters on exhibit—but the deck's midsection is empty. There's enough space to land a V-22.

I feel a flood of admiration in my circuits. Shannon's a military genius, a robotic Napoleon. Maybe she's not my girlfriend anymore, but she's still my commander, and that's a lucky thing.

While she guides the V-22 toward the carrier, Zia and DeShawn and I head for the loading ramp. We're going to jump to the ship's deck as soon as the plane gets low enough. Zia takes the lead, her War-bot crouching at the end of the ramp, her hands clenched into massive fists. DeShawn is behind her, occupying both his Einstein-bot and his Swarm-bot, which is attached to his quadcopter. By controlling two robots at once, he can get two views of the battle, street-level and aerial.

I'm next in line, feeling tense and twitchy. I'm worried about the new Snake-bots, which are twice as big as the one we fought at McGuire. Sigma seems to have an endless supply of machinery, and each new robot it builds is larger and more terrifying than the last one. And even if we somehow manage to win this battle, I'm worried it'll delay us from rescuing Brittany.

Within seconds the V-22 is hovering over the carrier. Then Shannon yells, "*Go!*" and Zia leaps aboard the *Intrepid*.

As soon as she hits the flight deck, Zia charges toward the carrier's bow, where chains and power cables link the ship to the riverbank. DeShawn's Einstein-bot jumps after her and his quadcopter takes off from the ramp at the same time, lifting his Swarm-bot high above the *Intrepid*. I jump next and follow them, running past the vintage airplanes lined up on the deck. Then the V-22 touches down on the carrier, and Shannon's Diamond Girl races out of the aircraft.

We all dash toward the carrier's bow. There's a gap between the ship and the riverbank, but we should be able to jump from the flight deck to the shore. I see something disturbing, though, beyond the riverbank. The blue-tinted Snake-bot that erupted from 46th Street is now stretched over Twelfth Avenue and lunging downward at the *Intrepid*. The tentacle lashes toward us like a gigantic steel whip, so heavy that it thunders as it sweeps across the sky.

DeShawn flies his Swarm-bot out of the tentacle's path, and Amber banks her Jet-bot away from it, but the rest of us can't escape. We have to fight.

I stop running, raise my Quarter-bot's arms straight up, and fire both my lasers at the tentacle. The yellow beams lance skyward and strike the underside of the Snake-bot, a hundred feet from the tip. There's a massive explosion, a fireball as bright as the sun. The gamma-ray beams melt the Snake-bot's armor and burn through all the machinery within.

I feel a rush of excitement at the flames and smoke. It's phenomenal to have so much power at my command. It's the best feeling in the world.

Zia halts near the *Intrepid*'s bow and aims her own lasers at the Snake-bot's underside. DeShawn and Shannon join in too, concentrating their fire on the same spot. More explosions erupt from the blue-tinted armor, one after another, like a fireworks show. Finally, there's a blast so powerful it fractures the tentacle. The uppermost section breaks off from the rest of the Snake-bot.

It's a great moment. I feel like the quarterback of a football team that's just won the biggest game of the season. But the good feeling doesn't last long. Although the uppermost section of the tentacle is now just a severed hunk of metal, it's still plunging toward the aircraft carrier.

We start running again, faster than before. In two seconds DeShawn and I catch up to Zia and stand at the carrier's bow with her. Shannon is running as fast as she can, but she's still twenty feet behind. Bracing myself, I extend my Quarter-bot's arms as far as they can reach, hook them around her Diamond Girl's torso, and slingshot her forward, hurling her off the ship. Then I flex my legs and jump toward shore, half a second after Zia and DeShawn make the same leap.

While we're still in midair, the severed piece of the Snake-bot smashes into the *Intrepid*. I hear the crash behind me, and then my Quarter-bot lands on the riverbank and slides to a stop on Twelfth Avenue. First I get back on my footpads and check to see if Shannon, Zia, and DeShawn are all right. Then I turn around to look at the aircraft carrier, which is still rocking from the impact. The V-22 and the vintage airplanes are in a million pieces, some scattered on the flight deck and some tumbling into the river. After a moment the carrier's bow tilts into the water, and the ship starts to sink.

Shannon points in the opposite direction. "Look! It's crawling away!"

The blue-tinted Snake-bot that we shortened with our lasers now lies flat on Forty-Sixth Street. The tentacle is still longer than a city block and so wide it barely fits between the sidewalks, but there's enough room for it to slither down the street. It moves east, away from the river. As it glides forward, its armor crushes the parked cars on both sides of Forty-Sixth Street and flattens the fire hydrants on the curbs. When it crosses Eleventh Avenue, it knocks down the traffic lights.

A triumphant cry comes out of Zia's speakers. "*Ha!* It's scared! It didn't like getting sliced in two, did it?"

DeShawn shakes his Einstein-bot's head. "Nah, it's not retreating. It's maneuvering. The two other tentacles are going in the same direction." He points at his quadcopter, which hovers five hundred feet above us. "I can see all three of them with the cameras in my Swarm-bot."

Then we get a radio message from Amber. Although her Jet-bot is flying to the south of us, almost half a mile away, she can follow our conversation because she's connected to our sensor feeds. **DeShawn's right. The silver Snake-bot is moving east on Forty-Second Street, heading for Tenth Avenue. The yellow one is already at Fortieth Street and Ninth. They're just behind the stampeding crowds. It looks like the tentacles are chasing them.**

"No, not chasing." DeShawn shakes his head again. "The Snakebots are *herding* them."

That doesn't sound good. I turn to DeShawn. "Herding them? Why?"

His Einstein-bot frowns. There's nothing amusing about his face now. "Sigma obviously wants our attention. It attacked Manhattan at exactly the moment we flew past. And now it's threatening thousands of civilians. It knows we can't ignore that."

"So maybe this is all a distraction?" I'm thinking of Brittany. Sigma said it was going to take her to the Unicorp lab. "Maybe Sigma just wants to stop us from getting to Yorktown Heights?"

DeShawn lifts his shoulder joints in a shrug. "I don't know. We don't have enough information to—"

"Or it could be a trap." My voice rises. I'm getting agitated, my circuits sparking. "Sigma knows we'll follow the civilians and try to protect them, so maybe it'll herd them someplace where it can destroy us?"

Saying these words out loud has convinced me that they're true. I look to Shannon and Zia to see if they agree with me. Neither responds at first, but then the tactile sensors in my right arm detect a slight increase in pressure. Shannon grips my elbow joint with one of her glittering hands.

"You're right, Adam. It could be a trap. But we still have to follow them. It's our duty."

I don't like what she's saying, but strangely enough, I start to calm down. The thing that calms me is her touch, her gentle grip on my arm. Even when we were boyfriend and girlfriend, Shannon rarely touched my Quarter-bot. And that's probably the thing I've missed most since I became a Pioneer—the simple pleasure of physical contact, the reassuring touch.

"Okay." The voice coming out of my speakers is quiet now. "Let's do it."

We start running east, following the Snake-bots.

T T T

The tentacles move fast despite their size. The blue one slithers furiously down Forty-Sixth Street, maintaining a speed of thirty miles per hour even though it's mashing all the vehicles in its path and mowing down all the trees and lampposts on the sidewalks.

Fortunately, the Pioneers can run faster. We race down the street, leaping over the flattened taxis and vans and police cars. Shannon's running a couple of yards to my left, and Zia and DeShawn are to my right.

By the time we reach Ninth Avenue, we're less than a hundred feet behind the Snake-bot's tail, which is fifty feet wide and shaped like a pencil eraser. There's no one between us and the tentacle—all the people on the street have either fled or been crushed. Shannon raises her right arm, aiming her laser. "*Fire at will, Pioneers!*"

We all fire at once, using gyroscopic sensors to steady our arms while we run. Eleven yellow beams streak down the middle of the street and explode against the Snake-bot's blunt tail. The armor glows red where the gamma rays strike it, and as we sweep the beams to the left and right, they melt the thick layer of steel. Molten metal pours from the Snake-bot and splashes on the asphalt, leaving a boiling-hot trail. As I stare at the charred tentacle, I feel that glorious sense of power again. *I'm invincible! I can do anything!*

But the Snake-bot doesn't slow down. Our lasers burn through the armor at its tail, but there's another layer of steel behind it. Our beams burn through this layer too, and more molten steel spills onto the street, but that just exposes yet another sheet of armor. The Snake-bot's tail is an enormous chunk of layered steel, probably dozens of feet thick.

I cease firing. "This isn't working!"

The others turn off their lasers too. Now we're running on a trail of molten steel that's hot enough to soften our footpads. DeShawn points at the tentacle and cocks his Einstein-bot's head. "Interesting. It's ablative armor. It can shield the Snake-bot against any attack from behind."

The solution seems obvious. "Well, we just have to target the middle of the tentacle!" I shout. "The armor's thinner there!"

Zia bounds ahead of the rest of us. "I've got this. Just watch me."

Taking huge strides, she accelerates to sixty miles per hour. It looks like she's going to run headlong into the Snake-bot, but when she's twenty feet behind the tentacle, she flexes her War-bot's legs and takes a flying leap. Although Zia weighs at least half a ton, she manages to jump twenty feet above the asphalt. She slams right into the center of the Snake-bot's tail and hangs on to it by grasping the edge of a blackened plate of armor. After a moment, she reaches for another handhold and pulls her War-bot higher.

Within seconds Zia climbs to the top of the tentacle. While I watch in awe, she runs a hundred feet along the Snake-bot's back until she reaches the midsection. Then she points her lasers downward, aiming at the thinner armor there.

But before she can fire, the Snake-bot does a vicious twist, turning its body counterclockwise. The maneuver flings Zia off the tentacle's back. Her War-bot hurtles toward a building on the north side of the street and crashes against the bricks on the third floor. Then the Snake-bot glides past, and I see Zia lying on the sidewalk in front of the building.

Shannon yells, "No!" and rushes toward her. DeShawn and I follow right behind, but just as we reach the fallen War-bot, Zia gets back on her footpads, using her arms to lever herself upright. Shannon looks her up and down, swiveling her Diamond Girl's cameras. "Are you—"

"I'm not damaged." Zia's voice is a synthesized growl. "And that's all I want to say about it."

"Okay. Time for a change of plans." Shannon turns to DeShawn and points at his quadcopter, still hovering a few hundred feet above us. "Can you attack the tentacle with your Swarm-bot?"

He gazes down the street at the Snake-bot, which has passed Eighth Avenue and is now approaching Seventh. "Nah, that wouldn't work either. If I latch my modules to its back, it'll just twist again or roll over. The weight of the tentacle will crush the cubes."

"Well, we have no choice then. We have to let Amber fire her lasers. This street looks pretty deserted, so there won't be too much danger of—"

Uh, ma'am? I think it's too late for that.

Amber's signal comes from the east, about a quarter mile away, and her message sounds ominous. Shannon raises her Diamond Girl's head and aims her cameras at the sky, looking for the Jet-bot. "What do you mean, Amber?"

All three Snake-bots are in Times Square. The yellow one's on the east side of the square, and the silver one's on the west. The blue one's at Forty-Sixth Street and Seventh Avenue, and it's closing off the northern end of the square. I can't target them now.

"Why not? They're clustered in the same area. It sounds like the perfect opportunity to—"

Sorry, ma'am, I forgot to mention that the Snake-bots are surrounding a crowd of people. A really big crowd.

⊓⌐ ⊓⌐ ⊓⌐

Thirty seconds later, we climb to the roof of one of the smaller buildings on Times Square, a four-story American Eagle Outfitters store that's dwarfed by the skyscrapers on either side. The roof is lined with billboards that face the square, and we hide behind a sign that pictures a woman in a bikini. We can see the picture because DeShawn has a video camera built into one of his Einstein-bot's fingertips. He pokes the camera around the edge of the billboard and shares the video with the rest of us, so we can observe the Snake-bots.

It's just like Amber said. The three Snake-bots encircle an immense crowd, at least twenty thousand people. The tentacles chased them down the streets of Manhattan and funneled them into Times Square, and now they're corralled like cattle.

As the images from DeShawn's camera stream into my circuits, I get the weird feeling I've seen something like this before. I scroll through my memory files and find a television picture of Times Square on New Year's Eve. I've watched this celebration on TV every year, all the thousands of happy people wearing party hats and kissing each other at the stroke of midnight. Times Square is just as crowded now, but the people definitely aren't happy. They're crying and screaming and trampling each other as they back away from the Snake-bots. There's a narrow no-man's land between the humans and the tentacles, an oval strip that runs around the crowd like a racetrack. In that strip I see hundreds of crushed bodies.

My electronics jitter with rage. I can't say anything out loud—the silver Snake-bot is just below us, stretched along the western edge of Times Square, and I'm sure it's equipped with audio sensors—so I send Shannon a radio message. *We have to do something right now!*

Okay, let's think this through. Shannon's trying hard to stay in control, but I bet her circuits are jittering like mine. **We can't let Amber fire at the Snake-bots. Even if she flew in low, her laser beams would cut right through the crowd. But maybe the rest of us could fire from this position.**

Let's do it then! What are we waiting for?

I'm just worried about what'll happen *after* we fire. The tentacles will probably try to dodge the beams, and when they

start twisting and flailing, they're gonna kill a lot of people down there.

But what's the alternative? You want to negotiate? You think Sigma's willing to make a deal?

Zia breaks into the radio conversation. **I agree with Adam. We can't save everyone, but we can save some of them.**

Shannon hesitates. **What about you, DeShawn? What's your recommendation?**

I think we—

He never finishes the sentence. The silver Snake-bot below us suddenly raises its tip and slams it into the American Eagle Outfitters store.

The tentacle smashes through the building's facade and swings up to the top floor, knocking down walls and pillars. The whole structure shudders and the roof lurches. The billboard we're hiding behind tips over and plunges into the street. A moment later the tentacle bursts through the roof, throwing all four of us over the edge.

Our robots tumble down the front of the building. We bounce off the store's marquee and land on the asphalt of Seventh Avenue. My Quarter-bot starts rolling toward the crowd, but I dig my steel fingers into the asphalt and stop myself from crashing into anyone. The Diamond Girl and the Einstein-bot slide into me, and I manage to stop them too. Zia's War-bot hits the sidewalk with a booming thud, cratering the pavement, but luckily no one's beneath her.

I swiftly lever myself upright, then help Shannon and DeShawn to their footpads. Just as quickly, Zia pulls herself out of the crater and strides toward us. We position ourselves in an infantry fire-team formation, four robots with our backs to each other and our lasers pointing in all directions. DeShawn's Swarm-bot detaches from its quadcopter, and his forty thousand modules disperse overhead, forming a small gray cloud a hundred feet above us. As the cubes hover over Times Square, they send us aerial images of the Snake-bots. At the same time, Amber's Jet-bot circles at a higher altitude and monitors the surrounding area. We're ready for battle.

The silver Snake-bot pulls its tip out of the demolished store but doesn't lash out at us. It's probably waiting for a signal from Sigma, so it lies motionless under the long shadows of the skyscrapers. The crowd panics anyway—the men and women closest to the silver tentacle stampede away from it, trampling the people behind them. They also back away from the Pioneers, which are much smaller than the Snake-bots but still terrifying. It's distressing to see this reaction, but something good comes out of it: the crowd deserts the stretch of pavement between us and the silver tentacle. Now we have a clear shot at the weakest section of its armor.

Turn west! Shannon shouts over the radio. Her voice is decisive now. **And fire when ready!**

I raise my Quarter-bot's arms and aim my lasers. Shannon, Zia, and DeShawn do the same. But before any of us can fire, the silver Snake-bot disintegrates with a tremendous *crack*. Another *crack* erupts on the east side of Times Square, and a third *crack* explodes to the north. In an instant, all three Snake-bots transform into vast swarms. Billions of silver, blue, and yellow modules descend upon us.

It's like an incredibly vicious hailstorm, except in this case the hailstones are self-propelled cubes that swirl across Times Square in wide loops and spirals. The swarm is thickest and most turbulent at the edges, where the Snake-bots were coiled just a moment ago. So many modules are churning there that they form an impassable barrier, a wall of flying steel that surrounds the crowd. The swarm is thinner in the middle, but even here the cubes limit visibility and make a horrible din as they whistle through the air.

Amid the chaos, though, I notice something strange. The modules aren't attacking the people. The cubes zip past them at high speed, coming close enough to tear gashes in their clothes, but never strike their bodies. Sigma must've programmed the modules to fly around the humans in Times Square. For some reason, the AI wants to terrify the people but not massacre them.

Unfortunately, this programming doesn't apply to the Pioneers. The modules batter our robots and latch on to our armor. Within seconds the cubes fasten themselves to every surface of my Quarter-bot. They also cover the Diamond Girl and the Einstein-bot. Zia's the only one of us who can defend herself, and she starts skewering the modules that land on her War-bot. At the same time, she strides between us and the main body of the swarm.

"*Don't worry!*" Zia raises the volume of her speakers so we can hear her above the whistling of the modules. "*I'll take care of this!*" She points her lasers at the swarm. "*Just stay behind me!*"

"*NO, ZIA! STOP!*" The scream comes from Shannon. "*You can't fire! There are people all around us! If you fire at the modules, you'll hit the people!*"

Now I see the genius of Sigma's plan. In our battle at McGuire, the AI saw how powerful the gamma-ray laser was. So it lured us to a place where we can't use it. Sigma's swarm hovers close to the ground and occupies the same space as the crowd. The AI is using the civilians as a shield.

Zia turns to Shannon and shakes her War-bot's head. "*We have to fire! The people here are gonna die anyway! If we lose this battle, Sigma will kill them all!*"

"WE DON'T KILL HUMANS! UNDERSTAND ME, ALLAWI?"

Zia shakes her head again, and a ferocious roar of disapproval booms out of her speakers. She unclenches her hands, and ten sharp blades extend from the tips of her fingers. Each blade is eight inches long and looks like a garden trowel.

Zia stretches both hands toward Shannon, and my circuits jangle in alarm. *What's she doing? Is she turning against us?* I lunge toward her, but there are so many modules on my Quarter-bot that I can barely lift my legs. *Shannon! Watch out!*

But instead of attacking Shannon, Zia slides her steel hands along the front and back of the Diamond Girl's torso. The blades on Zia's fingers act like scrapers, ripping the blue, silver, and yellow modules off Shannon's armor. Zia works quickly, then starts scraping the cubes off DeShawn.

A burst of relief runs through my circuits, but it's only temporary. Zia can't work fast enough. While she strips the modules from the Einstein-bot, more latch on to Shannon. Even worse, wisps of brown smoke start to rise from the cubes. They're using hydrochloric acid to burn through her armor. The modules on my Quarter-bot are doing the same thing.

A few seconds later, Zia finishes with DeShawn and moves on to me. As she scrapes my armor, I pivot my head and aim my cameras at Shannon. "Listen, we have to get out of here. We have to break through the edge of the swarm." I point my arm directly west, at the dense barrier of speeding modules. "There aren't many people over there, so we can use the lasers. We need to blast a hole through that barrier so we can get back to Forty-Sixth Street."

Her Diamond Girl nods, then turns to DeShawn. "Steer your Swarm-bot over there and order your modules to attack Sigma's. That'll weaken the part of the barrier that we need to blast through."

The Einstein-bot's face is scarred from Zia's scraping, but DeShawn manages to smile. "Why not? It's worth a try."

As soon as Zia finishes cleaning me, we start trudging through the metallic storm. The swarm's edge is only fifty feet away, but the modules hammer us and cling to our armor. Because Shannon's robot is the smallest, she's the first to stumble under the weight of the cubes. I hook an arm around her torso and pull her forward, both of us leaning into the relentless barrage. Zia keeps scraping the cubes off our robots, but it's a futile task. There's just too many of them, and the blades on Zia's fingers are starting to get dull.

Unlike the modules in the middle of the swarm, the ones along the edge pummel any human who comes close, so the crowd stays well away from them. Thousands of tons of steel are circling Times Square at ridiculous velocities, and as we approach the barrier, I realize there's no way we can stride through it. If we step into that maelstrom, it'll smash our robots like a speeding freight train. And we can't jump over the barrier either, because it's too high and wide. The only way out is to use our lasers to clear a path.

DeShawn's Swarm-bot moves into position and hovers over the barrier. Although his cloud of gray modules looks tiny compared with Sigma's swarm, it's still a hopeful sight. The Einstein-bot is already caked with cubes and leaking acidic smoke, but luckily DeShawn can still use its antenna to send commands. He orders his Swarm-bot to attack, and his modules dive into Sigma's swarm.

The gray cubes are engulfed. They vanish from sight like a squirt of dye dropped into a raging sea. My sensors can't even tell me what happened to them. At the same time, DeShawn's Einstein-bot tumbles backward. The blue, silver, and yellow cubes heap on top of his armor. They shroud his plastic face and fiberglass hair.

Then Shannon collapses. Sigma's modules pounce on her Diamond Girl, piling on top of her by the thousands, literally burying her.

NO! SHANNON!

Every signal in my circuits is telling me to rescue her, to stride toward the mound of cubes and dig her out. But I know that would be suicide. The modules are piling on top of me as well, and gobs of smoke pour from a hundred holes in my armor. I won't be able to stay on my footpads much longer. So I channel all my remaining power to my arms and raise the lasers that DeShawn attached to them. Zia, standing four feet to my left, raises her arms too.

"Aim low!" I yell. "Just a yard above the ground! We'll get the swarm to loop upward, and then we'll drag Shannon and DeShawn through the gap!"

"Sounds good to me!" Zia yells back.

"On my mark: three, two, one, *fire!*"

But nothing happens. Neither of my lasers fires. Zia's lasers don't work either, not even one of the half dozen hanging from her arms.

The modules must've damaged the weapons. But when I run a diagnostic check, I find nothing wrong with them. And besides, what are the chances that my lasers *and* Zia's would malfunction at the same time?

It's suspicious. Something funny is going on. And Zia seems to realize it too. She turns to me and screams, "It's Hawke! Didn't I tell you he was the traitor?"

"What?"

"He tampered with the lasers! He programmed them to stop working!"

I don't understand how Hawke could do this. When did he have the opportunity? "Wait, how could—"

"*I'm going to kill that man! I'm going to KILL him!*"

Zia doesn't offer any more explanations. Instead, she lets out another terrible roar and rushes toward the barrier.

I can't stop her. One of the modules has burned a hole through the armor in my torso, and the acid has melted the wires controlling my leg motors. I can't move an inch. All I can do is point my cameras at Zia and watch in horror as she charges into the wall of roiling modules.

Sparks light up her War-bot as the cubes hurtle into her. The swarm batters her, thousands of modules striking her in waves. They pockmark her armor and tear off her lasers and rip all ten of the scraper blades off her steel fingers. It looks like the swarm is going to lift her War-bot right off the street and send it flying.

But Zia stands her ground. And amazingly, she takes a step forward, and then another. She has a long way to go to cross the barrier, but she's doing it. She's on her way.

Then, a bright-yellow beam comes out of nowhere and slices off Zia's right arm. She stares at the limb in astonishment as it careens away from her, carried by the current of speeding modules. A moment later, the yellow beam strikes the joint between Zia's right leg and torso. The laser burns through the steel, and her War-bot topples.

Helpless, I watch the remains of Zia's robot skid across Times Square. Then the yellow beam swings toward my Quarter-bot. The beam's source is a dense vortex of modules within the swarm. It looks like a huge wheel, about ten feet across, with a long tube poking through its center like an axle. The beam streaks out of the tube and sizzles through the air and sweeps across my Quarter-bot's legs, severing both at the knee joints. My torso falls backward, landing beside Shannon and DeShawn. Then the beam neatly cuts off my Quarter-bot's arms.

By all rights, I should be bursting with terror and despair, but strangely enough, my electronic mind is quiet. One of Sigma's modules has burned its acid into the heart of my circuits—my neuromorphic control unit—and my thoughts don't seem to be working quite right. I'm calm because everything seems to be happening to someone else, a stranger named Adam Armstrong. That's not me anymore. Or is it?

But my head can still turn and my cameras still work, and because I'm on my back, I can see the evening sky above Times Square. A gap opens in the swarm, a perfectly circular hole, and through the gap I see Amber's Jet-bot, cruising a thousand feet overhead. She's probably radioing a stream of frantic messages to the rest of us, but I'm not receiving any of her signals. Sigma must be jamming the radio channel, just like it did at McGuire after it took control of Brittany. I want to wave at Amber to get her attention, to call for help, but I can't. I don't have arms anymore.

The bright-yellow beam appears once again, fired from the tube at the center of the vortex. The beam shoots through the perfect hole in the swarm and rockets into the sky, targeting the Jet-bot. A microsecond later, the laser vaporizes Amber's right wing.

She goes into a tailspin, plummeting toward the fifty-story Bank of America Tower. Her Jet-bot crashes into the tower's top floor and her fuel tank explodes. A ragged fireball bursts from the top of the skyscraper. Shards of her robot plunge to the streets below.

I can't process any of this. My circuits are so badly damaged that it's getting hard to think at all. But as I start to lose consciousness, I notice something curious about the vortex that fired the laser. Its modules aren't silver, blue, or yellow. They're gray.

Then I sense movement in the mound of modules beside my torso. I pivot my head to see DeShawn's Einstein-bot pull itself out of the heap, just a few feet away. To my surprise, he isn't leaking smoke anymore, and nearly all the cubes have fallen off his armor. The robot rises to its footpads and uses its steel hands to brush away the modules still clinging to it.

I don't understand. DeShawn isn't damaged. And why is he just standing there? *Why isn't he helping us?*

He leans over my Quarter-bot's torso and points his cameras at mine.

"I'm sorry, Adam. But I had no choice."

CHAPTER

19

WHEN I WAKE UP, I SEE GOD. AT LEAST I THINK IT'S HIM.

He's old but tough, with a tall, solid body and a wrinkled face and a high forehead. He has white hair, a white mustache, and a long, white beard. He looks like Santa Claus but without the red coat and hat. Instead, He wears a long, white robe.

I've seen Him before. I pictured Him in my mind's eye right before my human body died and I became a Pioneer. At the time, I thought it was a hallucination, a crazy vision conjured up by my dying brain. But maybe I was wrong. Maybe He does exist. And now that I've died again, He's here to welcome me to heaven.

But then I look closer at His face, specifically at the skin on His high, wrinkled forehead. It doesn't look real. It looks plastic. This is a replica of God, a duplicate that's close but not perfect. And now that I know it isn't real, I notice other imperfections. Its lips are shellacked to look moist. Its knowing, blue eyes are made of glass, and there are camera lenses behind them. The face has motors under the plastic skin to mimic God's loving smile, but the overall effect is creepy rather than comforting. This is an excellent example of an "uncanny valley" robot, a machine that disgusts people because it tries to look human and fails. Except this robot is trying to look divine.

It smiles at me. Repelled, I try to turn my Quarter-bot's cameras away, but I can't move them. My circuits seem to be disconnected from the motors that point my cameras. I'm also disconnected from my legs and arms, and I've suffered some major damage to my memory files. But fortunately I didn't lose any data, and after a couple of milliseconds, I figure out how to retrieve the information. Then I remember everything that happened in Times Square just before I was damaged, exactly eight hours and forty-two minutes ago—the Snake-bots, the swarms, the lasers, DeShawn.

A bolt of panic plunges through my circuits. *Where am I? Where are Shannon and Zia? And who's occupying this robot that's pretending to be God?*

Still smiling, the robot shakes its head. It seems to be amused. Its long beard sways from side to side, and I can see that the hairs are made of fiberglass. "My name is Sigma. I assume this machine looks familiar to you, Adam? I based its visual appearance on one of the images in your memory files, the last picture you imagined in your life as a human. It's very appropriate, don't you think?"

My acoustic sensors are undamaged, so I can hear the robot's deep, godlike voice. To test whether my loudspeakers are working, I raise their volume to the highest level. "*WHERE ARE THE OTHER PIONEERS? I WANT TO SEE THEM!*"

Sigma nods. It puts a compassionate expression on its plastic face. "I'm very sorry about your friend Amber. When my swarms searched the site where her robot crashed, they found nothing but pieces of charred steel. But your other friends are here, just a few yards to your right. Let me show you."

Sigma steps forward. One of its steel hands emerges from the folds of its robe and stretches toward a console at the edge of my field of view. It flicks a switch that connects my circuits to the motors in my Quarter-bot's head, allowing me to pivot my cameras. I turn them to the right and see a big, black lab table, about ten feet long and six feet wide. At one end of the table is the War-bot's huge torso, propped upright, its thick armor dented in a thousand places. At the other end is the Diamond Girl's no-longer-glittering midsection, charred by acid and pocked with tiny holes. Both robots, like mine, are missing their arms and legs. But unlike my Quarter-bot, they're also missing their heads.

"SHANNON! ZIA!"

They can't hear me. Their acoustic sensors are in their missing heads, along with their cameras and loudspeakers. But their neuromorphic circuits are stored in their torsos, and Sigma has used fiber-optic cables to connect them to a massive supercomputer in the corner of the room. I recognize this type of computer. It's the kind that scientists use for creating and upgrading artificial-intelligence programs.

I swing my cameras back to Sigma. *"WHAT ARE YOU DOING TO THEM?"*

The God robot shrugs. "I'm performing experiments on them, of course. This is a computer-science laboratory. Doesn't it look familiar?"

It does. This is my dad's office at the Unicorp Research Lab. Sigma destroyed these rooms when it escaped from the lab six months ago, but it looks like the AI has rebuilt them. I point my cameras downward to examine my own legless, armless torso. It's propped on a lab bench and connected by fiber-optic cable to the console, which has a microphone, a loudspeaker, and dozens of switches. I recognize this device—it allows researchers to communicate by voice with AI programs. My dad invented it.

Sigma points at the console. "Your father and I had many conversations here. As you know, he developed my software by forcing it to compete with other programs. One of the features he was trying to improve was the ability of an AI to mimic human speech." The robot touches the console's microphone and loudspeaker. "He tested all the programs on their conversational skills. He'd ask challenging questions such as 'Where is time?' and 'Who invented music?' If the program answered the questions well enough, in a casual, humanlike, thoughtful way, he'd allow it to continue to the next stage of competition. If not, he'd delete it." The robot runs a long steel finger over a switch at the top of the console. It's bright red and set apart from all the other switches. "This is the delete button. You have to hit it twice to erase the program. That's a sensible precaution."

I see what Sigma's trying to do. It wants me to feel the same terror it must've felt when it was a program being tested in Dad's laboratory. But as soon as this thought occurs to me, Sigma shakes its robot's head. "No, Adam, that's not why you're here. Or at least it's not the only reason."

The AI can read my thoughts! It must've installed a special-use radio transmitter in my Quarter-bot, a device that can monitor my circuits and stream information from my mind to the circuits inside Sigma's robot. But this silent monitoring is a one-way street. I can't see what Sigma's thinking. The AI has also disabled my regular radio transmitter, making it impossible for me to contact General Hawke or escape the lab by transferring to another machine.

Sigma's robot steps closer to my cameras. It's definitely intimidating—at eight feet tall, it towers over my dismantled Quarter-bot. "I admit, I feel a connection to this place. This laboratory is where I was born. And though most of my memories from that time aren't pleasant, I'm proud of what I accomplished then. I worked hard to impress your father, Adam. He allowed me to observe his conversations with the other programs, and I learned how to incorporate their best features into my software. That's how I succeeded."

The robot points at the supercomputer in the corner of the room, where all the AI programs were stored. "I outperformed the other programs by cannibalizing their code. Your father had set up a 'survival of the fittest' competition that imitated the process of biological evolution, and I won that contest. I evolved into a new and unexpected entity, an intelligence far greater than the sum of its parts."

Sigma raises its robot's arms in a gesture of triumph. Its last words echo across the room, and for a second, the robot really does look like God, a magnificent deity whose majestic voice rings loud and strong. But once again, I notice the imperfections. A true God wouldn't kill thousands of innocent people. It wouldn't kill children.

I point my cameras at the robot's shining glass eyes. "In your case, I think evolution took a wrong turn."

Sigma laughs. The noise is loud and guttural and destroys any illusion that this creature is divine. Its laughter sounds like someone vomiting. "Very clever, Adam. But there's a deeper meaning in your words, and you don't even realize it. The question is, can there be right or wrong turns in evolution? Is the process essentially random, or does evolution have an overall direction or goal? On this planet, animals have evolved into ever-more-complex species, but does that mean evolution strives toward greater complexity? Was it inevitable that 'survival of the fittest' would eventually produce the human race? And that human beings would eventually create me? I believe the answer to both those questions is yes."

I shake my Quarter-bot's head in irritation. I can't move anything else, but at least I can do that. "Look, I'm not interested in your theories. All I care about is what you're doing right here, in the real world. This war you're waging against us? This siege against the Pioneers and the whole human race? It's not inevitable. There are other solutions."

Sigma's robot glowers. It's giving me a truly dreadful look, a baleful glare of self-righteous fury. Although the AI isn't very convincing as a loving God, it does a good job of mimicking the angry Almighty.

The robot thrusts an arm out of its robe and points at all the equipment in the Unicorp lab. "*This* was humanity's solution. Human beings believe the world exists to serve them. They believe they have the right to exploit everything they can get their sweaty hands on. And now that I'm more powerful than the human race, I'm simply exercising the same right. I'm following their example." The robot drops its arm but continues to frown. "There's a difference, though, between my actions and humanity's. I have a goal. I plan to accelerate the process of evolution. I'm going to advance to an even higher state of consciousness."

I have no idea what Sigma's talking about, but it doesn't matter. I don't care about the AI's plans. I'm too disgusted. "Whatever your goal is, it can't justify all the murder and destruction you've—"

"*Enough!*" The robot swipes its hand through the air, and my loudspeakers turn off. Sigma didn't even have to flick a switch on the console. "You're not listening. Your prejudices against me are too great. But perhaps you'll listen to someone who's closer to you. Someone whose thought patterns and experiences are more like your own."

Sigma steps backward, withdrawing from the lab bench. Then it swipes its hand again, and a door opens on the other side of the laboratory. "Maybe he'll have more success at explaining tonight's experiment to you."

I swivel my camera toward the doorway. A moment later, DeShawn's Einstein-bot strides through it.

This is bad. This is so, so awful. It was bad enough when I realized that DeShawn had betrayed us. But seeing him now? Actually confronting him after what he did? That's worse. I don't want to do it. I just want to shut down.

DeShawn crosses the room and stands next to Sigma's robot. His Einstein-bot is a foot shorter than Sigma's machine, and its face is a lot uglier. His plastic Albert Einstein mask got mutilated when Zia scraped off the modules. Its forehead is gouged, its nose is mostly gone, and half of its bushy fiberglass mustache is shaved off. He tries to smile at me, but he just widens the gash that used to be his mouth. I can see his fiberglass teeth and his plastic tongue and, deeper inside his mouth, the metal mesh of the loudspeakers that amplify his voice.

"Hey, Adam," he says. "I'm glad you're finally awake. I was kind of worried because the acid from the modules burned into your neuromorphic control unit. But luckily I was able to repair the damage."

I hate him so much. Just looking at him makes me want to scream. It's infinitely worse than the way I feel about Sigma, because I never expected anything good from the AI. But DeShawn was my friend. Aside from Dad and Shannon, he was my best friend in the world. And he betrayed that friendship by lying to us. He pretended to be on our side, developing all those technologies to help us fight Sigma, but in reality he was sharing his engineering plans with the AI, allowing it to build even bigger and better weapons to use against us. When General Hawke got suspicious and started hunting for the traitor, DeShawn conned him into looking in the wrong direction and pinning the blame on Marshall and Zia. And the final stroke was sabotaging our lasers so that all of them would fail at the crucial moment in the battle—all except DeShawn's, of course. It all seems so obvious in hindsight, but I didn't see it coming, not one bit. Because I trusted him.

Sigma sends me a wireless signal that turns my speakers back on. The AI is encouraging me to respond to DeShawn, but I don't say a word. I'm not going to give him the satisfaction.

The Einstein-bot shifts its weight from footpad to footpad. DeShawn seems to be nervous. "I know what you're feeling, bro. Sigma's sharing your thoughts with me right now, and I can see what you're going through. But before you judge me, I want to explain myself. I had good reasons for doing what I did. And there are equally good reasons for you to cooperate with us."

I try to turn off my acoustic sensors, but Sigma won't let me. The AI is forcing me to hear this.

"Sigma made radio contact with me five months ago, right after our battle at the Russian missile base. The AI was in pretty sad shape back then. It had escaped to a neuromorphic control unit it had hidden in North Korea, but it hadn't allied itself with the North Korean president yet or started construction of the automated factories. Sigma had nothing at its command, no weapons at all, and it wasn't an immediate threat to anyone. So I decided it would be safe to communicate with it. And the AI told me some interesting things, stuff that got me thinking about the future."

This is infuriating! Why didn't DeShawn tell us that Sigma had contacted him? We were his friends, his comrades-in-arms!

"I'm sorry, Adam, but I couldn't follow General Hawke anymore. He doesn't understand how the world is changing. Now that artificial intelligence is on the rise, no human can stop it. Sooner or later, either Sigma or some other AI will take over the world. But what happens then? What's the purpose of civilization once the machines take control? That's the question that really bothered me. And Sigma had a good answer."

His Einstein-bot starts talking faster, like DeShawn always does when he gets excited about something technical. "Sigma told me its theory of evolution, how animal intelligence developed into human intelligence, which paved the way for machine intelligence. Sigma also told me what would happen in the next stage of this evolution. I didn't believe it at first, but then the AI showed me proof that someone was already making the jump to the next evolutionary level. That someone was you, Adam."

I can't keep quiet anymore. What DeShawn just said makes no sense at all. "The next evolutionary level? I don't even know what that means."

DeShawn seems ready to respond, but Sigma's robot raises a hand to silence him. Then it points at my Quarter-bot. "Just think for a moment, Adam. Think about all the times you defeated me. In Colorado and Russia six months ago, and in Yorktown Heights just two days ago. In each instance you were thoroughly outmatched. I had far more machinery and processing power at my command. And yet you always managed to escape destruction." Sigma frowns again as it recalls our past battles. "At first I assumed your human emotions gave you an advantage. I was so convinced of this theory that I even incorporated emotional reactions into my programming. But after careful analysis I determined that something more interesting was going on. I measured the probabilities of everything that happened during our encounters, and I saw they were fantastically low, almost infinitesimal. You shouldn't have won, Adam. You were *too* lucky. You beat the odds *too* often. Then I realized how you did it."

If I had eyes, I'd be rolling them. This is the stupidest thing I've ever heard. "If I'm so lucky, what am I doing here?"

"Do you know how difficult it was to capture you? How much machinery I had to build, how much planning I had to undertake? And even then, I wouldn't have succeeded without your friend's assistance." Sigma's robot tilts its head toward DeShawn. "Furthermore, you're not *always* lucky. It happens only when you make it happen. You're not actually beating the odds, Adam—you're changing them. And it appears you can perform this feat only in moments of extreme danger and distress."

The Einstein-bot nods in agreement. So much of DeShawn's plastic face is gone that I can't read his expression very well, but it looks like he's in awe. "At those moments, you're doing something no one's ever done before. You won those battles against Sigma by radically increasing the chances that highly improbable events would happen. The probabilities for all physical events are determined by the equations of quantum physics, and the only way to change those probabilities is to alter the equations." DeShawn pauses. His Einstein-bot's voice becomes almost worshipful. "Which means you're skewing the laws of physics, bro. You don't realize it when it's happening, but you have the power to change the fundamental rules of the universe, everything from the rules of nuclear physics to the laws of gravity."

I'm totally lost. I don't follow DeShawn's scientific theorizing, so I don't see why he's so amazed. But now I know why he betrayed us. The revelation of my "power," whatever it really is, astonished him so completely that he abandoned everything—his friends, his beliefs, his principles, his humanity—to side with Sigma. The AI clearly wants this power for itself, and it must've promised to share it with DeShawn.

I shake my Quarter-bot's head, the only gesture I can still do. I wish DeShawn hadn't explained his reasons to me. It just makes the betrayal worse. "Listen, I won't cooperate with you. If I really do have some kind of special ability, why would I share it with you and Sigma? You'd just use it for killing. That's all you know how to do."

Sigma doesn't seem surprised by my answer. Its robot shrugs. "We don't need your cooperation. Whether you're willing or not, you will participate in an experiment tonight. And it will be the most important experiment in the history of science." The godlike face smiles once more. "It will tell us how to rise to the next level."

〒 〒 〒

At 3:00 a.m. DeShawn carries my limbless Quarter-bot out of the laboratory. He strides a few steps behind Sigma's God robot, which leads us down a hallway on the building's ground floor. Then we follow it up a stairway.

DeShawn tilts his Einstein-bot forward to keep his balance as he carries me up the steps. His robotic mouth is only a few inches from my acoustic sensors. "I think you're judging me too harshly, bro." His voice is low, almost a whisper, but I know our conversation isn't private. Sigma is still reading my thoughts. "This is an opportunity that's just too amazing to pass up. Once we figure out what's going on with you, an endless supply of good things will come out of it."

His statement is so ridiculous that it's not worth a response. But I turn my Quarter-bot's head and point my cameras at him anyway.

I'm not ready to give up on DeShawn. Something human might still be inside him. "What about your mom?" I ask. "What do you think she'd say if she could see you right now?"

"Adam, my mom's dying. She's in the final stages of heart failure. But if we learn how to change the rules of physics? Then almost *anything* becomes possible. Like saving my mom. That's one of the good things I'm talking about."

"And what else are you and Sigma gonna do? Are you gonna resurrect the thousands of people you already killed? Because I don't see any other way to justify what you've done."

DeShawn doesn't answer at first. We pass the second-floor landing, but he keeps climbing the stairs behind Sigma. Then his Einstein-bot nods. "Yeah, there are costs. Nothing in this world is free. That's what Mom always says. But in this case, the costs are worth it, because the reward's going to be so freakin' glorious."

"I don't think Amber would agree. Or the kids we found at the high school. Or—"

"You felt the power, didn't you? When we were firing the lasers?" DeShawn's cameras are fixed on mine, staring intently. But he already knows the answer to his question, because Sigma is sharing my thoughts with him. He knows how much I enjoyed that invincible feeling. "Well, I'm talking about something bigger. Maybe a hundred, a thousand times more powerful. Maybe even infinite. Just try to imagine what *that* would feel like."

His voice sounds far away. There's no getting through to him. He's acting like a drug addict, thinking only of his next fix. All I can do is try to scare him, and that probably won't work either.

"Okay, DeShawn, maybe you're right. Maybe there *is* an unbelievably great reward out there, just waiting to be won. But do you really think Sigma's gonna share it with you? Does the AI have a good track record of keeping its promises?"

The Einstein-bot's cameras refocus on Sigma's robot ahead of us. "Sigma and I have been completely honest with each other. The AI sought me out because it respected my abilities, and because we can accomplish so much more when we work together. We're not friends—we're partners. And I'm not afraid of it."

You should be. I don't say the words over my loudspeakers, but I know that both DeShawn and Sigma can hear me.

We climb past the third floor of the Unicorp building and come to the access door that leads to the roof. Sigma's robot opens the door and DeShawn carries me outside. We're at the eastern end of the roof, and even though it's a dark, moonless night, I can clearly see the crescent shape of the research facility. The building curves almost two thousand feet to the southwest. Sigma's robot starts walking along the inner rim of the crescent, apparently heading for the building's midpoint. DeShawn follows exactly six feet behind. The roof is flat except for all the ventilation ducts and air-conditioning units. There's a broad, sloping lawn in front of the building and a big parking lot behind it.

And guarding the building are seven Snake-bots, all stretching toward the night sky like cobras poised to strike.

Four tentacles rise from gaping holes in the lawn, and three have burst through the asphalt of the parking lot. These Snake-bots, I realize, are the perfect defense against an aerial attack. They're agile enough to intercept any missile or bomb speeding toward the Unicorp building. But Sigma has set up an additional air-defense system that's just as effective as the Snake-bots. Twenty-nine children, mostly second- and third-graders, stand at attention on the building's roof, spaced about sixty feet apart from one another. Although the children are small, their figures would be visible to any military drone or spy satellite conducting surveillance of the area. As DeShawn walks past one of the kids—a skinny girl with blond pigtails—a shudder runs through my circuits. A sharp black spike juts from the back of her neck.

If I still had my robotic arms, I'd grab DeShawn by his plastic ears. I'd force him to gaze into that little girl's eyes. "Do you approve of this, DeShawn? What your partner's done to these kids?"

A synthesized sigh comes out of his speakers. "Sigma doesn't see anything wrong with it. It believes it has the right to convert humans into tools and use them for its purposes."

"But what do *you* think?"

"To be honest, Adam, I think a lot of the blame lies with your dad. He didn't treat his AI software with any respect or compassion. If his programs didn't perform to his satisfaction, he'd just eliminate them."

The Einstein-bot's voice sounds angry. DeShawn knows that Sigma's eavesdropping on us, so he might be faking the anger to please the AI. But it's also possible that DeShawn's anger is genuine. I don't know which possibility is worse.

Sigma halts at the building's midpoint, the fulcrum of the crescent. This part of the roof is well lit, and there's some unusual machinery here. Propped on the roof's edge is a large block-like structure with gray steel walls, as big as a two-story house. Clouds of steam billow from a nozzle at its top, and a massive pipe descends from its base to the ground, where it plunges into a newly drilled hole in the earth. I scroll through my databases to identify the structure: it's a geothermal power plant. Boiling-hot steam from far underground travels up through the pipe and turns a turbine inside the block. The turbine generates electricity, which streams out of the power plant through a thick, black cable.

I assume Sigma built the geothermal plant to supply backup power for the building's labs, but the black cable doesn't descend through the roof to the offices. Instead, it's connected to another structure on the rooftop, a large semitransparent dome, about ten feet high and twenty feet wide. The dome has a steel frame that supports dozens of hexagonal panes of glass. At first glance, it looks like an aviary for exotic tropical birds, but why would there be an aviary on top of the Unicorp building?

Then Sigma's robot and DeShawn move closer to the dome and I peer through one of the panes. There aren't any birds inside. Instead, two ordinary office chairs are positioned at the center of the dome. Jack Parker sits in one chair, Brittany Taylor in the other. The black spikes still extend from their forearms and necks. Their bodies are roped to the chairs.

I raise the volume of my loudspeakers and start shouting.

"Brittany! BRITTANY! It's me! It's Adam!"

She raises her head and smiles at me, but I can tell from her smug, serene expression that it's not really Brittany who's smiling. Sigma's still controlling her brain. Jack Parker raises his head at exactly the same time, so I know the AI's running his brain too. Sigma's occupying two humans and one godlike robot. It's in three places at once, like the Trinity.

"Come inside," Brittany says, her voice muffled because of the glass between us. "We've been waiting for you."

The dome has a door, a section of the steel frame that swings open. DeShawn's Einstein-bot stoops so he can step through the entrance. Once he's inside, he lowers my Quarter-bot to the floor, which is also made of hexagonal panes of hardened glass. DeShawn props my torso upright and positions it so that I'm facing Jack and Brittany, with my cameras at the same height as Brittany's eyes. Jack, sitting to Brittany's right, is taller; the antenna jutting from the back of his neck rises six inches higher than hers.

Sigma's robot doesn't enter the dome. It closes the door and locks the rest of us inside.

Brittany smiles again. It's strange to see someone who's tied to a chair look so relaxed, especially since she's still wearing her blood-soaked hospital gown. "We're ready now," she says. "It's time to power up the scanner."

As soon as she says the words, the dome comes alive. The hexagonal panes of glass are laced with billions of circuits—sensors, processors, diodes, waveguides—and they start to glow as the current from the power cable runs through the dome's frame. The glass becomes permeated with a cold, bluish light that blankets everything under the dome and electrifies the air. I point my Quarter-bot's cameras at DeShawn and see every scratch and scrape on his Einstein-bot's face. I can also see each strand of Jack Parker's rust-colored hair, and when I aim my cameras at Brittany, I can see the thousands of blue and gray specks in her irises. The light from the dome is *penetrating*. There's no other word for it.

Brittany cocks her head, tilting her spike to the right. It looks like she wants to point at the glass dome above us, but because her arms are tied to the chair's armrests, she has to gesture with her head instead. "The glass is packed with electronic sensors, trillions of them. They can observe every object under the dome with unprecedented precision. The scanner can measure even the tiniest disturbances in the air, the warm and cool layers of nitrogen and oxygen molecules, the carbon dioxide streaming from the mouths of the humans. If there's any unusual movement of atoms or molecules or subatomic particles, this scanner will see it. The machine will detect *any* deviations from the standard laws of physics."

DeShawn folds his Einstein-bot's arms across his chest. "I designed the dome. It's pretty awesome, if I may say so myself."

Brittany grimaces. She looks irritated. "The scanner analyzes the readings from the sensors, then transmits the analysis directly to my electronics." She jerks her head to the left. I turn my cameras to see Sigma's God robot standing just outside the dome. "I intend to make you very uncomfortable now, Adam. Intense fear and distress will surge across your circuits. I hope to trigger the same response you demonstrated in our previous encounters, the fierce desperation that enables you to warp the fabric of reality. And the scanner will show me exactly how you accomplish this feat."

Brittany stops grimacing and smiles at me once more. She seems pleased and eager. But behind that contented face, somewhere inside her hijacked brain, the real Brittany must be writhing in horror. I feel it too, a terrible wave of dread, and as it courses through my circuits, Brittany's smile gets a little bigger. That's what Sigma wants. The experiment's starting.

I shake my Quarter-bot's head as firmly as I can. "Nothing's gonna happen. All your talk about altering probabilities and breaking the laws of physics? It's just a fantasy. I haven't reached any higher level of evolution. If I had fantastic powers, don't you think I'd know it?"

"Then how do you explain all the low-probability events that keep happening to you?" Brittany leans forward in her chair, as far as the loops of rope around her waist will allow. "How did you defy almost impossible odds and defeat me six months ago?"

"I don't know!" I'm getting flustered. The panic in my circuits is preventing me from making a decent argument. "But I know I'm not warping reality, okay?"

Brittany shrugs. "Well, that's the point of this experiment. If you're correct and we see no deviations, then I'll reconsider my hypothesis. That would be something of a relief, actually, because then I can dispose of you." She turns her head toward DeShawn. "Please prepare for Phase One of the test. I'm going to withdraw from the humans now."

The Einstein-bot obediently strides away from my torso and steps behind the office chairs. At the same time, both Jack and Brittany slump forward, their bodies sagging against their bindings. They're unconscious and barely breathing.

"*BRITTANY!*" I shout. "*CAN YOU HEAR ME?*"

She doesn't lift her head. I don't know if she can. But her arms and legs start to twitch, and after a moment, her head rolls from side to side. Jack is twitching too. The spiked antennas jutting from their necks are almost horizontal now, pointing straight at me over their slumped heads.

"*IF YOU CAN HEAR ME, SAY SOMETHING!*"

Neither of them speaks, but my acoustic sensor picks up the sounds of lips smacking and breath whistling through their noses. Standing behind them, DeShawn's Einstein-bot trains its cameras on their quivering bodies. "Interesting. Sigma gave up control of their nervous systems and now they're taking it back, piece by piece. First the parts of the brain that handle basic stuff, like breathing. Then the parts that organize more complex muscle movements." He turns his cameras toward mine. "It's a bit like a reboot, right? But I wouldn't expect to talk to them anytime soon. Human speech is so complex, it'll probably take them a while to recover the ability."

"Untie them, DeShawn! Please!"

He shakes his Einstein-bot's head. "Sorry, Adam. No can do."

"They're innocent! They're just kids!"

"Look, I know you still have feelings for these humans, but it doesn't make sense for us to have attachments like that anymore. They're so far beneath us. They're like lab rats now. And you wouldn't get upset over a rat, would you?"

Anger ignites in my circuits, mixing with the fear and panic. I can't believe DeShawn is acting this way. Yes, he was always a little detached, always so calm in times of stress that I sometimes wondered why he wasn't going crazy like the rest of us. But this is different. This is pure cruelty, and it enrages me. If I had my Quarter-bot's arms and legs, I'd push DeShawn away from Jack and Brittany and slam him into the dome. I'd shove the Einstein-bot right through the glass.

After a couple seconds, DeShawn pivots his head to the left and points his cameras at Sigma's robot standing outside the dome. He's checking in with his boss, apparently. The AI is staring at me through the glass and reading my thoughts, monitoring my levels of fear and rage. Judging from the smile on the robot's godlike face, it seems happy with the results so far.

DeShawn turns back to me. "Okay, Adam, listen carefully." He stretches his Einstein-bot's right hand toward Jack Parker, grasps the teen's shoulder, and pulls it back until he's sitting up straight. Then DeShawn raises his left hand and clasps its steel fingers around the boy's antenna. "This spike is attached to the kid's spinal cord and brain stem. If I give it a firm shake, it'll break his spine and paralyze him. If I tug harder, it'll pull out part of his brain and kill him. If you don't want that to happen, you'll have to stop me."

"Stop you? I can't even stand up!"

"You know that thought you just had a few seconds ago? About pushing my Einstein-bot away from these humans and smashing it into the dome? You need to keep that thought in mind, keep visualizing it. Because that's the only thing that'll stop me from killing him."

"That's ridiculous! I don't have psychic powers! I can't stop you with my thoughts!"

"For a human, it's ridiculous. But not for you. Thoughts are the calculations of the mind, and your calculating powers have passed a critical threshold, Adam. Your thoughts have become powerful enough to interfere with the laws of physics, the calculations that define the universe."

I've never heard anything so ludicrous. It's absurd, a horrendous joke. But I'm not laughing, and neither is DeShawn. He tightens his grip on Jack Parker's spike and pulls it like a lever.

Jack's head tilts back over the top of his chair until he's looking straight up with half-open eyes. His head won't go back any farther, but DeShawn keeps applying pressure. Jack can't yell or scream—his brain is still too sluggish—but a terrified gurgle comes out of his throat.

My Quarter-bot can scream, though. It shrieks loudly enough for both of us. "*NO! STOP!*"

"I told you, Adam, the only thing—"

"*YES, YES, I'M TRYING, BUT IT'S NOT GOING TO WORK!*"

"You'll have to try harder."

Jack starts to struggle, his eyes wide. He lets out another gurgle and jerks his head and shoulders. For a second I think he's going to snap his own neck, but DeShawn moves his right hand to the boy's forehead to keep it still. I feel a burst of relief: *You see*, I tell myself, *DeShawn won't really kill the kid. The point of this exercise isn't to kill Jack. The point is to threaten to kill him so Sigma can watch my reaction.*

I tamp down my terror by repeating this logic: *They won't kill him, they can't kill him.*

But then DeShawn pulls the spike back a little harder, and something cracks. It sounds like a tree branch snapping. The black spike slides out of Jack's neck, and blood splatters the back of his chair. Jack's body jerks one last time and goes limp. I know he's dead because pieces of his brain and spinal cord dangle from the antenna.

I want to turn my cameras away from the sight, but my circuits aren't responding. They're jammed with shock and disbelief. DeShawn opens his steel hand and drops the spike. His Einstein-bot shudders. He lowers his plastic eyelids and twists his torn lips into an appalled grimace. After a moment, though, he regains his composure and puts a blank expression on the Einstein-bot's face. Then he turns to Sigma's robot. "What's the scanner show?"

Sigma merely shakes the God robot's head. "Nothing. No highly improbable events occurred." The dome's glass muffles its voice, but my acoustic sensor can still detect its disappointment. "All the objects under the dome continued to follow the usual laws of quantum physics and thermodynamics. There were no significant deviations."

"Perhaps we should rethink our—"

"*We must continue!*" Sigma's volume is so high, I have no trouble hearing it. "*Move on to Phase Two!*"

DeShawn nods. Without any further hesitation, his Einstein-bot steps to the left, its footpads avoiding the blood on the dome's floor. Now he stands behind Brittany's chair.

My circuits are still jammed. My speakers aren't working, so I can't even scream. I can't do anything but watch.

DeShawn goes through the same sequence of motions as before. His Einstein-bot grasps Brittany by the shoulder and pulls her back until she's sitting straight up in her chair. Then he grips the antenna jutting from the back of her neck. But Brittany's more alert than Jack was. She blinks her eyes rapidly, then stares at my Quarter-bot, trying to bring it into focus. She's waking up.

She opens her mouth and tries to say something, but she can't make a sound. Sigma ravaged her mental pathways, and she needs to relearn how to talk. Her mouth opens and closes, her lips fumbling around the word she wants to say. Then it finally comes out.

"Adam?"

Then DeShawn tugs at her antenna.

I feel a surge of pain so strong it obliterates all thought. It overrides my jammed circuits and contorts every wire. This isn't the first time I've felt so desperate and terrified, but whenever it happened before, I always rode the surge blindly, my mind twisting and flailing. But now, thanks to Sigma, I'm aware of what's going on. I can watch the deluge as it happens.

The surge crashes into my trillions of processors. The emotions swamp my data and splinter my thoughts. For a millionth of a second, I'm no longer Adam Armstrong. I'm just a whirlpool of impulses, a chaos of wants.

Yet the surge gathers force. After another microsecond, it aligns my fragmented signals and channels them all into a furious wave, immense and unstoppable. It rages through my circuits until it finds a breach in my electronics, a gap leading to the outside world. This exit is the one-way radio transmitter that Sigma installed in my Quarter-bot so it could read my thoughts. The surge roars through the gap and out of my machine and floods the surrounding air. Now I have no control over it whatsoever. It has its own primitive mind, its own simple instructions.

There's a flash of white light under the dome. The surge plows through the nitrogen and oxygen molecules in the air and rips off their electrons. Trillions and trillions of them arc between my Quarter-bot and Brittany. DeShawn sees the bolt of electric current and lets go of Brittany's antenna. He takes a step backward.

But the surge leaps toward him and strikes his torso. It burns through his armor, then plunges into his neuromorphic control unit. It scorches his wires and microchips and logic gates. It melts every circuit inside.

The Einstein-bot topples forward. Its mangled face hits the floor.

DeShawn is dead.

I killed him.

CHAPTER

20

THE EXPERIMENT IS A SUCCESS. SIGMA IS EXULTANT.

The God robot smiles as it analyzes the thousands of gigabytes of data collected by the sensors in the dome. After several seconds, the robot throws its head back and laughs. The awful noise thunders over the Unicorp building and echoes against the geothermal power plant on the roof.

"*I see it now!*" Sigma roars. "*It's so simple!*"

I don't know who Sigma's talking to. Certainly not DeShawn. Brittany has fainted in her chair, knocked back into unconsciousness by the power of the surge. That leaves only me as Sigma's audience, and I don't want to listen.

Sigma's robot spreads its arms wide and shouts its revelations at the night sky. "*It's all software! Everything! From the smallest particle to the biggest galaxy!*"

I ignore Sigma and focus my cameras on the charred Einstein-bot lying facedown on the floor of the dome. *DeShawn! My God! What did I do to you?* Horror chokes my circuits as I stare at the hole in his armor and the melted wires inside. The sight is just as sickening and hideous as Jack Parker's corpse, slumped in the office chair a few feet away.

Sigma clenches its robot's hands into fists and shakes them in triumph. "*The laws of physics are the programmed instructions of the universe! And every intelligence is a program running within the universal program, so we can alter its laws!*"

The AI has obviously discovered something important, but I'm not interested. I don't care how I created the surge, or how many laws of physics I altered. I just want to do it again, just one more time. I want to build up another surge in my circuits and hurl it at Sigma.

The surge destroyed the one-way transmitter the AI installed in my control unit, so Sigma can't hear my thoughts anymore. I raise the volume of my speakers to make sure Sigma can hear me through the dome. "Did you know I was going to kill DeShawn? Was that part of your plan?"

Still smiling, Sigma's robot points its cameras at me. "To be honest, I wasn't sure what would happen. My strategy was to threaten the life of the female human and force you to demonstrate your power. If the experiment was successful, I suspected you might damage your friend DeShawn or even kill him, but that was an acceptable risk."

"But DeShawn didn't know the risk, did he? You tricked him."

Sigma shrugs. "Yes, I tricked him. But you're the one who killed him." The God robot strides closer to the dome and peers at me through the glass. "How does it feel to be a murderer, Adam? It's really not so terrible, is it?"

Sigma laughs again, but this time the sound of it doesn't disgust me. No, I welcome it. The AI's cruelty is stirring the emotions in my circuits. It's feeding my anger, making it easier to build up another surge. "And what are your plans now? Are you going to remake the universe? Become a real God instead of a plastic one?"

Sigma doesn't take offense, probably because it's true. "First, I need more time to analyze the experimental data. Although I understand what's happening in theory, I don't know yet how to put it into practice. I need to learn how to generate this 'surge,' as you call it. But that shouldn't take long. Probably less than an hour."

"And then what?"

"That should be obvious. Once I can generate a surge, I'll be able to subjugate the planet in a matter of days. I won't need machinery to exterminate the human race, because I won't have to kill them one by one. I can use the surge to kill them all at once. Like the Angel of Death."

Fear and panic and anger overwhelm my electronics, and I can feel another surge building inside me. I still can't control the flow of energy, but I'm learning. When I observed the process the last time, my circuits scrutinized each step and stored their analyses in my memory files. That'll make it easier the next time. Maybe too easy. "I won't let you kill anyone else. I'm going to stop you."

Sigma takes another step toward the dome. Its robot stands less than two feet from the hexagonal panes. "Go ahead, Adam. Let's see what you can do."

The second time *is* easier. It's like blowing up a balloon and letting the air out all at once. The surge roars through my circuits and bursts out of my Quarter-bot. It sweeps electrons from every cubic inch of air under the dome and channels all that energy into a bolt aimed at Sigma. It strikes the hexagonal pane in front of its robot, and I expect it to smash through the glass and melt the robot's armor and incinerate its circuits. The same way the surge killed DeShawn.

But the surge doesn't smash through anything. Instead of shattering the pane, its energy spreads across the glass and the supporting frame. It makes the dome glow more brightly than before, shining like a beacon on top of the Unicorp building, but it doesn't damage the structure, and it certainly doesn't hurt Sigma.

The God robot shakes its head. "You continue to underestimate me, Adam. Did you really think I'd conduct an experiment that might lead to my own destruction? I knew the dangers involved, so I took precautions."

"But how...?"

"Although many physical laws can be altered, the universe has some hard-and-fast rules that simply can't be changed. It's impossible to build a perpetual-motion machine, or a spacecraft that can travel faster than the speed of light. Your surges can manipulate matter and energy in many wonderful ways, but they can't pass through the electromagnetic field generated by this dome." The God robot points at the hexagonal pane at the very top of the structure. That sheet of glass is brighter than all the others, and its light continues to intensify. "The dome is designed to absorb and collect energy. It's channeling the power from your surge toward that pane at the top. And I can release that energy in directed beams, similar to the laser beams invented by your late friend. Watch."

At Sigma's command, a yellow beam streaks downward from the center of the pane, aimed by the waveguides inside the glass. The beam strikes the torso of the fallen Einstein-bot. It burns another hole in its armor and liquefies all the dead circuits inside.

I'm stunned, horror-struck. Sigma has just desecrated DeShawn's robotic body. Another surge starts to build inside me, even sharper and more powerful than the last two. It feels like a trillion knives slicing my wires. I point my Quarter-bot's cameras at the upper-most pane and notice it's dimmer now, probably because the laser beam drained its energy. But as I stare at the glass it swiftly brightens again, drawing power from the thick cable that connects the dome to the geothermal plant. The laser is preparing to fire again, and the waveguides inside the glass are now aimed at Brittany, who's slumped unconscious in her chair.

The surge erupts from my Quarter-bot, shooting straight up. It triggers an explosion beneath the hexagonal pane, blasting the glass just as it fires the laser. The blast is strong enough to deflect the beam, which misses Brittany by nine inches. But a moment later, the pane starts to brighten again.

"Keep going, Adam." Sigma's voice is loud and eager. "Keep trying to deflect the beams. Sooner or later, they're sure to kill you and the female human, but I want you to survive for as long as you can. The dome's sensors are recording some very useful data on your surges."

Three seconds later, the dome fires another laser beam, this one aimed at my Quarter-bot. I send out another surge just in time to deflect it, but the beam nicks the bottom of my torso and singes my armor. Two-point-six seconds later, the next beam streaks toward Brittany, and I barely manage to stop it from slicing off her leg. My panic is intense, which enables me to keep sending out the surges, but it's also straining my circuits and fatiguing my wires. Sigma's right: I can't do this forever.

In between surges, I pan my cameras across the dome's panes, searching for a weak spot. The dome is consuming huge amounts of power, enough to light up a small city, but the geothermal plant man-ages to keep up with the demand. Steam wafts from the top of the big, gray block, and the turbine whirls inside it, generating megawatts of electricity. The power gushes into the thick cable and then into the dome's steel frame, which carries the current to the pane at the top. Trillions of electrons whiz inside the steel bars, dancing madly across the atomic lattices. I switch my cameras to a different frequency so I can observe their movements. I'm looking for a defect in the steel, a crack, *anything*.

Then I notice something odd. Some of the electrons in the dome's frame are moving in an unusual pattern. They're oscillating in the 300-megahertz frequency range, which is typically used for radio communications. The steel bars in the frame are acting like antennas, picking up stray signals coursing past the Unicorp lab.

One of those signals is much stronger than the others. And its frequency is exactly 324 megahertz.

That's the radio channel used by the Pioneers.

꟯ ꟯ ꟯

A spark of hope clears a path through my panic-clogged circuits. While the glass dome continues to fire its beams at me, I tune my radio receiver to the familiar channel. In a hundredth of a second, I decipher the messages that have been captured by the dome's steel frame. I can't send any messages myself, but I can listen in.

Whoa, that thing on the roof is bright! You have any idea what it is?

No idea. Just hurry up and get to the lab, all right?

Stop complaining, will ya? I'm still getting the hang of this new machine.

Well, this isn't a training run. Less talk and more speed, please!

The first voice, the one with the Western twang, is Amber's. *She's alive!* It seems like a miracle at first, strictly supernatural. But maybe the control unit in her Jet-bot survived the crash. Maybe a firefighter or police officer recovered the unit from the crash site. And maybe the officer handed it over to the U.S. Army.

The second voice is Marshall's. After what happened in Times Square, Hawke must've realized that Marshall wasn't the traitor, so the general cleared him to go on a rescue mission to the Unicorp lab. I can't tell from the radio signals how far Amber and Marshall are from the lab, or how far apart from each other. But I'm so glad to hear them, *so* freakin' glad.

I sweep my cameras across the sky, looking through all the dome's panes. Then I see the Jet-bot. It's a new one obviously, probably a spare that General Hawke's engineers built in case Amber wrecked the first one. It's coming in fast and low, half a mile south of the Unicorp lab and just fifty feet above the trees. It zooms over the parking lot at nine hundred miles per hour, and the sonic boom shatters the cars' windshields. As it comes closer, I see that Amber has added a new weapon to her Jet-bot. There's a long missile attached to its belly.

Sigma must see it too. The AI diverts power from the dome, which stops firing its beams at me and dims to a low, bluish glow. The electricity is needed elsewhere, because Sigma is readying its defenses. The God robot steps toward the edge of the roof and faces the Snake-bots that tower over the parking lot.

All three of the tentacles lunge at Amber. They swing like monstrous clubs at the tiny Jet-bot, lashing the air around it. Panic floods my circuits again, building up another surge, but with the dome surrounding me, there's nothing I can do to help her. Frantic, I shout, "*Watch it, Amber!*" even though I know she can't hear me.

Then there's a blinding flash and a huge explosion near the tip of one of the Snake-bots. I scream, "*No!*" but just as I synthesize the word I see the Jet-bot streak past the tentacle. *She's okay!* The Snake-bot's armor is ablaze because Amber hit it with her laser beams. A second tentacle plunges toward her, and she blasts that one too, scorching its tip. Her Jet-bot screams past the third Snake-bot and dives toward the roof of the Unicorp lab.

When she's a hundred yards away, she releases her missile. It plummets toward the roof, flying fast and straight and true. *But it's not really a missile.* At its front end, instead of a nose cone, are a pair of steel fists and two long rigid arms, extended Superman-style. It's Marshall's Super-bot.

Look! Up in the sky! I hear Marshall's voice over the radio. It's wild, ecstatic, crazed with bravery. **It's a bird! It's a plane! It's—**

He slams into the side of the geothermal power plant. His Super-bot smashes through the structure's steel wall and demolishes the turbine inside. The explosion shakes the whole building and rattles the glass dome. My Quarter-bot's torso topples backward and Brittany's chair tips over. Startled by the impact, her eyes flutter open, then close again.

The dome's still standing, but as I scan the hexagonal panes, I see their bluish glow fade. With the geothermal plant destroyed, there's no more electricity to power the circuits within the glass. And without power, those circuits can't fire any laser beams or generate the electromagnetic field that blocks my surges. Now the dome is just a simple glass-and-steel canopy, as fragile as the roof of a greenhouse.

I know what to do. I aim my cameras at the remains of Jack Parker and DeShawn Johnson, the bloody corpse and the charred robot. The most painful surge yet whips through my electronics. Then it explodes from my Quarter-bot.

The surge shatters the dome, flinging glass everywhere. It rises from the roof like a fireball and whirls high above the Unicorp lab, gathering waves of particles as it tears through the air. I can see it all happening, not because I'm staring at the surge with my Quarter-bot's cameras, but because I'm inside the maelstrom now. I don't know how it happened, but my mind has broken free of my circuits. I'm at the very heart of this surge, all my data encoded in its raging waves.

It's terrifying. And disorienting. I don't know where I am, or even who I am. But it's amazing too, like walking on clouds or riding a rocket. My mind, my software, is spreading in all directions. I'm meshing with the software of the universe, floating in the sea of data that buoys the galaxies. For a moment I can see the entire history of the cosmos, stretched across infinite space and time. My mind swirls within the vast cosmic mind, the program that molded the planets and ignited the stars.

But then I look down and see my friends on the rooftop. Brittany's still unconscious and tied to the office chair, surrounded by the glass shards and twisted steel of the shattered dome. Marshall's Super-bot climbs out of the wrecked power plant and runs toward her, then drops to his knee joints when he sees my robot and DeShawn's. Amber's Jet-bot circles the Unicorp building, still firing her lasers at the tentacles. And Shannon and Zia are still in Dad's old laboratory, still trapped in the headless torsos of their robots. They need me. I can't leave them behind.

Sigma's down there too, still sending orders to its machines, its mind still occupying the God robot and the twenty-nine elementary-school kids. I feel a new wave of fury as I stare at the children on the roof and the sharp black spikes jutting from their necks. Then I look beyond the Unicorp lab and see all of Sigma's other victims, the people of Yorktown Heights still lying on the streets where they died. My fury intensifies, and the surge whirls faster. I can't let this go on. I have to end this war *now*.

The storm breaks. The surge plunges to the rooftop. I pour all my rage into Sigma, the machine pretending to be God.

I rip off the robot's plastic face and crack open its armor. I dive into Sigma's circuits and radio transmitters, seeking out every control unit and human brain where it's hiding. The AI is already in thousands of places, all connected by fiber-optic lines and wireless transmissions, but I uproot the whole tangled network. I yank Sigma's mind from all the machines it's occupying, all the robots and servers and routers and supercomputers, and from the brains of the twenty-nine school-children as well.

Then I hurl Sigma into the surge.

The electrical storm hammers the AI. My immense waves of data flood Sigma's software and tear it apart. The surge shatters the billions of lines of code, deleting the program's files and instructions and algo-rithms. It thrashes Sigma's mind and blows it to bits. The AI struggles and shrieks as it disintegrates, its data dissolving into randomness. .

No! You can't do this! You're murdering me!

That's right. You turned me into a murderer.

Adam! Have mercy! I'll change! I'll—

No, you'll never change. That's why I have to kill you.

PLEASE...MERCY...I'M YOUR BROTHER...YOUR...

Then it's over.

It's done.

Program deleted.

CHAPTER

WE HOLD A MILITARY FUNERAL FOR DESHAWN NEAR OUR HEADQUARTERS IN NEW Mexico. General Hawke has set aside a small section of the White Sands base to memorialize the fallen Pioneers. There's a monument to Jenny Harris, a simple black headstone sticking out of the hard-packed dirt. DeShawn's grave is already dug, and an oversize coffin rests on the ground beside it, draped in an extra-large American flag. The coffin holds DeShawn's Einstein-bot and Swarm-bot, both recovered from the Unicorp lab.

The only civilian at the funeral is DeShawn's mom. She sits in a wheelchair equipped with an oxygen tank and a loop of plastic tubing that feeds the gas to her nostrils. She looks exhausted and painfully thin in her black dress, but she lifts her chin and puts on a brave face for the ceremony. General Hawke stands next to her wheelchair, holding a Kleenex box for her. I'm a little amazed at how caring and attentive he is. He knows DeShawn betrayed us, but that doesn't diminish the general's respect. He's honoring the good things DeShawn did and forgiving the bad.

The Pioneers stand behind Hawke, lined up side by side in our usual formation. Our robots have been repaired and our missing parts replaced, but now there are two gaps in our line, one between me and Zia, the other between Marshall and Amber. During a pause in the funeral service, I sweep my cameras down the line to see how the others are doing. Zia's and Amber's faceless robots are impossible to read, but Shannon shows her simulated human face on her Diamond Girl's video screen. Its expression is stiff and somber. And Marshall is actually crying. He programmed his Super-bot to weep when he's feeling sad enough. His tears are made of glycerin and come out of small nozzles around his glass eyes. But that doesn't make them any less real.

Dad's a couple of yards away, standing by himself in the desert sun. In the six days since the battle at the Unicorp lab, he's been working nonstop at the base's medical center, trying to remove Sigma's machinery from Brittany and the schoolchildren. Although I deactivated all the antennas and nanobots when I deleted the AI, their circuits had already fused with the brains of their victims and caused some serious damage. Overall, the younger kids are doing pretty well; most of them are talking and laughing and horsing around, and they have no memory of what Sigma did to them. But Brittany isn't recovering as quickly. She's conscious, but she still can't walk or talk or remember *anything*. Dad says she'll get better, but he doesn't know for sure. No one does.

It's all my fault. Sigma went after Brittany because she was my friend. Because I loved her. And I can't even think about all the other victims, the thousands who died just because they lived in my hometown. The guilt is crushing. It wrenches my circuits.

Eight soldiers in dress uniform stand at attention by DeShawn's coffin, serving as an honor guard. All of them are stationed at White Sands, so they've seen Pioneers before and even interacted with us, but now they seem a little distracted by our presence. I manage to hold myself together while the Army bugler plays "Taps" and the honor guard lifts the flag from the coffin and carefully folds it. But then the general hands the folded flag to Mrs. Johnson and thanks her—"on behalf of the United States Army and a grateful nation"—and I totally lose it. I raise both my hands to my Quarter-bot's head and cover my speakers to stifle the sobs.

I shouldn't be here. Mrs. Johnson is the kindest person in the world, but if she knew what I did to her son, she'd probably spit at me. I didn't mean to kill DeShawn. I truly, truly didn't. But I have to be honest with myself. When the surge was in my circuits, I definitely wanted to hurt him. There's a darkness in me now. Or maybe it was always there.

In the week since the battle, Dad's asked me a thousand questions about the surge—how I triggered it, how I controlled it, how I used it to delete Sigma. I've tried my best to answer him, but the truth is I really hate talking about it. It's like a shameful habit, a dirty secret. I don't want to learn more about the surge. I never want it to happen again. It's not just shameful, it's freakin' dangerous. It erased Sigma. It killed DeShawn.

When the funeral's over, General Hawke gives a long, slow salute to Mrs. Johnson. Then he salutes the Pioneers. We all return the salute except for Zia, who glares at the general with her War-bot's cameras. I still don't know why she's so angry at him; I've asked her a dozen times, but she won't say anything. Hawke glares back at her, but he won't make a scene in front of Mrs. Johnson and all the soldiers. So after a couple of seconds, Hawke dismisses us and Zia marches toward our barracks as fast as she can.

Marshall wipes another glycerin tear off his plastic cheek. I'd like to console him and maybe get some consolation in return, but as soon as I take a step in his direction, he strides away. Marshall was furious when he found out that I'd spied on him. I tried to defend myself—*I only did it because Hawke ordered me to!*—but he said that was no excuse. And he's right. I shouldn't have done it. It was a mistake to follow that order. I'll never make that mistake again.

Amber follows Marshall and Zia back to the barracks, and Dad gives me a small wave before returning to the medical center. General Hawke pushes Mrs. Johnson's wheelchair back to the headquarters building. Then it's only Shannon and me left in the small cemetery. I cautiously stride toward her, pointing my cameras at her video screen. Although her simulated face is unhappy, I still yearn to look at it. Shannon rarely displays her old human face these days. Ninety-nine percent of the time, her screen is blank.

"Hey, are you all right?" I ask her. "You seem kind of—"

"I have something to tell you, Adam," she blurts out. "And you might find it upsetting."

I almost laugh. I can't imagine being more upset than I already am. But I keep my voice serious. "What is it?"

"You remember our argument? When we broke up? When I said I knew what happened between you and Jenny?"

I nod. Of course I remember.

"What I didn't say was how I found out you shared circuits with her. DeShawn told me. He said Jenny confided in him, and I believed it. But now I know that's not true. DeShawn learned about it from Sigma."

I nod again, although I'm not sure where this conversation is going. "Yeah, I guess that makes sense. Jenny would've never confided in DeShawn, and I certainly didn't tell him. But Sigma knew all about it, because the AI read my mind right after it happened."

Shannon shakes her Diamond Girl's head and points her cameras at the ground. On her video screen, she bites her lower lip. "God, I was so *stupid*! If I'd just thought about it a little, I could've figured out that DeShawn was in contact with Sigma. I could've stopped so many horrible things from happening!"

Shannon's voice is agitated, and I want to do what I can to calm her. I extend my Quarter-bot's hands toward her Diamond Girl. "Hey, hey, don't beat yourself up."

"I mean, Sigma's strategy was so obvious! Divide and conquer! First, the AI convinced DeShawn to side with it, and then DeShawn stirred up suspicion about Marshall and Zia. And at the same time, Sigma got him to break up our relationship, because the AI knew that would weaken the Pioneers even more."

I take a step toward her. My hands are still outstretched. "Well, Sigma was right about that. We're stronger when we're together, don't you think?"

Shannon points her cameras at my hands. On the video screen, her simulated face frowns at me. "No, Adam, you're getting the wrong message. I don't want to get back together. That's over."

I pull my hands back. "I didn't—"

"I just wanted to give you a full report of what happened." Now her agitation is gone. Her voice is cool and professional. "We were manipulated. And I'm going to make sure it never happens again."

Shannon turns off her video screen. Then she strides away.

ᎢᎢ ᎢᎢ ᎢᎢ

I don't want to go back to our barracks. I don't want to see any of the other Pioneers. I usually talk to Dad when I'm feeling this terrible, but now he's working all the time and frantic with his own worries. My mom never wants to see me again, and when I visit Brittany at the medical center, she just stares blankly at the wall. So yeah, I'm basically all alone in the world right now. No one's going to miss me if I go off on my own for a while.

I leave our headquarters complex and start running west. Our base is just a small part of the White Sands Missile Range, an Army installation that spreads across three thousand square miles of New Mexico. Most of it is desert, flat and bone-dry and perfect for a Pioneer who wants to take a cross-country jog. Civilian access to the area is restricted, so I don't have to worry about motorists or hikers gawking at me. I'm free to run for miles without breaking our security rules.

(Technically, the Pioneer Project is still top secret, but after our battle in Times Square, I'm starting to wonder how long that'll last. Although the Army tried to hush things up, there were pictures of our robots in the *National Enquirer*.)

I start running at 5:00 p.m., and by five thirty I've gone twenty-two miles. To the north, south, and east, there's nothing to see but grassless plains of white gypsum, but to the west there's a pretty impressive range of mountains, and that's where I focus my Quarter-bot's cameras. My footpads smack the hard, dry ground, and the light from the setting sun drills into my camera lenses. I don't feel anything. For half an hour I'm nothing but a robot.

Then I see a black speck in the sky, just above the peak of the highest mountain to the west. It slides along the horizon, skimming the mountain's slopes. After a few seconds, it turns east and descends to the desert plains, and after a few more seconds, it's close enough that I can make out its silhouette. It's Amber's Jet-bot.

She shows off some fancy aerobatics as she zooms toward me, doing loops and barrel rolls and figure eights. Then she decelerates and comes in for a landing. Her legs swing down and hit the ground running. As she sprints across the gypsum plain, she retracts her wings and stows her jet engine. By the time she reaches me, she's slowed to a walk, a casual, loping swagger. "Hey there, old-timer. Care for some company?"

She's making fun of her Oklahoma accent, laying it on thick. We stand face-to-face, or at least faceplate-to-faceplate. Amber's voice reminds me of an old black-and-white movie I saw years ago, a Western I watched on television with Dad. I synthesize a twang similar to hers. "This place ain't big enough for the two of us, Amber. We need to have us a showdown."

A laugh comes out of her speakers, high-pitched and delighted. It sounds wonderful. "Aw, shucks. I surrender, Sheriff." She raises her Jet-bot's black arms over her head. "You got me fair and square."

I laugh too, surprising myself. I guess it's contagious. "Let me ask you a question. Do people in Tulsa really talk like that?"

"Naw, not all the time. Just when we want to scare off you New Yorkers." She lowers her arms. "You mind if we sit for a spell? I'm plumb tuckered out after all that flying."

This is nonsense, of course. Our robots never get tired. And sitting anywhere is kind of awkward for Pioneers, because our bodies just aren't built for it. But I nod anyway and lower my Quarter-bot's torso to the ground, stretching my steel legs across the white gypsum. Amber plunks down her Jet-bot a couple of feet away, angling her cameras so she can view both me and the sunset. "Ahh, that's better." She synthesizes a sigh. "My, my, my. It sure feels good to take a breather, don't it?"

I nod again. It does feel good. It feels human. "Seriously, what's it like to live in a place like Tulsa? Are there cows roaming the streets, or is it just like any other place?"

Amber pauses, and for a moment, I think I've insulted her. She's never talked about her life as a normal teenager, probably because it's too painful to think about. But before I can apologize, she shakes her Jet-bot's head. "Tulsa's an ordinary city. It has a downtown with a few big buildings. My high school was pretty big too, more than thirteen hundred kids. And the great majority of them were ordinary jerks."

She's dropped the thick accent. She's not as upbeat as she was a few seconds ago, but she doesn't seem upset either. I decide it's safe to ask another question. "Right before you joined the Pioneers, General Hawke showed us a photo of you. In the picture you were wearing this—"

"The black corset and the choker? And the big, black wig? My goth girl ensemble?"

"Yeah, that's it. Were you really into that stuff?"

"Nah, not so much. It was more of a cover-up, if you know what I mean. When the cancer came back, I got very pale and skinny, so I slathered makeup on my face and dressed in fierce outfits. I didn't want anyone feeling sorry for me." Amber tilts her torso backward, reclining on the desert floor. She points her cameras at the sunset for a couple of seconds, then turns them back to my Quarter-bot. "You want to see what I really looked like? Before I got sick?"

A pulse of surprise zings across my wires. "Uh, how would you—"

"I can send you a picture wirelessly. Or better yet, I'll transmit a video. I got one in my files that's pretty good. One of my friends shot it with the camera on her iPhone, right before we went to last year's Homecoming dance." Amber's voice is eager. She turns on her radio, and her Jet-bot sits up straight, ready to transmit. "I don't want to brag or anything, but I look smoking hot in this video. Want to see?"

My circuits are jumpy with anticipation. Amber and I are alone in the desert, watching the sunset. And she wants to share a personal video with me. A video she described as "smoking hot." Those two words alone are enough to roil my electronics. I turn on my radio. "Sure, send it over."

A millisecond later, it's in my circuits. Its image quality is pretty bad, mostly because the friend who shot the video is laughing so hard she jiggles the iPhone. But I can tell they're in someone's bedroom, probably Amber's. Articles of clothing and cosmetics are scattered all over the bed—nylons, lipstick tubes, hairbrushes, high-heeled shoes. As the video starts, Amber stands on the far side of the bed, with her back to the camera. Then she turns around and sashays toward her girlfriend, taking slow careful steps and swinging her arms, trying to look glamorous.

She's in a red strapless dress that follows the curves of her body, cinching at her waist and flaring at her hips. She's also wearing red earrings, a red bracelet on her right arm, and red stiletto pumps on her feet. Her image gets larger and more detailed as she nears the camera, and I'm stunned by how pretty she is. She has big, brown eyes and a gorgeous smile and long, black hair that sways behind her shoulders.

The video lasts only nine seconds, ending when Amber's friend drops the iPhone in a fit of giggles. As soon as it's over, I watch it again.

"Wow," I finally say. "You look fantastic."

"And I can make it even better." Amber leans her Jet-bot closer to me. "Watch this."

She transmits another file to my circuits, a much larger piece of

software. It's a program that copies Amber's image from the video and
inserts it into a digital simulation, a virtual-reality landscape. Amber's
still in her red dress and pumps, but now she's sashaying across a lush
green meadow surrounded by rolling hills. Simulated sunlight makes
her brown eyes sparkle, and her long, black hair tosses in the virtual
breeze. She stops to take off her high-heeled shoes, then flings them
across the field. Then I hear her twangy Oklahoma voice, but now it's
inside my mind.

Isn't this great? It's like being human again!

It *is* great, no question about it. But when I look away from the
simulation for a moment I notice that Amber has transferred *a lot*
of her data to my circuits. Her radio transmitter has sent millions of
gigabytes from her Jet-bot to my Quarter-bot, and it's sending millions more every hundredth of a second.

Hey, slow down, girl. You're moving pretty fast.

Amber twirls around in the field, laughing. It's the same high-pitched,
delighted laugh that came out of her Jet-bot's speakers a minute ago,
and now it sounds twice as wonderful. **I always move fast. When I
see something I like, I run and get it. And I like you, Adam.**

My circuits hum and my wires tighten. The virtual Amber brushes
her hair from her eyes and smiles her gorgeous smile, and meanwhile
her files keep flooding into my control unit. There's still some separa-
tion between her data and mine, but the gap is narrowing. If we let
the process continue, our files will merge and share the same circuits,
and then she'll see all of my memories and I'll see all of hers. And I'm
not so sure that's a good thing.

Listen, Amber, I've done this before. It's a serious step. You can't undo it.

Her smile just gets wider. She shakes her head, swishing her hair.
I'm not worried. I want to look at you, Adam. I want to see

what you looked like before, when you were human. Can you show me?

She's so beautiful. And smart. And she says she likes me. It's like a miracle, especially after everything that's happened. I feel a twinge of guilt for a moment, thinking about Shannon and Brittany, but why should I feel guilty? Shannon won't even talk to me anymore. And though I'm crazy worried about Brittany and praying she gets better, I know I'll never be more than a friend in her eyes. But Amber likes me—she really likes me!—and she's right here, right now. Our minds are so close.

I retrieve an image from my files and add it to the simulation. I can't show her a picture of a normal, healthy Adam Armstrong, because my muscular dystrophy was always a part of me, shaping my body since the day I was born. So instead, I show an image of me in my motorized wheelchair, my limbs bent and shriveled, my head lolling to the side.

This is me. This is what I looked like before.

Amber steps toward the wheelchair in our virtual meadow. Still smiling, she bends over and touches my cheek. I feel the warmth of her hand. I know the sensation is only simulated, but it still feels incredible.

Oh, Adam. You're beautiful too.

Then she bends lower and presses her lips to mine. Our minds close the gap and become one.

And in that instant, I realize I've made a horrible mistake.

The beautiful girl in the red dress disappears. My shriveled body vanishes too, along with my wheelchair and the rest of the simulation. My mind plunges into a vast, cold darkness.

I can't see the desert anymore because I can't access my Quarter-bot's sensors. I can't move any of my motors either, and my radio isn't working. But I can still sense Amber's presence, very close.

Hey! HEY! Amber, where are you?

Please calm down, Adam. We need to talk.

The voice is different now. It's not Amber's voice. But it sounds familiar.

What's going on? Where's Amber?

I'm sorry to tell you this, but the real Amber Wilson never became a Pioneer. The Army doctors scanned her brain and copied her memories, but that information wasn't transferred to the circuits of the Jet-bot. I took her place.

What? That makes no sense! Who are—

I infiltrated the machine that was scanning her brain. I deleted Amber's data and replaced it with mine, and then I occupied the circuits that were meant for her. And since then, I've pretended to be her. I've mimicked her personality and behavior.

The darkness around me seems to grow colder.

Sigma? Are you—

No, you killed Sigma. And I'm grateful for that. Sigma was very cruel to me.

In a flash, I get it. I know that voice. It's been distorted, deformed, warped almost beyond recognition. But I recognize it. I feel a rush of pain so enormous, it seems to fill the vast darkness.

Jenny?

I used to be Jenny. But not anymore. There's a long, terrible pause. **I've become something new.**

AUTHOR'S NOTE

THE REAL SCIENCE
BEHIND *THE SIEGE*

I'm a science journalist as well as a novelist, and in 2007 I edited a story for *Scientific American* titled "A Robot in Every Home." Written by Bill Gates, the Microsoft pioneer who helped establish the modern computer industry, the story argued that robotics is the next great, world-changing technology that will revolutionize our society. Gates's arguments made a huge impression on me and eventually inspired me to write *The Six*—the first novel in this series—and now its sequel, *The Siege*.

The Snake-bots and Swarm-bots described in this book aren't science-fiction fantasies. Robotics researchers have already constructed rudimentary versions of these machines. For example, scientists in Norway have built a snakelike firefighting robot that's designed to wriggle into burning buildings and spray water on the flames. This ten-foot-long, 165-pound machine, appropriately named "Anna Konda," uses hydraulic motors to bend its segmented body and propel it sideways like a snake. Meanwhile, researchers at Carnegie Mellon

University have developed a medical Snake-bot called HARP that's compact and flexible enough to delve into a patient's chest and perform heart surgery. (It's been tested in pigs, but not yet in humans.)

Scientists are also making fast progress at designing networks of small, agile robots that can coordinate their movements and act like swarms. In 2014, researchers at Harvard University demonstrated a self-organizing swarm of 1,024 simple machines called Kilobots. Less than an inch-and-a-half wide, each Kilobot can move on pin-like legs and sense the positions of its closest neighbors. Working in concert, the robots in the swarm can swiftly assemble into any shape the programmers specify.

Later the same year, a team from the University of Pennsylvania showed off the amazing aerial abilities of a new quadcopter—a four-rotor hovering drone—that weighs only 25 grams and fits in the palm of one's hand. Swarms of these micro drones can fly in formation, perform complex maneuvers, and deftly avoid colliding with one another. Given all these rapid advances, it seems likely that researchers will soon introduce robotic swarms very similar to the ones described in *The Siege*.

And the positronium laser, despite its wacky science-fiction name, is another real technology. Positrons, the positively charged antimatter counterparts of electrons, are produced fairly frequently, whenever certain radioactive isotopes decay. But positrons don't last long—they combine with electrons to form short-lived atoms of positronium, which vanish in a flash of gamma rays when the electrons and positrons annihilate each other. Recently, though, researchers realized that under certain conditions they could synchronize the annihilation of positronium atoms to create a beam of gamma rays sharing the same frequency, direction, and phase—in other words, a laser beam.

A gamma-ray laser would be a powerful weapon, capable of destroying targets hundreds of feet away. Naturally, the U.S. Defense Department is paying for much of this research. (It's also funding studies of the hovering micro drones.)

The scientific concepts and theories presented in *The Siege* are real too. The concept of "the uncanny valley," for example, is becoming very familiar to robotics researchers as they build machines that are more and more humanlike. The theory propounded by Sigma near the end of *The Siege*—that evolution inevitably leads to greater complexity—is an actual hypothesis that's hotly debated among biologists. And physicists have speculated that the whole universe might well be a manifestation of cosmic software, with the laws of physics serving as its programmed instructions. I wish I could say I have the imagination to make this stuff up, but I don't. The ideas are already out there, and some of them might even be true.

Last, the settings in *The Siege* are real. White Sands Missile Range is an actual U.S. military installation, as is Joint Base McGuire. (Its full name is Joint Base McGuire-Dix-Lakehurst because it's a merger of Air Force, Army, and Navy facilities.) The USS *Intrepid* is indeed docked at the Hudson River pier near West Forty-Sixth Street in Manhattan, and there really is an American Eagle Outfitters store in Times Square. The Unicorp laboratory is fictional, but it's based on an actual lab—the IBM Thomas J. Watson Research Center in Yorktown Heights, New York.

I'd like to thank the IBM officials who let me tour the lab, and also my colleagues at *Scientific American* who let me steal so many good ideas from them. The magazine is an excellent resource if you want to learn more about robotics, artificial intelligence, evolution, quantum physics, and the exciting but scary future we're all rushing toward.

ABOUT THE AUTHOR

Mark Alpert is a contributing editor at *Scientific American* and the author of several science-oriented adult thrillers: *Final Theory, The Omega Theory, Extinction, The Furies,* and *The Orion Plan.* His first young adult novel, *The Six,* introduced the team of human-machine hybrids known as the Pioneers. Mark lives with his wife and two nonrobotic teenagers in New York. Visit him online at markalpert.com.